Detective Frank Tripp was not a happy man.

Certain situations just got under his skin . . . and when that happened, he was about as much fun to be around as a polar bear in a sauna. At the moment, he was surrounded by a hundred such situations—and all of them were named Santa.

"Hey, Frank," Wolfe said. "I didn't know the North Pole was your jurisdiction."

"Okay, get it out of your system now," Frank growled. "You wanna know how many Santa jokes I've heard already?"

"Hmm." Wolfe looked past Frank, at the milling crowd of Santas behind the yellow crime-scene tape. "A sleighful, I'd say . . ."

"Yeah, well," Frank said, "in anticipation of your next question, no, nobody's grandma got run over by a reindeer. The vic's back here."

CSI: MiaMi™

HARM FOR THE HOLIDAYS
PART ONE: MISGIVINGS

DONN CORTEZ

CSI: MIAMI produced by CBS Productions, a business unit of CBS Broadcasting Inc.
and Alliance Atlantis Productions Inc.
Executive Producers: Jerry Bruckheimer, Ann Donahue, Carol Mendelsohn, Anthony E. Zuiker, Jonathan Littman
Series created by Anthony E. Zuiker, Ann Donahue, and Carol Mendelsohn

POCKET
BOOKS

LONDON • SYDNEY • NEW YORK • TORONTO

An *Original* Publication of POCKET BOOKS

Published by
POCKET BOOKS, a division of Simon & Schuster, Ltd.
Africa House, 64–78 Kingsway, London WC2B 6AH

ISBN-13: 978-1-4165-2633-9
ISBN-10:   1-4165-2633-1

This Pocket Books paperback edition December 2006

10 9 8 7 6 5 4 3 2 1

Art and design by Patrick Kang

Printed and bound in Great Britain

A CIP catalogue record for this book is available
from the British Library

For my agent, Lucienne Diver, for all her hard work, dedication and belief.

1

CHRISTMAS IN MIAMI, HORATIO THOUGHT, *was almost redundant.*

He glanced out the window of the Hummer as he cruised down the Rickenbacker Causeway. On the other side of the guardrail, out in Biscayne Bay, the sailboats had their masts decorated with strings of Christmas lights, and he could see at least one cruise ship with a big inflatable pine tree on its deck. Those sorts of details, he had to admit, only showed up once a year . . . but conceptually, the city was Christmas all year round. Miami Beach was a great big Santa's workshop for grown-ups, dispensing booze and food and sex and music; sure, the trees were palm instead of evergreen, the lights neon instead of twinkling, the crowds lined up outside clubs instead of inside malls—but everybody still had a list of what they wanted. Bouncers kept track of who was naughty or nice, and nobody complained when their present showed up in a *mojito* glass or wrapped in a thong instead of paper. Miami even got snow . . . but it usually arrived in kilo-size packages of tightly bound plastic, stashed in the hold of a Cigarette boat.

And of course, Horatio thought, *there was the occasional Grinch.*

The crime scene was a convenience store in Liberty City, not one of Miami's better neighborhoods. He parked in front, beside the two black-and-whites, and got out. By the time he ducked under the yellow police tape barring the front door, he had already gloved up; Horatio went through more latex than a sex-trade worker moonlighting as a paramedic.

Calleigh Duquesne was already there, kneeling beside a pool of blood on the floor. Horatio took a quick look around, noted the security camera, the closed till, and a toppled rack of potato chips.

"Hey, H," Calleigh said. She used the camera in her hands to snap a quick couple of pictures. "What brings you out on this cheery holiday night?"

"An attempted robbery, apparently," Horatio replied. "I understand the vic is still alive?"

"And his attacker—problem is, we don't know which is which. A customer found two men, both unconscious, both sprawled out on the floor. It looks like one clocked the other one with this." She held up a large glass bottle of malt liquor; the bottom edge was matted with blood and hair. "Both men were in their thirties, of Middle Eastern or Hispanic descent. One had ID, the other didn't. Ambulance took them to Dade Memorial."

"So how did they both wind up unconscious?"

"Check this out." Calleigh pointed at the floor, where a short red smear jutted from the edge of the pool of blood. "Believe it or not, it looks like the second one slipped in the first one's blood—or maybe vice versa. Cracked his skull on the floor."

"So we have a clumsy criminal or an unlucky clerk," Horatio mused. "And if the security camera is working, we should be able to tell which is which . . ."

Horatio walked behind the front counter, Calleigh right behind him. There was a small video monitor mounted on the underside of the counter, out of sight of the customers. It cycled between two views: the front of the till and the back door.

"I've got blood spatter on the counter," Calleigh said. She snapped off a few pictures. "Looks like this is where the fight started."

Horatio found the recording unit and fiddled with the controls. "Okay, here we go," he murmured.

The monitor showed them the back of the clerk's head. A tall, dark-skinned man wearing a long black coat entered the frame, holding a magazine in one hand and gesturing wildly with the other. A scarf obscured the lower part of his face.

"Too bad there's no sound," Calleigh said. "Wonder why he's so agitated."

"As near as I can tell, it has something to do with that magazine," Horatio said.

The attacker tossed the magazine away and struck the clerk in the face with his fist. Blood poured from the clerk's nose. The man's hand suddenly shot out and grabbed the clerk by the throat. Using only one arm, he dragged the clerk across the counter and in front of the till.

"Strong," Calleigh said.

"And violent . . ." The fight was no longer in range of the camera, but they could see the rack of potato chips fall into the frame. There was no movement after that.

"So the blood pool was from the punch in the nose," Calleigh said.

"And presumably right afterward is when our poor besieged clerk grabbed the bottle and got in a lucky shot." Horatio reached down and stopped the recording.

"Lucky is right," Calleigh said. "Did you see how fast that guy moved? And hauling the clerk across the counter like that, one-handed—what do you figure, H? Martial arts, military training, or drugs?"

"I guess we'll have to wait until one of them wakes up to hear the whole story," Horatio answered. "But at least we know who did what."

"Yeah." Calleigh walked over to one corner of the store. She bent over and picked up the magazine in question from the floor, flipped it open, and examined it critically. "I can see why he was so upset. Those boots she's wearing really don't go with her hat."

Horatio stepped over and took a look. "At least they don't clash with anything else," he pointed out.

"H, she's not *wearing* anything else. Nothing but a smile, anyway."

"Quite the contrast to the rage in our perp's eyes," Horatio said. "If looks could kill, we'd be investigating a murder instead of an assault . . ."

She heard them before she saw them.

Luisita worked at Excolo Hotel, a four-star Miami Beach hotel with an art deco exterior that always reminded her of a cross between Flash Gordon and Fred Flintstone—something about the combination of terra-cotta color scheme and streamlined design elements, she supposed. Luisita was studying to be an architect, and she paid her tuition by manning the front desk at the Excolo on weekends. She was used to dealing with tourists, drunken college kids, and eccentric locals . . . but she'd never experienced anything like *this.*

"Ho, ho, ho! Ho, ho, ho! Ho, ho, ho!"

The sound was coming from the street. It was getting closer, and louder—a lot louder.

Luisita glanced at the other desk clerk, a gangly guy in his twenties who always looked vaguely surprised. "Stuart, what is that?"

"Um," Stuart said. "Him?" He pointed at the front door.

There, framed in the doorway, was Santa Claus. Sort of.

He wore the traditional red suit and had a big white beard—but he held a megaphone in one hand, and what appeared to be a bottle of window cleaner in the other. He gave the hotel staff a cheery wink, raised the megaphone to his lips, and shouted, "Santa! *Into the lobby!*"

And suddenly, Santa wasn't alone.

They poured through the door like a crimson flood, Santas of every size and description. There were tall Santas and short Santas, fat Santas and skinny Santas, male Santas and female Santas.

And then there were the mutant Santas: Santas in fishnets and high heels, Santas in sequin-covered suits, Santas with horns, Santas in clown makeup and gorilla masks and Groucho glasses. For every identical Kris Kringle there was another, warped version, dressed in a fur bikini or leading a leather-clad elf on a leash. There were reindeer as well as elves, and at least one Easter Bunny. Every single one of them was chanting, "Ho, ho, ho!" at the top of their North Pole lungs.

Luisita glanced at Stuart. Stuart appeared to be in shock; the customary amazed expression on his face had frozen there like the screen of a crashed computer.

And they just kept coming. The security guard,

talking to the bell captain, was caught completely by surprise; by the time he reacted, at least a dozen Santas had strolled through the door.

And they kept coming.

They filled the lobby, laughing and *ho*-ing and hoisting flasks aloft. The security guard held up his hands, but they ignored him, streaming past in a merry, white-furred swarm.

Luisita stared, and realized she was grinning. It was impossible not to.

A bunch of Santas formed a ring around the Christmas tree in the center of the lobby, joined hands, and started singing. At first Luisita thought the song was "Deck the Halls," but realized after the first verse she'd never heard this particular version before—especially the part about "Don we now our rubber panties."

One of the Santas bounded up, reached into his red sack, and pulled out a brightly wrapped present. He handed it to Luisita with a big smile and a cry of "Merry Christmas!"

She took it hesitantly, and he bounded away again. Luisita stared around the lobby; how many Santas *were* there, anyway? She was sure there were over a hundred already, with more pushing their way inside every minute.

"Are you going to open it?" Stuart asked.

Luisita laughed. "Sure, why not?" She tore off the paper, revealing an old shoebox. She pulled off the lid—

"SANTA LOVES YOU!" one of the Santas screamed.

Inside the box was a toy—a very odd toy. It had the torso of a Barbie doll, the head and arms of a cartoon tiger, transparent fairy wings, and one cybernetic leg. Little kernels of unpopped popcorn were glued on as nipples.

"I think Santa made this one after a few too many eggnogs," Luisita said, smiling. She propped it up behind the counter, where the staff could see it but guests couldn't.

And just as quickly as they'd swirled into the hotel lobby, they were gone, marching out into the warm Miami night. They left a trail of candy canes and stickers that read "Naughty!" or "Nice!" behind them, and several bewildered staff members. On closer examination the Christmas tree was discovered to have had several ornaments added to it, ranging from the ludicrous to the pornographic, and someone had spray-painted a large HO! on every elevator door in artificial snow. Luisita couldn't stop grinning for the rest of the night.

Until she got home after her shift and saw the news.

Detective Frank Tripp was not a happy man.

Not that he was unhappy in general—underneath his gruff exterior, he was actually a pretty friendly and easygoing guy. But certain situations just got under his skin . . . and when that happened, he was about as much fun to be around as a polar bear in a sauna.

At the moment, he was surrounded by a hundred such situations—and all of them were named Santa.

Ryan Wolfe strolled up, CSI kit in one hand. The kid was dressing well these days, Tripp noted—a sharp tan blazer, pin-striped shirt underneath it open at the collar. Tripp himself had a grand total of five suits, which he rotated on the basis of which one had accumulated the least number of coffee stains. *Kid keeps dressing like that,* Tripp thought, *people are gonna start callin' him little H.*

"Hey, Frank," Wolfe said. "I didn't know the North Pole was your jurisdiction."

"Okay, get it out of your system now," Frank growled. "You wanna know how many Santa jokes I've heard already?"

"Hmm," Wolfe said thoughtfully. He looked past Frank, at the milling crowd of Santas behind the yellow crime-scene tape. "A sleighful, I'd say . . ."

"Yeah, well," Frank said, "in anticipation of your next question, no, nobody's grandma got run over by a reindeer. The vic's back here."

Tripp led Wolfe around the side of the building to a parking lot. In one corner there was a white pile, around three feet high, with a body-shaped outline cut into it. At the base of the figure, a pair of black boots jutted out.

"Is that *snow*?" Wolfe asked, setting down his kit and opening it.

"Not exactly," Tripp said. "It's shaved ice from the rink inside; apparently Santa likes to cut a few figure eights during his downtime. Zamboni driver found him when he came out here to dump a load."

Wolfe snapped on a pair of gloves, then approached the artificial drift. The boots sticking out of it belonged to a mostly naked man—besides the boots, he wore a pair of red pants pulled down around his knees, a fake white beard, and a Santa hat.

"Looks like he melted right into the drift," Wolfe said. "Our Santa was giving off a lot of heat."

"Think Santa was tryin' to make a snow angel?" Tripp asked.

"If he was making an angel," Wolfe said, "she was on top." He pointed to two depressions in the snow on either side of the Santa's hips. "And it looks like she left a bootprint, too—it's way too small to belong to the vic."

"Better get a picture of it quick. The way this stuff is melting, it'll be gone in no time."

"I can do better than that." Wolfe rummaged in his kit and brought out a spray can. He shook it up, uncapped it, then carefully misted a layer over the bootprint. "Aerosol wax. Perfect for making casts in snow."

"Something specially designed for casting footprints in snow—and you just happen to have it in your kit?"

"I like to be prepared," Wolfe said defensively. "Besides, it's also good for sand or mud—and regular casting materials heat up as they set. The exothermic reaction can cause details to get lost."

"What do you figure killed him?"

Wolfe began to examine the body carefully. "I don't know. No visible trauma to the body; skin is flushed and still warm. I can see traces of vomit in his beard. We might be looking at a heart attack or stroke."

"Maybe frolicking in the snow with a playmate was a little too jolly for him?"

"Maybe," Wolfe said. "Or maybe this is just what happens when you only come once a year . . ."

Tripp frowned. "ME's on her way. Maybe she can firm the COD up—and do it without making any bad jokes."

"Oh, come on, Frank. I can't believe you can look at this with a straight face. I mean, it's a naked Santa." Wolfe peeled the wax impression off the snow carefully.

"It's not the vic that's got me in a bad mood. It's all the suspects we've got to interview. Over a hundred, and not one of them sober. It's going to be a long night—and not a silent one, either."

"You've got a point." Wolfe inspected the body's fingernails, then took out a pair of tweezers and an evidence envelope. "Well, you better get started— I've still got a ton of trace to collect. I've got fibers under his nails, the vomit, what look like beard hairs on his groin, and possibly even DNA from sexual activity. . . . I'm going to be here a while."

"Wonderful."

Chester Cypress liked to hunt. He didn't use a gun or a bow or a dog, and his hunting trips all took place when the sun was down. He would go deep into the 'Glades on a flat-bottomed skiff, just him, a bucket, and a six-foot-long pole that ended in four razor-sharp, barbed tines.

Chester Cypress was a Miccosukee Indian, one of maybe five hundred left. He worked at the Miccosukee Village, a settlement that had been there long before the Tamiami Trail. Chester was a cook in the restaurant there, which featured genuine Miccosukee dishes like fry bread, pumpkin bread, catfish—and frog's legs.

Chester had been taught how to gig frogs by his father, and he planned on teaching his own son one day. His father had used a carbide lantern to spotlight the big bullfrogs and freeze them in place, but technology had improved since then; Chester used a tiny, extremely bright halogen light strapped to his forehead. If you used this method on deer, it was called jacklighting—and was highly illegal—but when used on frogs it was considerably more sporting. All you had to do to bag the deer was aim and shoot, but to get your frog you had to get close to him without making a sound, then spear him with one quick thrust. You also had to keep an eye out for gators and water moccasins at the same time, and one frog didn't make much of a meal; you couldn't call it a good night's hunting until you had a bucketful, and sometimes that meant you didn't get to bed until dawn.

Still, the tourists paid well for the privilege of tasting something exotic—though really, what they were getting was no more exotic than what they probably had in the local pond back home. It was all in the presentation, Chester supposed. That was what they'd taught him in cooking school, anyway.

Tourists—the few that came out to the swamp after dark—were always amazed at how loud it was. The insects alone generated a constant background cacophony, punctuated by the occasional roar of a bull alligator or the cry of a chuck-will's-widow. As his boat glided along, Chester's ears were listening for something else: the basso croak of his prey.

He turned his head methodically from left to right as he poled the boat along, looking for the golden flash that would mark the reflection of a frog's eyes. Most people went gigging in groups of two or more—one to pole the boat, one to spotlight the frogs, and one to gig them—but Chester preferred to do it solo. He knew it was just ego, but he liked that he could tell people he'd caught and cooked them himself.

The beam of his halogen winked off something floating in the water ahead. It wasn't a frog's eyes, though; it was more like a piece of metal. He poled closer.

The metal was a length of shiny silver chain, the kind used for dog leashes. It was wrapped around the torso of a human body, though it took Chester a moment to recognize it for what it was; the head, lower legs, and hands were missing.

Chester stared at the body for a moment, then sighed and looked for a nearby tree to mark. "So much for a good night's hunting," he muttered. "By the time I get through talking to the cops, the sun'll be up. And this was such a good spot, too . . ."

He studied the body, and shrugged. "Well, for some of us, anyway . . ."

They used the rink's bleachers to hold the Santas. The Santas had apparently decided to make the best of the situation; about half of them had jumped onto the ice and were now playing some sort of improvised game that involved kicking a stuffed toy reindeer from one end of the rink to the other. Wolfe thought he heard it referred to as "ho-hockey."

He and Tripp had commandeered the booths of the concession stand to hold interviews. Wolfe had done a dozen already, and all thoughts of Christmas-related humor had been banished from his head.

A uniformed officer led the next interviewee over and sat him down. This one was a traditional Claus, except that his beard covered his entire face; only his bloodshot eyes were visible.

"Name? And *please* don't say—" Wolfe said.

"Santa!"

"Do you have any identification?"

"Santa doesn't need ID! *Everybody* knows who Santa is!" The Santa's voice was cheerfully slurred.

"Yeah, okay . . . look, a man died tonight. One of you guys. We're just trying to find out what happened, all right?"

The Santa blinked at him owlishly. "Poor Santa . . ."

"Yeah, poor Santa. You know the deceased?"

Santa shrugged. "If he was with us, he was Santa. What kind of Santa was he?"

Wolfe resisted the urge to say, *The naked, dead kind.* "In appearance, he was a pretty standard Santa. Midthirties, Caucasian, around five foot eleven." Wolfe slid over a picture he'd printed off his digital camera. "We think he may have been having sex out in the parking lot."

The Santa studied the picture. "Nope, doesn't ring any sleigh bells. He was obviously a *naughty* Santa, but that narrows it down to . . . pretty much all of us. Who was Santa showing his North Pole to?"

"We don't know," Wolfe said. "Any Mrs. Santas you think might be responsible?"

"Sorry, Officer—Santa doesn't kiss and tell."

"Right. Well, I'm also going to need samples of the fibers from your clothes and your beard, and I'm going to need your boots."

"My boots? But—Santa can't spread holiday cheer in his *socks*."

"Sorry, Santa. But I don't have the resources to take casts of a hundred pairs of boots here, so they'll have to go with me back to the lab. If you want them back, you can give your real name to an officer. You're going to have to eventually, anyway."

"Hey, does this concession stand sell beer? Santa needs a *drink*."

Wolfe sighed.

The next Santa was dressed in a kilt trimmed in white fur, a jacket of red serge, and a tartan Santa hat. His bushy white beard appeared to be entirely natural, and he was, if anything, even more drunk than the last Claus.

"Ho, ho, ho!" he bellowed, sitting down with a thump. "And what do *you* want for Christmas, little boy?"

"A new job," Wolfe muttered.

"'Scuse me," the new Santa said politely, bent over, and threw up on the floor.

"And a mop," Wolfe said gloomily.

2

HORATIO PULLED THE HUMMER into the parking lot of the Miami-Dade Pre-Trial Detention Center, a tall, orange-red building that could house over seventeen hundred inmates. This was Miami's main jail, where arrestees were taken after being charged. Horatio's job was generally to make sure the right person ended up in one of those cells—but today, he was there in a more advisory capacity.

He checked in at the front desk, went through the various security procedures, and eventually wound up in a small office on the second floor. The officer who stood up to greet him was in his forties, with short dark hair, a large, crooked nose, and a wide smile. His name was Calvin Selmo, and he and Horatio had known each other back when Horatio was on the bomb squad.

"Horatio! Good to see you!" Calvin said, putting out his hand.

Horatio shook it and smiled. "You, too, Calvin. How's Rose and the kids?"

"Fine, fine. Manny's going through puberty and my life is a living hell. The usual." He sat back down and Horatio pulled up a chair and joined him. "Anyway, I hate to bother you with what, I admit, is a relatively minor problem—not to mention a problem I should be able to solve myself—but I thought you might have a little insight to spare for an old friend."

"Absolutely," Horatio said. "What's the problem?"

"Well, there's this guy downstairs in holding. Brought in last night after he tore up a convenience store and attacked the owner. The owner fought back, got lucky, and conked the guy on the head with a bottle."

"I know," Horatio said. "I was at the scene, afterward. Security camera caught the whole thing—seemed pretty straightforward to me."

"Well, once the arresting officers cleared up which was which, it should have been. But since both guys were out cold, they took both to the hospital to get checked out. The clerk is still in a coma, but the perp woke up in the ambulance. He's fine—in a strictly medical sense, anyway."

"Oh?" Horatio cocked his head to the side, his blue eyes intent.

"But when they got him down to processing, he balked. We got his mug shots done, no problem.

Then he saw the fingerprint pad and refused. Made a fist—two of 'em, actually—and wouldn't open up for anything."

Horatio started to reply, but Selmo cut him off. "I know, I know—every rookie knows those pressure points that'll *make* him open those hands. Been tried. Either this guy's central nervous system is wired up different, or he's got a pain threshold somewhere around Jupiter. Now, I know we could get those prints eventually—it's just an engineering problem, really—but I have never seen someone put up this much resistance. I mean, it took six guys to just hold him down to where we could even start to pry his hand open. I thought, 'By the time we're done we're gonna wind up breaking a few of his fingers just by accident'—and you know what that'll look like in the press."

"Uh-huh," Horatio said. "Breaking a suspect's fingers while printing him doesn't really read as plausible, does it?"

"Not remotely. But when it comes to implausible, my friend, you're the expert."

Horatio smiled. "The forensics lab does encounter the occasional strange situation," he admitted. "And we've gotten our share of prints from unusual sources, too. Is that what you want—us to find something this guy has touched and lift a print?"

"I'm hoping you'll have better luck than us," Selmo said. "See, the guy's wearing gloves. Tight-fitting, expensive leather gloves. Wouldn't take 'em off at the hospital, either. Which not only makes his fingers hard to get a grip on, and means we have to cut them off—which is a lot harder than it sounds—but also means he hasn't left many fingerprints lying around."

Horatio nodded. "He must have put the gloves on at the hospital, too—I don't remember seeing them in the security video. We have the magazine he handled, though; there's a good chance we can lift a print from that. And if that doesn't work—well, he's got to sleep sometime."

"Yeah, but the longer this takes, the worse I look. And this guy's already called a lawyer—for all I know, he's setting us up for some kind of civil suit. I keep expecting news crews to suddenly appear on my doorstep."

"Wait a minute—how did he call a lawyer when you didn't even get him through processing?"

"Not sure—we think he got hold of a cell phone in the hospital. In any case, the lawyer's down there now, talking to him. I was hoping maybe you'd be next."

"Oh? Let me guess—you want some of his DNA."

"If that's what it takes. But first, I thought you might try some of the famous Caine charm."

Horatio chuckled. "I'm not a professional negotiator, Calvin."

"Maybe you don't have a piece of paper that

says so, H, but you're still the most persuasive cop I know. Anybody that can keep their cool while making small talk to a maniac with two dozen sticks of dynamite strapped to their belly is *my* go-to guy in a negotiation. Y'know?"

Horatio studied Calvin for a moment before replying. Selmo had been the kind of cop who sometimes took chances when he shouldn't—that was one of the reasons he was now helping process traffic offenders instead of defusing high explosives. Horatio, when asked to evaluate Selmo by a superior, had been honest; there was very little margin of error on the bomb squad, and no room at all for hurt feelings. A bad evaluation would hurt Selmo's career, but a bad decision on the job would end it— as well as Calvin's life, and who knew how many others.

Apparently Calvin had learned a little about caution since then. Calling Horatio in was a smart move; since the objective was to ID a suspect, it technically fell within the crime lab's purview, and any political fallout—such as a civil suit—could be directed at his department instead of Selmo's.

Calvin's smile was open and guileless, but Horatio could detect just a touch of smugness as well. Still, he couldn't hold it against the man; Horatio had helped put him behind that desk, after all. He'd never felt he owed Calvin an apology—but he did owe him something.

"I'll do my best," Horatio said quietly.

3

DELKO SNEEZED.

"Bless you, honey," Doctor Alexx Woods said. "You coming down with something, Eric?" She walked briskly over to the wall of stainless steel drawers that held her clientele and consulted the clipboard in her hands.

Delko shook his head. "I hope not. Man, Christmas colds are the worst." He followed Alexx over, but made sure he stood well out of the way of the sliding drawer as she pulled it open.

"You think it's bad here, you should try it when it's twenty below," Alexx said. "And anyway, at least you're still in one piece—which is more than I can say for our John Doe."

"Yeah, he's in pretty rough shape. A Miccosukee found him in the 'Glades last night. Unfortunately, not being familiar with CSI protocol, he just pulled the vic into his boat and brought the body out himself. I processed what I could there—including the chains wrapped around the body—but I'm going out today to take a look at the actual spot where the DB was found. Just thought I'd drop by and get your opinion first."

"Well, opinion is about all I'm prepared to give at the moment," Alexx said. "And you *know* I don't like doing that, right?"

Delko held up his hands in defense. "I know, I know—you haven't got a chance to even look at him, yet. But if I'm going to be diving in a swamp, I'd like to know what I'm looking for."

"Hmmph. Well, I can't tell you that, but I can tell you what you probably *won't* find—his head."

"Why's that?"

She pointed at the stump of the neck. "See how the bone is fractured? No tool marks, but plenty of charring and torn flesh on the shoulders. This guy's head was blown off—literally. You might find fragments, but that's about it."

"What about his hands and legs? Same thing?"

She inspected both sites carefully before replying. "No, they're both different. I can see teeth marks on the flesh of the lower legs—looks like predation, probably by alligators. And the hands . . . the hands are something completely different." She picked up one of the corpse's forearms gently and examined the stump of its wrist. "These look like chemical burns to me."

"Getting a positive ID is gonna be hard. No

prints, no dental, no wallet—if his DNA isn't in the system, we're at a dead end."

Alexx looked down at the body and shook her head. "Not as dead as his," she said, and shut the drawer softly.

The guard standing beside the door of the interview room, a tall black man wearing steel-framed glasses, shook his head and grinned. "You ain't gonna believe this, Sarge," he said to Selmo.

Selmo snorted. "Wait, lemme guess—you finally got the gloves off and it turns out the guy's an alien, right?"

"Well, you got it half-right. He's taken the gloves off himself. Says he's ready to cooperate—but I wouldn't call that an accurate description of his attitude."

"Oh?" Horatio said. "He's still being difficult?"

"Hell, no. He's gone past cooperating to being downright helpful. His lawyer just left—I don't know what the guy told him, but whatever it was, it spun his whole outlook a hundred and eighty degrees. I mean, he's gone from Mister Hyde to Doctor Jekyll."

"He give a statement yet?" Selmo asked.

"No, just his name and address. We figured you'd want to hear his story yourself."

"Well, looks like I wasted your time, Horatio," Selmo said.

"If you don't mind, Calvin, I'd like to sit in," Horatio said. "I'm curious as to what exactly our gloved friend is going to say."

Selmo shrugged. "Sure, I don't mind. I dragged you all the way down here, after all." He nodded to the guard, who unlocked the door.

The man manacled to the interview table sat with his back erect, staring straight ahead. His skin was a light brown, his eyebrows dark and thick, his nose prominent. He was clean-shaven, with a small scar at the point of his chin. He was still wearing the clothes he was arrested in, a long black coat over a nondescript gray sweatshirt, jeans, and sneakers. The gloves were gone.

Selmo took the chair across from him, while Horatio remained standing. "So," Selmo began, "I understand you've had a change of heart, Mister—?"

The man smiled, showing a mouthful of brilliant white teeth. "Pathan. Abdus Sattar Pathan, at your service. I would shake your hand, but . . ."

"An hour ago, you wouldn't even *open* your hand," Selmo snapped. "What gives?"

Pathan's smile instantly faded into embarrassed self-effacement. "I do apologize for that." His voice was cultured, with just a trace of a British accent. "I believe I may have suffered a mild concussion."

"You seem all right to me," Selmo said. "Why didn't you want us to take your prints?"

"Arab-Americans must be careful these days. I know it must seem absurdly paranoid to you, but I was convinced you were trying to frame me for some sort of crime. I'm not a doctor, but I believe a concussion can sometimes produce such neurological symptoms."

"We don't have to frame you for anything, Abdus. We've got you dead to rights—video surveillance, blood on your clothing, and pretty soon your prints. That's not paranoia, that's reality."

Pathan frowned. "I don't understand. I went into a convenience store, saw a man lying in a pool of blood, and rushed over; then everything went blank. I woke up in the back of an ambulance with a lump on my head."

"Are you kidding me?" Selmo growled. "That's your explanation? You didn't do it? You just happened along and it's all just a big misunderstanding?"

"I'm afraid that's the truth. The real attacker must have hit me over the head and run away."

"And I suppose," Horatio said, speaking for the first time, "that you and he just happened to be wearing the same scarf, too."

Pathan gave Horatio an apologetic smile. "That does stretch credibility, doesn't it? No, I imagine he placed his own scarf around my neck after he knocked me out. That doesn't contradict the evidence, does it?"

"Technically, no," Horatio said. "However, we do have video of the attacker holding a certain item. You say you rushed right over to the clerk once you entered the store?"

Pathan didn't hesitate. "Yes, that's correct."

"Then you didn't have time to handle anything in the store, did you?"

Pathan shook his head. "I assure you, Officer . . . ?"

"Lieutenant Caine."

"I assure you, Lieutenant Caine, I have never been in that store before. You will not find my prints on anything."

Horatio regarded him coolly. "You seem very sure of that. What if the attacker planted your finger-prints the same way you claim he placed the scarf around your neck?"

Pathan met Horatio's eyes calmly. "That seems a trifle hard to believe, doesn't it, Lieutenant? After all, this is a convenience-store robbery we are talking about, not some criminal mastermind."

"Actually, the store wasn't robbed," Horatio said. "Which seems odd, don't you think? That our mystery man would go to all the trouble to frame you, but leave the cash behind?"

Pathan nodded. "Yes, it does. But the workings of another's mind are always a mystery, wouldn't you agree?"

"Maybe so," Horatio said. "Fortunately, I have something much more concrete to rely on; I have evidence, Mister Pathan . . . and believe me, what it has to say won't be mysterious at all."

Pathan's smile widened, ever so slightly. "Well, then, Lieutenant Caine," he said softly, "I can only hope the truth will set me free . . ."

*   *   *

"Morning, Wolfe," Frank Tripp said. He finished off his cup of coffee and motioned toward the waitress for a refill.

"Morning." Wolfe yawned and slid into the booth across from the detective. After interviewing Santas late into the night, he had gone home and caught a few hours' sleep, agreeing to meet Tripp for breakfast to compare notes. They were at Auntie Bellum's, an old-style art deco diner close to the crime lab. Wolfe stared at a menu and tried to get his eyes to focus.

"What's the matter—didn't get your beauty sleep?" Tripp sounded in a better mood than last night.

"Mm," Wolfe said. "I'm fine. Think I dreamt about fat guys in sleighs all night, though."

"Yeah? I decided not to take the chance. Haven't been to bed yet." The waitress, a pretty young Cuban girl, delivered Tripp's breakfast with a smile. He smiled back and dug into his eggs with a fork and knife.

"Just coffee, please," Wolfe told her. "Maybe I should have stayed up, too. Feel like I've got a head full of . . . whatever the opposite of brains is."

Tripp dunked a triangle of toast in the yolk of his eggs. "Better get in the game, son. We've got a lot to go over."

"I know, I know. Man, I must have talked to fifty Santas last night."

"Fifty-two. I talked to seventy-three, myself."

"Okay. What do we know?"

Tripp finished chewing and swallowed before answering. "Well, apparently this is an annual thing—they call it Santarchy, or Santacon. Started around ten years ago. Groups get together and go on what they call a rampage—basically, an excuse for an extended bar crawl. They sing naughty Christmas carols, give away mutant toys, indulge in public nudity—"

"I'm sorry—mutant toys?" Wolfe added cream and sugar to his cup.

"Yeah. They chop up a bunch of old toys, then glue 'em back together. Teddy bear heads stuck on top of G.I. Joes, that kinda thing."

"And this has been going on for a decade? How come I've never heard of it?" Wolfe took a sip of his coffee.

"I said it's been going on for ten years—I didn't say in Miami. Started in San Francisco—big surprise—and spread from there. From what I understand, the so-called Red Menace has made appearances in Barcelona, Helsinki, Bangkok, New York, London, Vancouver, Tokyo—even the Antarctic. They've only started up in our neck of the woods recently."

Wolfe stared at Tripp blearily over the rim of his coffee cup. "That's . . . impressive, Frank. So I guess you'll be handling the information on this case and I'll be arresting the bad guys?"

Tripp chuckled. "What, you think only you CSI guys know how to do research? In case you didn't notice, my badge *does* say detective."

"Okay—point noted. So what else can you tell me about our jolly gang of suspects?"

"Let's see . . . well, despite all the drunken tomfoolery, they've actually got a pretty strict code of conduct."

"You're kidding."

"Nope. They call it the four effs. As in, don't eff with the cops, don't eff with store security, and don't eff with the kids."

"Yeah? What's the fourth eff?"

"Don't eff with Santa. Guess somebody decided to break that one."

"And now they're effing with us," Wolfe said.

"Not all of them. Actually, they're a fairly reasonable bunch, once they understand you're not out to ruin their good time."

Wolfe frowned. "Did you and I talk to the same group last night, or were you interviewing a *different* bunch of drunk Santas?"

Tripp took a swig from his glass of OJ. "Well, there's drunk, and then there's *drunk*. You may have encountered a few more of the second kind than I did—one of the uniforms that rode herd on the crowd is an old friend of mine."

Wolfe nodded his head ruefully. "Gotcha. So you accumulated useful information, and I accumulated vomit. Terrific."

"Well," Tripp said, polishing off his last piece of toast, "not everybody's a people person."

"Okay, so now we know what all the Santas were doing there. How about our vic?"

Tripp wiped his mouth with a paper napkin and leaned back. "Not a lot to go on. None of the other Santas seemed to know him, though by all accounts he was enjoying himself. He spent most of his time flirting with the female Santas."

"Any of them admit to more than flirting?"

"Sure. He played a little tonsil hockey with a few of them and was more than happy to spank the naughty ones. That's another thing that's big with Santas—spanking."

"That I could have told you," Wolfe said. "I had one show me her paddle. She was very proud of it."

"Nobody would admit to jumping our vic's bones. Nobody caught his real name, either, but that's no surprise—during the rampage, everyone refers to everyone else as Santa. There are individual variations—Spanky Claus, Santa Ho—but those are generally used between friends. Our vic apparently went by the name Santa Shaky."

"He get into trouble with any of the other Santas?"

"If he did, nobody's talking."

Wolfe signaled the waitress for more coffee. "Well, hopefully we'll know more once we figure out who this guy is. Could be his death had nothing to do with the other Santas."

Tripp nodded. "Might not even be a homicide.
Guy could have just stroked out—maybe even in
midstroke."

"And his partner either didn't notice or freaked
out and ran away," Wolfe said. "Either way—not
very nice."

"How's it going on the forensic front?"

Wolfe stirred his coffee and suppressed another
yawn. "Well, I'll be heading straight to the lab after
this—I've got a lot of material to go through. Fiber
samples, beard samples, boot casts, plus I found evidence of sexual activity so I've got to talk to Valera
about DNA. And we won't have a cause of death
until Alexx performs the autopsy."

"I'm gonna take a closer look at our list of suspects, run 'em for priors, see if any of 'em stands
out." Tripp stood up, pulled out his wallet, and
tossed a few bills on the table. "Coffee's on me. I'll
see you later, all right?"

"Sure." *I'll be the one*, Wolfe thought as Tripp
strode out the door, *draped over the microscope,
asleep.*

Chester Cypress used an airboat to ferry Delko to
the spot where the Miccosukee had found the
body. "I guess I could have left it where I found it,"
he told the CSI, speaking loudly to be heard above
the racket of the boat's prop, "but what if a gator
stole it before I got back? I'd look like I was making
up stories."

"You sure you can find the exact same spot?" Delko asked.

Chester Cypress just nodded. Delko supposed he'd have to trust him.

The channel they'd been following through the saw grass led into the undergrowth, the knobby knees of cypress roots jutting up like the black legs of giant, half-submerged crabs. It was cooler in the shade, but the temperature was still in the high seventies and climbing.

Even in the bright sunshine of midmorning, the swamp felt haunted. Spanish moss hung from the dead branches of trees like decaying lace shawls draped over bone, as they moved slowly through thick, silty black water that gave no hint to its depth. The racket of the airboat's fan obscured all natural sounds, providing a kind of surreal white noise that buried insect chatter and birdsong. Brilliant shafts of sunlight would occasionally break through the overhead canopy, dazzling the eyes and deepening the surrounding shadows.

Eventually, Chester Cypress killed the engine. After the roar of the prop, the silence seemed overpowering.

The boat bumped against a dead log jutting from the bank. "See that mark, right there?" Chester pointed to a cut emblazoned on the log. "That's where I found him, floating right next to that log."

Delko nodded. "Okay. I just want to take a look

around, see if there's anything obvious. If not, I'll have to dive."

"Ah. You want me to do anything?"

"You have a rifle, right?"

Chester nodded.

"I'd appreciate it if you'd keep an eye out for gators while I'm in the water," Delko said. "My superiors tend to get a little upset when one of us gets eaten."

Chester shrugged. "I can do that. Seems kinda strange, though. Shouldn't you have a partner watching your back?"

"What can I say—it's the holidays. Everybody's busy. And no offense, but riding shotgun on a swamp boat isn't that high on anyone's list of priorities."

Delko looked around, trying to envision what had happened. Was it a body dump, or had the John Doe died here? If the vic had been taken out here in a boat, there was no way to backtrack it . . .

Delko unpacked his camera gear, then clambered out of the boat and onto the shore. He bent down and examined the surface of the log. A muddy footprint was barely visible on the mossy surface; he took a picture of it.

"You didn't get out of the boat when you retrieved the body, did you?" he asked Chester.

"Nope."

Okay, so someone—maybe the vic, maybe someone

*else, stood here. Let's assume it was John Doe, and he's
got some kind of explosive around his neck or stuffed into
his mouth. The bomb goes off, the body falls in the water.*

He checked tree trunks at head-height, looking
for blast damage. Nothing obvious, but the closest
tree was a good fifteen feet away; a small charge
might not have left any visible charring.

Shrapnel, though, was another matter . . .

He started a closer examination of all the trunks
in the immediate vicinity, working outward in a
spiraling radius. Anything that had gone into the
water, the mud, or the undergrowth was probably
gone forever, but the solid wood of a living tree
was a much better medium.

He found what he was looking for around six
feet off the ground in the bole of a mangrove tree.
He took a few pictures, then pried it out carefully
with a small knife.

"Whatcha find?" Chester called out. "Bullet?"

Delko put his discovery into an evidence envelope. "Not sure. Might be an incisor, might be a
molar."

"A *tooth*? For real?"

"Unless the guy wore dentures, yeah," Delko
said, grinning.

"Wow. How'd you know it was up there?"

"Sorry, I can't really discuss details of the case.
I probably shouldn't have told you that much."
Still, he thought, *I'm about to trust the guy with keep-
ing me safe from large carnivorous reptiles. Better not to*

tick him off. "Let's just say I used deductive reasoning and a knowledge of blast mechanics, all right?"

"Yeah? Wow," Chester said again. He sounded impressed.

So the vic had his head blown off here. And his hands, too? Alexx said she thought his arms had chemical burns on them, but was that done pre- or postmortem? Was it a result of the explosion, or something different?

He peered down at the water and sighed. It was going to be next to impossible to see anything down there, but he had to try.

"All right, I'm going to suit up," he told Chester.

A few minutes later he slid into the water. Chester had poled its depth to around ten feet, but the amount of debris and algae in the water blocked a great deal of the light. What filtered through was green and murky; by the time he was on the bottom, he felt as if he were a hundred feet from the surface.

Shadows and silt swirled around him like a living particulate cloud. The bottom was littered with dead logs and rocks; he picked his way through carefully, shining his wrist-mounted light into every hollow and crevice.

He came upon the boat around twenty feet from the bank. It was a battered aluminum skiff, with a jagged hole in its bottom and charring around the edges. Delko could tell it hadn't been there long.

The boat itself held nothing except a long pole

wedged under one seat and a few rocks that looked as if they'd been placed there for weight.

Maybe the bomb that destroyed John Doe's head also sank the boat. So it might not be a murder—it could be an accident.

Delko didn't know. What he did know was that he'd have to get the sunken skiff back to the lab and take a closer look at it. *Hope Chester doesn't mind helping me haul this up; not really his job, after all.*

But then, guarding a CSI wasn't, either, and so far he hadn't seemed to mind that. Chester Cypress was at home in the swamp, but Delko was showing him things he hadn't seen before; no matter how much you thought you knew, a CSI could always reveal something you didn't . . .

4

THE MOST IMPORTANT PIECE OF EVIDENCE against Abdus Sattar Pathan, Calleigh knew, would be the fingerprint he'd left on the magazine. By waving it around in front of the security camera, Pathan had provided visual evidence he'd handled it just before the assault; once she had his fingerprint from the magazine itself, Pathan wouldn't be able to claim he was being framed by some unknown criminal.

There were a number of techniques for lifting prints. Often, the method employed was dictated by the surface the print was on. For high-gloss paper like that of the magazine, Calleigh knew just what was called for.

The device she selected resembled a slim Maglite flashlight, made of black anodized aluminum. A short cylinder projected from the flared end, like an oversize metal bulb; it held a powerful rare-earth magnet inside. A small, inverted cone projected from the opposite end of the device.

She poured a small amount of Magneta Flake, an iron powder coated with amino acids, onto a piece of paper, then stuck the cylinder end of the applicator into it. Immediately, a spiky head of particles formed around the cylinder. She lifted it off the paper, then carefully dusted the print with it, barely grazing the surface with the fuzzy metallic brush she'd created. When she was done, she held the applicator over the small pile of powder she'd first drawn from and pulled the cone-shaped handle on the butt end. The spring-loaded internal magnet moved away from the tip, causing the powder to drop from the cylinder.

She got a gel-lifter from the lab's fridge—gel was better for materials like printed paper, where a stronger adhesive might lift ink as well as the print, but it needed to be kept refrigerated. Once she'd lifted the print, she used the lab's scanner to enter it into the system.

And suddenly, her day got a lot worse.

"H," Calleigh said, "you are not going to believe this."

Horatio glanced at his CSI and raised his eyebrows. "Oh? What's going on?"

He and Calleigh were in the main lab, looking at the fingerprint data from the Pathan case.

Calleigh had the information up on one of the big flat-screen monitors.

"Okay, I dusted the magazine from the convenience store for prints. I ran the security video again, and you can clearly see Pathan's right thumb pressed against the page. The magazine is open at that point, and the image is fairly clear."

"Not to mention revealing," Horatio said.

"Yes, the young lady in question doesn't seem to have a problem with shyness. Her turn-offs include narrow-minded people, polyester, and men who chew with their mouths open. I doubt if any of those things inspired the attack, though."

"And the problem is?"

"The problem is that I matched the image on-screen to page one seventy-three of the magazine and found a nice big thumbprint right where it should be. No other prints on the page."

"And?"

"And it's not Pathan's."

Horatio frowned. "How is that possible?"

"I don't know. Maybe I picked up the wrong magazine from the scene."

"No. There was only one magazine on the floor, and it was the same one we saw in the video."

"Could the magazine have been switched after the fight? It wasn't in the frame of the camera while it was on the floor."

Horatio rubbed his jaw with one hand, thinking. "So while Pathan is lying there unconscious, someone else sneaks in and replaces a key piece of evidence? That makes even less sense."

"Maybe Pathan is telling the truth. The man in the video is someone else."

"That's certainly what his lawyer is going to claim . . . and right now, we can't prove otherwise." Horatio shook his head. "Something about this is very wrong. Our suspect refuses to have his finger-prints taken, then has an abrupt change of heart at the same time a fingerprint clears him of the crime?"

"Yeah. It stinks, doesn't it . . ."

"Yes, it does. Tell you what—let's take a look at the other evidence, shall we? The scarf, for in-stance. Maybe it can tell us something."

"All right—but if he's claiming the scarf was planted, then linking it to him won't necessarily do us much good."

Horatio narrowed his eyes. "You let me worry about that . . ."

"He recovered consciousness a few hours after he was brought in," the nurse behind the station said. She was Asian, with a broad, friendly face and rec-tangular, gold-rimmed glasses. "Broken nose, bruised windpipe, mild concussion. Some internal swelling of the brain tissue, but no bleeding. Skull is still in one piece, no stitches. We're keeping him a few more hours for observation, then he can go home."

"Has an officer been by to take his statement yet?" Horatio asked.

The nurse shook her head. "No. He got a phone call from his family, but no one's come by."

"Thank you. I'll try not to take too long."

Horatio walked down the hall to the room that held Talwinder Jhohal, the clerk who had been attacked in the convenience store. Jhohal was lying propped up in bed, a large white bandage covering his nose. Both his eyes were blackened, and dark purple bruises were visible on the brown skin of his throat.

"Are—are you the police?" he croaked in a rough-edged whisper.

Horatio produced his badge. "Lieutenant Horatio Caine, Mister Jhohal. I was wondering if you could tell me about last night."

Jhohal blinked, then shook his head. "I wish that I could. I can't remember anything about it."

"Really? Well, I understand you put up quite a struggle. Thanks to you, we have a suspect in custody. All we need to do is have you identify him—"

"No," Jhohal said curtly. "I'm sorry, I don't remember. Not a thing. I was working, and then I woke up here."

He glared at Horatio. Horatio met his eyes calmly, then dropped his gaze. He didn't want to antagonize his only witness.

"All right, Mister Jhohal. Partial amnesia isn't uncommon in these circumstances; hopefully, a little bed rest will restore your memory. But I should caution you—sometimes, once a witness starts to remember, they start thinking about taking matters into their own hands. That's never a good idea."

The look Jhohal gave him was more incredulous than offended. "You think I—? No. No, Lieutenant Caine. Believe me, the last thing on my mind is revenge. I will—I *would*—fight to defend what is mine, but that is all. I am not a warrior, and I do not wish to be one."

And beneath Jhohal's bitter tone Horatio heard something else, something that radically altered his line of reasoning.

Talwinder Jhohal wasn't angry.

He was *terrified*.

"Mister Jhohal, I can understand your reluctance—but as I said, we have the man who assaulted you in custody. And I can assure you, if you identify him he will stay there."

"I know you are only doing your job," Jhohal said, "and for that I do not fault you. But this"— he reached up to touch his bandaged nose—"will not kill me. It is not important. I must concentrate on the things that *are*—my life, my job, my family. You understand?" It came out almost as a plea.

"Not yet," Horatio said. "But I will . . ."

Delko showed up in the autopsy room wearing a pair of bright orange coveralls. Alexx frowned and said, "Excuse me? What *are* you wearing?"

Delko gave her an embarrassed grin. "Sorry. I was down in the garage looking at a boat I pulled out of the swamp—it's pretty mucky. When I got your call, I came straight up, didn't bother to change."

"Well, you can bother now. Show some respect—this isn't an auto shop."

"Okay, okay." He shucked out of the coveralls; his street clothes were underneath.

"If we're done with the fashion show?" Alexx said.

Delko slipped on a fresh pair of gloves. "All set."

Alexx pulled back the sheet that covered the body on the autopsy table—what there was of it. One leg ended at midthigh, the other just below the shin. The arms were both truncated at the same spot, halfway down the forearm. There was no head, no neck, and the flesh on the shoulders was charred and torn.

"Our John Doe is probably Hispanic, approximate age midforties. No visible tattoos or significant scars. COD was the explosion that removed the head; the extremities were all altered postmortem. The legs by animal predation, the hands by a chemical agent—an acid or corrosive of some kind. I've sent a sample to Trace."

"How about fragments of the bomb?"

"There were a few bits of plastic and metal embedded in the tissue of the trapezius; I collected them for you." She picked up a small plastic bag from the tray next to her and handed it over.

"Not much shrapnel." Homemade bombs frequently used nails or other bits of metal to increase the amount of damage they did.

"Didn't need it, I guess. Getting your head blown off by a bomb in the middle of a swamp—what a way to die."

"At least it was quick. Time of death?"

"Recent; a few days, maybe less. You want something more accurate, talk to an entomologist—I don't do bugs."

"Tox screen?"

"Not back yet. I didn't find any evidence of chronic disease or drug use—he was perfectly healthy as far as I can tell. Stomach contents were too degraded to identify visually, but I'm having them analyzed."

"All right. The bomb fragments should tell me what kind of explosive was used." Delko shook his head. "Won't tell me why, of course. Though it's starting to take on a certain South American flavor."

"You think it's drug-related?"

"I wouldn't be surprised. Colombian guerrillas have been known to use necklace bombs; someone in the cocaine trade could have borrowed the technique. It's the kind of thing drug lords like to use to send a message."

"But Eric, he was found in the middle of nowhere. We still don't know who he is. Who's supposed to get this message—the alligators?"

"I don't know, Alexx. But somebody, some-where, has to be looking for this guy."

Alexx covered the body up again. "Yes," she said quietly. "But they're not going to have much of a Christmas when they find him."

Horatio punched in the number of the county pros-ecutor's office by memory, then asked for the proper extension.

"Hello?"

"Alison? Hi, it's Horatio Caine." Alison Schoen-hauer was a prosecuting attorney who Horatio had worked with before. She was good at her job, pos-sessed boundless energy and was bluntly honest. Horatio stared down at the report in his hands, then tossed it onto his desk. "You're handling the Pathan case, aren't you?"

"Uh, haven't had a chance to look at the file, yet. Just a sec."

Horatio waited while she rummaged around.

"Okay, I got it . . . sorry, it's been kind of crazy around here. I'm going to the Bahamas for Christ-mas and I'm trying to get my workload organized before I leave. Anyway, what's up? Looks like a slam dunk to me."

"Well, something's come up. The perp's claim-ing he didn't do it—that he was knocked out from behind by the real assailant, who then planted in-criminating evidence at the scene."

Alison chuckled. "Sure. The file says the security camera caught the whole thing—wait. Tell me you still have the footage."

Horatio pinched the bridge of his nose between a thumb and forefinger. "We have the footage, but the face of the assailant is hidden by a scarf—"

"Which you *also* have, right?"

"Yes—"

"And, being a scarf, it's picked up all kinds of things, right? Hairs, fibers, bits of leftover breakfast? Maybe even some of his DNA?"

"He claims the scarf was planted on him while he was unconscious."

"So? He can claim any dumb-ass thing he wants in court—I'm sure the judge has heard every screwball story there is. C'mon, Horatio, I've got things to do."

So he told her about the fingerprint, Pathan's reluctance and sudden reversal of attitude.

There was a long pause while she considered it, then a loud expulsion of breath. "Hoo, boy. So what happened?"

"I honestly don't know," Horatio said. "But I was at the scene myself, and I can tell you one thing for sure: no mistakes were made in gathering or processing the evidence."

"That's a shame. Because losing that fingerprint, in light of all the other evidence, is not exactly the worst thing that could happen."

"I won't tamper with evidence, Alison."

"Of course not. But if our friend Pathan is

pulling a fast one, then he certainly understands the significance of that fingerprint and won't hesitate to use it in court. And if you can't prove it was faked, we don't have a case. Actually, it's worse than that—the fingerprint proves Pathan's innocent. Which, despite the unlikelihood of his story, I have to consider."

"He's not," Horatio said. "I talked to the man he assaulted, but apparently not soon enough; the victim refused to give a statement, claimed he couldn't remember anything. Somebody got to him first, Alison—he was scared out of his wits."

"So even our vic won't come forward? Horatio, I can't put this in front of a judge. He'll kick it so fast the guy'll bounce all the way to civil court. Then we're talking lawsuit for false arrest, and that's not going to do either of our careers any good."

"I know, I know. But his story is thin, we still have the security footage, there may even be blood on the scarf—"

"Not good enough, Horatio. If the clerk won't ID him, then the fingerprint is more than enough to create reasonable doubt. Let him go."

Horatio paused.

"You still there?" Alison asked.

"Yeah," Horatio said quietly. "Have a good time on vacation."

He hung up.

*   *   *

In the basement garage of the crime lab, Delko went over the aluminum skiff carefully. The seat of the blast was in the stern, and the direction the metal had buckled in clearly showed that the bomb had been inside the boat when it detonated.

He scraped samples from the charred edges of the hole. It would probably match the explosive used on the vic, but it was always best to be sure. As with the first bomb, there was little evidence of shrapnel damage.

The sophistication of the device would tell Delko a lot about the person who'd made it. One of the simplest bombs to make was a pipe bomb, which you could build by pouring the black powder from a few shotgun shells into a pipe, closing off the ends, and adding a fuse. When the powder ignited, it quickly produced a large volume of gas, which was compressed inside the pipe. But only for an instant—once the walls of the pipe gave way, the compressed gas expanded, generating a shock wave that moved at close to seven thousand miles an hour. A black-powder bomb was classed as a low explosive; while it was sensitive to heat and friction, making it somewhat dangerous to transport or store, it didn't require a primer and almost anyone could make one.

High explosives—such as TNT, PETN, or RDX—could generate a shock wave that moved at nearly seven thousand meters per second. They were harder to obtain and required a primer to deto-

nate, but were more stable to handle. He didn't
think he was dealing with that kind of firepower,
though; the damage just wasn't extensive enough.

Chemical analysis would tell him, one way or
the other. He was more interested in the activation
device, what actually set the bomb off. Almost all
bombers came up with their own unique variation,
which they tended to use over and over; this was
known as their signature.

Unfortunately, between the swamp and the explosion, little of the activator had survived the
blast that had sunk the boat. He would have to
concentrate on the fragments that Alexx had retrieved from the DB.

First, though, he did his best to find any kind of
identifying marks on the boat. An aluminum boat
had to have been manufactured; therefore, there
should be the equivalent of a serial number somewhere on it.

He found it stamped into the port gunwale, near
the oarlock. There was no manufacturer's name,
though, just a number.

*Looks like I'm hitting the nautical databases. At least
it's something . . .*

When Abdus Sattar Pathan walked out the front
doors of the Miami-Dade Pre-Trial Detention Center,
Horatio was waiting for him.

"Mister Pathan," Horatio said coolly.

"Lieutenant Caine." Pathan had his coat draped

over one arm. "Are you here to offer an apology?"

Horatio's smile barely justified the word. "I don't think so. I just came by to tell you this isn't over."

"I'm glad to hear it. Whoever attacked me—and that poor shopkeeper—certainly must be brought to justice."

"I couldn't agree more. At the moment, he's no doubt congratulating himself on how clever he is—but that won't last."

"No?"

"No. You see, I've dealt with his kind before. He's thinking he's gotten away with it. The witness isn't talking, the evidence won't stand up in court—besides, it's not like anyone was killed, right? All he has to do is keep his head down, and all this will blow over."

"I hate to contradict you, Lieutenant—but that sounds like a fairly accurate assessment to me."

"It's not." Horatio pulled his sunglasses out of his pocket, unfolded one arm of them, then the other. He paused, holding the shades in both hands, turning them over as if they were a rare artifact he was studying. "You see, I'm not satisfied. A man wound up in the hospital, through no fault of his own, and the criminal that put him there is now walking the streets. That kind of arrogance and contempt for human life is not something I take lightly."

Horatio looked up and met Pathan's eyes. Pathan stared back steadily, his expression unreadable.

"I applaud your commitment, Lieutenant. I'm sure you will need it for an opponent as devious as this . . . *criminal* . . . seems to be."

"He's not an opponent, Mister Pathan. He's just another felon who thinks he can beat the system. They've got a word for people like him in Vegas."

"Which is?"

"A loser, Mister Pathan." Horatio slipped on his sunglasses. "A loser."

Horatio turned and walked away. He'd only taken three steps when Pathan called after him. "Lieutenant Caine!"

Horatio turned halfway, glanced over his shoulder.

"I'm not unfamiliar with Vegas myself; I've played there many a time. I don't gamble, of course."

Horatio waited.

"I'm sure you'll want to keep me updated on your progress." Pathan unfolded his coat and slipped it over his shoulders. "You have my address, but my personal cell number is on my business card."

"That won't be necessary."

"Just in case. Right-hand pocket," Pathan said briskly, then strode down the steps and away.

Horatio stared after him for a moment, then reached into the right-hand pocket of his suit jacket.

The card he pulled out was black, the printing in silver.

"'The Brilliant Batin,'" he read out loud. "'Amazing feats of skill and prestidigitation. Cruise ships a specialty . . .'"

He glanced up sharply.

Pathan was gone.

The rowboat turned out to be manufactured by a small company named Effundo Enterprises. Delko traced the serial number to the boatyard that had sold it, over twenty years ago, to a man named Christopher Silverbeck. Silverbeck had died two months ago, and his estate had sold the boat through the marina where Silverbeck had a live-aboard. When Delko tried calling the marina, all he got was voice mail. He wasn't surprised; over the holidays, some businesses ran on a skeleton staff, while others were so overworked they didn't have time to answer the phone. A marina, he supposed, could be either—residents and employees might be visiting relatives, leaving the place deserted, or it could be crammed with tourists looking for a tropical Christmas vacation.

"Uh—hello?" The speaker was a young man with short brown hair, standing in the doorway. He wore a lab tech's white coat with L. FRANKEL stitched on the breast and had large, worried-looking eyes.

Delko was examining a fragment of the bomb under a microscope. He looked up and said, "Yeah? What can I do for you?"

Frankel stepped inside and held out a file folder. "Trace told me to bring these to you. Results on that explosive you wanted analyzed?"

"Thanks." Delko took the folder and flipped it open. "Hm. That's what I thought."

"Pipe bomb, right?"

Delko gave the tech a friendly nod and smile. Frankel was new, and a little overeager, but he seemed like an all right guy. "Yeah, straight black powder. The kind of thing kids make out of firecrackers or ammo they stole from their dad's closet."

"Yes. Munitions are very interesting," Frankel said, his head bobbing nervously. "When Alfred Nobel created dynamite in 1866, he used twelve percent nitroglycyerin and seventy-eight percent sodium nitrate, which of course is nothing like today's dynamite, or more properly, gelignite, so-called because it's a gel composed of ammonium nitrate mixed with guar gum, or a hydrocarbon base with added resin, glass, or ceramic microspheres. It can give you a headache. If you absorb it through your skin."

After this outburst, Frankel suddenly went quiet. He blinked at Delko with large, watery eyes, reminding him of a dog convinced he's done something wrong, but not sure what.

"Uh, yeah," Delko said, his smile even wider. "You know a lot about explosives?"

"I do. I was directing a great deal of my energy

toward a career on the bomb squad, as a matter of fact."

"Really. What changed your mind?"

"Oh, I just lost interest. I didn't find it challenging enough."

"Right . . . well, there's more than enough challenges around here. Welcome aboard."

"Thank you. Good-bye." Frankel spun around and left.

Makes Wolfe seem normal, Delko thought.

He went back to studying the fragments of the bomb. Either the timer hadn't survived or there hadn't been one; he had some metal shards that looked as if they came from the pipe, a shred of duct tape, a tiny piece of plastic with no discernible purpose.

Pretty low-tech. Whoever made this, they probably didn't have a lot of experience in blowing things up.

The next thing he took a look at was the chemical residue from John Doe's arms. He ran it through the mass spectrometer, which identified it as a mix of hypochloric acid and sodium hydroxide, with trace amounts of cellulose.

"Lye and a sodium salt," he murmured. "Household drain cleaner, in other words." Again, easy to get—but highly effective. Lye was strong enough to eat through a metal can in a few hours and could easily corrode a corpse's hands away. With all the plant matter in a swamp, trace amounts of cellulose were to be expected.

Next, he pulled out the length of chain that had been wrapped around the vic's body. It looked like the kind you could buy at any hardware store by the foot, and there was a lot of it; obviously, it was supposed to have kept the body weighted down and on the bottom. *Some of the coils must have slipped off when the gators took an interest,* Delko thought. The links were too small to hold a print, and the links on the end—where he hoped to find a tool mark—weren't cut at all. The last link must have dropped off, or maybe it was still back at the hardware store.

He went over every link anyway, hoping to find something, anything, that might give him a clue. He found mud, bits of vegetation, and three fibers: the mud matched the area the vic was found in, the plant matter ditto. The fibers all came from the clothes the vic had been wearing, a nondescript T-shirt and cheap jeans.

So far, John Doe was keeping his secrets.

5

"HEY, RYAN," CALLEIGH SAID BRIGHTLY, strolling into the lab. "How's it going?"

Wolfe lifted his head from where he had slumped over the light table. "Too. Much. *Santa*," he groaned.

"So I heard. H told me to come by and give you a hand. And I promise, I will resist making any comments on the festive nature of the evidence."

"Don't make promises you can't keep," Wolfe said. "I mean, don't get me wrong, I appreciate the help—but so far, *nobody*'s been able to resist making Santa cracks. It's like some kind of highly contagious *virus*."

"Like Ebola, but jollier?"

"Exactly." He eyed her suspiciously. "You'll succumb. No one is immune."

"Not even Horatio? I can't see H making bad puns about reindeer."

"If he does, my head'll explode," Wolfe said gloomily.

"Well, hopefully things won't go that far. What are you working on right now?"

"Fibers. Between Santa suits, Santa beards, and various Santa accessories, I've got a few hundred to process. I'm about halfway through the suits."

"All right. How about you finish those up, and I start on the chinwear?"

"Fine by me."

They got to work. Every sample had to have a single strand isolated for comparison; it was a long, tedious process, and Wolfe was glad for the assistance.

"So, Ryan—any plans for the holidays?" Calleigh used a pair of tweezers to carefully pick out a strand from a sample.

"Not really. See the family, open presents, eat too much unhealthy food—you know, the usual." He yawned. " 'Scuse me."

"Sure. I'm gonna spend it with my dad, I guess."

"I guess? You don't sound too sure."

"Well—holidays are one of the times recovering alcoholics tend to fall off the wagon, you know? I don't really look forward to spending Christmas trying to stay between him and the eggnog."

Wolfe stopped what he was doing and looked over at Calleigh. "Must be hard."

She shrugged. "It's family. You do what you have to."

There was an uncomfortable pause. "Uh—man,

haven't these Santas ever heard of natural fabrics?" Wolfe said. "All I'm getting is polyester and nylon."

"Yeah, I'm getting a lot of artificial fibers myself. I suppose it's too much to ask for our suspect to have worn a beard made of real hair?"

"No, the hairs I pulled off the body were a synthetic polymer called Kanekalon, a modacrylic often used for wigs, toys, or fake fur. But I also found fibers of viscose rayon—and something I haven't identified yet."

"Well, there are only twenty-seven kinds of fibers that compose fabric," Calleigh said. "Four natural—silk, wool, cotton, and linen—and twenty-three man-made. If it came from an article of clothing, it has to be one of those."

"Yeah, but those twenty-seven kinds can be blended in any number of combinations," Wolfe said. "I can ID it, no problem—I just haven't had the time yet."

"We'll get there. Even Santa can't get away with murder."

"Especially since they passed that antistocking law."

"Ryan!"

"Sorry. Guess I'm not immune, either . . ."

The marina was called Barry's Boathome, on the north side of Biscayne Bay. No one was in the trailer that housed the office, but Delko found someone out back, in the Hurricane-fenced dry dock area.

Boats of all sizes and shapes were stored there, from two-person skiffs to sixty-foot cabin cruisers. A squat, gray-haired man wearing a stained pair of bib overalls was jockeying the prongs of a large forklift under the hull of a Boston whaler when Delko walked up.

"Excuse me," Delko called out.

The driver of the forklift stopped what he was doing and squinted at Delko. He had the kind of broad, bulging features that looked as if he'd gotten his head caught in a vise at some point; apparently, the experience had soured his outlook as well. "What?" he demanded.

"Miami-Dade Crime Lab," Delko said, holding up his ID. "I'd like to ask you a few questions."

"Yeah, yeah, just a sec." The man adjusted the forklift's controls, then shut it off. He climbed down from the seat, pulled off a greasy pair of gloves, and stuck them in a pocket of the overalls. "Whatta ya want?" he asked brusquely.

Delko refrained from retorting, *A little civility would be nice.* "I understand you sold this boat recently," Delko said, pulling out a photo. He handed it over.

The man studied it, then grunted. "Yeah, sure, Silverbeck's boat. Unloaded it a few days ago. Why?"

"I'm trying to track down the person you sold it to. Who was it?"

"Don't know. Some guy that answered the ad.

Only relative Silverbeck had was a sister on the West Coast, and she didn't want an old skiff. Got a hundred bucks for it."

"The person I talked to said you didn't provide a receipt."

"So? Guy paid cash. Mattera fact, he told me he didn't *want* no receipt. I didn't argue."

Course not, Delko thought. *Guy probably paid you extra to skip any paperwork, and that went straight into your pocket.* "Sure. Want to know something interesting about the State of Florida?"

"I ain't got time for a history lesson—"

"Lot of people retire here, everybody knows that. What most people never think about is that means a lot of people *die* here, too. A lot of wills go through probate in Florida—and as a result, our rules and regulations about that are pretty detailed. You want to know how much trouble you can get in for breaking any of those rules?"

"Hey, I wasn't . . ."

"See, people tend to be pretty sensitive about things like that. They've just lost a loved one, they're all charged up emotionally, and then someone comes along and tries to take advantage? It can get pretty ugly. . . . Of course, I'm sure you didn't do anything wrong."

The man glared at him, but Delko could sense his anger was mainly there to hide his nervousness. "I woulda gotta receipt, I'd known it was such a big deal."

"Well, it doesn't have to be," Delko said. "All I care about is finding the person you sold the boat to. The sooner I get to talk to him, the less likely you are to ever see my face again."

It was amazing how much more cooperative the man became after that—though it didn't do Delko that much good. The man had been Hispanic, in his midforties, dressed in a well-to-do middle-class sort of way, and had paid cash. He hadn't given his name, and he'd taken possession of the boat by simply rowing it away. He'd headed south, but there were any number of beaches or marinas in that direction where he could have transferred it to a vehicle without anyone noticing—the boat was small enough to fit in the back of a pickup or even on the roof of a car.

Other than that, the forklift driver had given him only one other piece of information, and Delko wasn't sure how useful it was going to be. "He looked kinda—unfocused," the driver told him.

"Unfocused? You mean intoxicated?"

"Nah, it wasn't like he was on anything. Just not really there, y'know? Like he had a lot on his mind. Distracted, I guess. Maybe he forgot to do his Christmas shopping."

Maybe, Delko thought. *Or maybe he was thinking about something a lot more deadly . . .*

Horatio hated being played.

He was used to being lied to; that just went with

the job. He dealt with people who thought they could get away with murder all the time. But that wasn't the same—they were all trying to beat the system, and he just happened to be the representative they'd been unlucky enough to attract. His job was to separate fact from fiction, and with the assistance of his team that was exactly what he did.

But every now and then, someone made the mistake of trying to manipulate Horatio himself.

Usually, they failed. Horatio's intellect was surpassed only by his self-control; trying to get him to lose his cool was like trying to burn through a bank vault with a magnifying glass.

But he could be fooled.

It didn't happen often, and never for long. Proof was proof, and sooner or later he or his team would uncover what there was; if there was one unshakable principle Horatio based his life on, that was it. Evidence could be tampered with, but you couldn't destroy the truth. He believed that, he really did.

But he was only human. And unlike the truth, sometimes human beings got things wrong.

Pathan had tricked him. And what was worse, he'd used the evidence to do so. Horatio's own work had freed the man, a man Horatio now suspected was guilty. And that was—almost—the worst part; that he only *suspected* Pathan was guilty. It meant Horatio not only had to question his own judgment, but his competence, too—*and* Calleigh's.

Casting doubt on Horatio was one thing. Casting

it on a member of his team was another thing altogether . . . a very, very *bad* thing.

And then there was the business card.

It had been very slick, how Pathan had managed to get it into his pocket without him noticing. And it had conveyed a message far more profound than Pathan's phone number or address. What it had said, simply, was this: *I'm smarter than you are. And I don't care whether or not you know it.*

Horatio sat behind the wheel of his Hummer, the motor idling, holding the card in one hand. Just looking at it.

He smiled. "Okay," he said softly.

The card went into his breast pocket, next to his sunglasses. He put the Hummer in gear and drove away.

Calleigh and Wolfe tackled the footwear last, and it didn't take long. They eliminated a bunch simply by size or tread, leaving only a few to actually examine.

"And the lucky Mrs. Claus is . . ." Wolfe said.

"Valerie . . . oh, no. This can't be right."

"What?"

Calleigh handed the list over with an apologetic look, and said, "I know what it looks like, but I *swear* I didn't put this in as a joke—"

Wolfe ran his finger down the list. "Valerie . . . Blitzen. You *can't* be serious."

Calleigh put her hands palm-up and gave an exaggerated shrug.

"Our dead Santa was mounted by a *reindeer*?" Wolfe said. "If this is Tripp's idea of funny—"

"Oh, come on," Calleigh said. "You know as well as I do that Frank would never mess around with evidence. And Blitzen is a perfectly good surname. Life imitates art, right?"

Wolfe sighed. "I guess . . ." He checked the list again and frowned. "But something doesn't add up. Blitzen wasn't wearing a wig—but there are definitely artificial hair fibers here."

"From what I've heard, the Santas are a pretty touchy-feely bunch," Calleigh said. "Lots of hugging and lap-sitting. Our vic could have picked up transfer from all kinds of sources."

"That's true," Wolfe admitted. "I guess the next step is to bring Ms. Blitzen in for questioning."

"Yes. Let's do that."

He stared at her suspiciously.

"That's it," she said. "Bring in the suspect. Interview her."

"All right, then."

"And if she has an alibi, there's always Donner and Dancer and Prancer and . . ."

"I knew it," Wolfe said, throwing up his hands in despair. "No one is immune. Excuse me while I go find some tinsel to hang myself from."

"Vixen, can't forget about her—I hear she's a real tramp—Comet and Cupid and of course Rudolph— *he's* probably the ringleader . . ."

Wolfe walked out the door while she was still ticking them off on her fingers.

Doctor Alexx Woods had a love/hate relationship with Christmas.

On one hand, she loved spending time with her family. She loved the look on her kids' faces as they opened their presents, and she loved the little rituals and traditions that she and her husband had created over the years—like watching the old, black-and-white version of *A Christmas Carol* over the holidays, the one with Alastair Sim. The scene where he danced around, ecstatic that he's been given another chance, never failed to make her laugh. "Now *that*," she was fond of saying to her husband as Scrooge stood on his head, "is one *seriously* happy man. He may be crazy, but he's having a ball."

And her husband would smile and put his arm around her and say, "He ain't got nothing on me, baby."

What she didn't love was the mess. Christmas wrapping, pine needles, nutshells, orange peels, cookie crumbs, and spilled eggnog. She hated a messy house almost as much as she hated a messy workspace, and the holidays meant she was always either cleaning or telling somebody else to. She always heaved a small sigh of relief when January finally arrived, even though it made her feel a little Scrooge-like herself.

But Scrooge hadn't valued the important people in his life. Alexx did, and she never let herself forget how important they were. Every corpse that crossed her autopsy table reminded her of how precious life was, and how easily it could be lost.

Looking through her notes on the John Doe found in the 'Glades, she was suddenly, acutely aware of just how much it was possible to lose. John Doe hadn't just lost his life, he'd lost his identity, his history; those who might mourn him didn't even know he was dead. He was as disconnected from humanity as Scrooge had been, a ghost without even a tombstone to gaze at.

She left her office, walked over to the body drawers and opened John Doe's. Most people would have seen the headless torso with its mutilated stumps as grisly, but to Alexx it just looked sad.

"Nobody should be *this* alone," she said. "I'll bet you have a family somewhere, don't you? I'll bet there's presents under a tree right now, with your name on them. I sure wish I knew what it was . . ."

Tripp and Wolfe conducted the interview of Valerie Blitzen. She was a young, attractive brunette with long, curly hair, a nice tan, and a hangover. She stared at them through bloodshot eyes, taking slow, careful sips from the water bottle she clutched in one hand. She was dressed in pajama pants and an oversize gray sweatshirt, and huddled in her chair with her knees drawn up.

"Miss . . . do you mind if I call you Valerie?" Wolfe began. Tripp was already hunched forward in his seat, elbows on the table, staring at his suspect like a hungry bulldog at a bone.

"Whatever," she said weakly. "Let's just get this over with, okay?"

"Not feeling too good?" Tripp asked. "You look a little queasy."

"I'm all right." She tried to smile. "Just waiting for the painkillers to kick in."

"Too much holiday cheer can do that to you," Wolfe said. "Especially on an empty stomach."

"Oh, there was plenty to eat. We always make sure we have a food stop scheduled along the way. We stopped at this great deli place—they *love* Santa there. I just overdid it on the Elf Steroids."

"Elf Steroids?" Wolfe asked.

"Shots of pure grain alcohol and eggnog. Short but powerful."

"Uh-huh," Tripp said. "Guess a few of those would loosen you right up, huh?"

She blinked and managed to give the impression that her eyelashes hurt. "You could say that, yeah."

"So much so that you found yourself in a snowbank with a dead man?" Wolfe asked. "We matched a bootprint next to the dead Santa with the boots you were wearing—and we found DNA from a sexual encounter. When we test yours, are we going to find a match?"

She put her hands over her face and groaned. A muffled "Yes" escaped.

"You want to tell us about it?" Wolfe prompted.

"Not really, no . . ."

"Would you prefer to go to jail?"

Her hands came down. "Look, it was just a spur-of-the-moment thing. All the Santas were partying, we were at the rink, and me and Santa Shaky had been sort of flirting for a while. Then he comes up and says he's found some actual snow—so I followed him out a side door. Next thing I knew, we were rolling around in it. He ripped off his top and started rubbing snow all over his chest—kept telling me how *good* it felt."

"Guess those Santa suits are pretty warm, huh?"

"Oh, yeah. It's worse for the guys in the full getup—at least I got to wear a skirt. He was so hot that when he lay down in the snow, steam came off him . . ."

"So one thing led to another."

"Yeah. But I guess he'd had too much to drink, because he—well, he threw up. Right in the middle."

"He threw up while you were engaged in intercourse?" Wolfe asked.

"Yeah. If he'd been on top, it would've been—I don't even want to think about it."

"So you just got up and walked away?"

"More like staggered. I was pretty wasted."

"And you weren't worried he might have asphyxiated on his own vomit?" Wolfe asked.

"Is—is that what killed him? Oh, God. I swear, he was alive when I left. I could hear him puking when I went back inside—I thought he'd be okay. I didn't tell anyone else because . . . well, it's embarrassing, you know? I never had a guy do *that* before."

"I wouldn't take it personally, if I were you," Tripp said.

"And as for cause of death, we haven't determined that yet," Wolfe said. "So no one else knew you and he were outside together?"

"I guess someone could have seen us leave. I'm pretty sure nobody saw me come back in, though."

Wolfe and Tripp glanced at each other, and Tripp shrugged.

"Okay, that about wraps it up for now," Wolfe said. "We'll be in touch once the autopsy's finished and the lab results have come back." He hesitated. "Just one thing, though. Why Santa?"

She gave him a wary look. "You mean, why did I . . ."

"Get jolly?" Tripp offered.

"No, no," Wolfe said. "I mean, the whole Santarchy thing. Why do you do it? Is it just an excuse to put on a costume and get drunk?"

She studied him for a second, then decided he was genuinely interested. "That's not it. Well, some of it, sure, but not all. The real reason is simple: *everyone* loves Santa . . ."

"You would know," Tripp said under his breath.

"But what about the kids?" Wolfe said. "I mean, doesn't it bother you that you're portraying Santa as a drunken pack of party animals?"

She sighed. "First of all, we don't mess around with kids. Any of the mutant toys we give to children are kid-friendly. Second, we only get really crazy late at night or in bars, where there shouldn't be any kids, anyway. And third—how old were you when you found out Santa wasn't real?"

The question caught Wolfe off guard. "I don't know—seven or eight, I guess."

"You remember how you felt?"

"Actually, I do. At first I was angry and wouldn't believe it, and then I was really sad."

"That's how a lot of people remember it. See, we have all these little myths about Santa we tell our kids, all these rituals—putting out stockings, leaving milk and cookies, making a list—and all of it is really designed for just one thing: to convince us he's real. But he *isn't.* And there's no corresponding ritual to let us know that, no ritual to let us know that Mommy and Daddy have been fibbing to us our whole lives. Don't you think that's kind of screwed up?"

Wolfe frowned. "I never really thought about it like that before."

"Yeah, well, I'm not saying that's the purpose of Santacon. I'm just saying that as far as sacred cows go, a fat guy in a red suit that symbolizes spending lots of money while lying to your kids isn't an icon I think deserves a lot of respect. Of course, a lot of pagans would disagree with me—but that's a whole 'nother rant, and I just want to go home and go to bed. Okay?"

"You're free to go," Tripp said. "Merry Christmas."

She stood up and gave him a weak but genuine smile. "Merry Christmas to you, too."

Natalia Boa Vista was lead scientist for the Justice Project, a federally funded program designed to re-examine cold cases in the light of DNA evidence and new technology. The project was headquartered out of the Miami-Dade Crime Lab, and government money had paid for refurbishing much of the building as the scope of its responsibilities expanded. That made Natalia both popular and unpopular; while most of the lab's workers appreciated the new facilities and equipment, the DNA lab was now a much bigger player in the internal politics that went, inevitably, with any bureaucracy. Natalia was, by nature, outgoing and friendly, but she was passionately dedicated to her cause and wouldn't back down from a fight. She'd already ticked off several people in the power structure, which usually caused Horatio to give her an amused nod when he passed her in the hall. She got the sense he enjoyed how she was stirring things up.

One person she didn't have a lot of experience

with, though, was Alexx Woods. Alexx dealt almost exclusively with the recently deceased, while Natalia's purview was cold cases. So she was somewhat surprised when Alexx came over and sat down across from her in the break room.

"Can I talk to you for a minute?"

"Sure," Natalia said with a smile. "What's up?"

"Well, I'm not sure if you can help or not. I'm having trouble identifying a body—no fingerprints, no hits through CODIS. You're specialty is cases everyone else has given up on—I was hoping you might have some advice."

Natalia took a sip of her bottled water and thought about it. "Well, I generally use standard DNA techniques to examine old evidence. I do have access to more and more databases every day, though; I could reach out to some agencies that are just coming online, including some international ones. If your vic is from another country, we might get lucky."

"Well, skin tone suggests he might be Hispanic, but that's hardly definitive. He might be Native American, Asian, or even an Eskimo for all I know."

"Well, there are certain genetic markers associated with indigenous people from the Americas. If the Q3 haplogroup shows up, we can at least narrow down where he's from, genetically speaking."

"Well, that would help. Thank you." Alexx shook her head. "I don't know. More than likely, this guy was just on the bad end of a drug deal and wound up in the swamp—but for some reason, it's bothering me more than usual."

"Maybe it's because he's a blank slate," Natalia suggested. "When you don't know anything about a person, you tend to project characteristics onto them. It's like when you're walking along and you see the back of someone's head; you form a picture in your mind of what their face looks like, even though you really don't have enough information to do so."

"Maybe. You can't get much blanker than this poor guy; he doesn't even have a face, let alone a name."

"You really get attached to them, don't you?" Natalia said curiously.

"They're my patients. I feel the same responsibility to them as I would to someone living."

"I get that," Natalia said. "It's how I feel about my cases, too. Nobody deserves to be forgotten."

"No. They don't. But at least your subjects get a second chance; by the time mine reach me, all their chances have been used up."

"Yeah. One of the guys I just helped to free referred to me as the Ghost of Christmas Past."

"What?" Alexx looked startled.

"You know, Scrooge? Revisiting your own history, getting a second chance?"

"Sure, I know, it's just—I was just thinking about that earlier."

"Well, 'tis the season, right?"

Alexx got up from the table. "For some of us, anyway. Thanks, Natalia. Merry Christmas."

"Merry Christmas, Alexx. I'll run that DNA as soon as I can."

6

CRUISE SHIPS WERE ALWAYS HUNGRY for entertainment. Most ships had more than one lounge or theater, and while the bigger rooms often featured musical reviews and floor shows, the smaller ones favored comedians, singers—and magicians.

"The Brilliant Batin," as Abdus Sattar Pathan billed himself, had carved something of a niche for himself in this particular world. As Horatio discovered, many cruise ship talent bookers knew his name, and almost all of them recommended him highly.

Almost.

"Well, he's very talented, there's no doubt about that," one booker told Horatio over the phone. "His close-up stuff is phenomenal, his patter is smooth, he's young and good-looking and extremely dedicated to his craft."

Years of experience had taught Horatio to hear

a certain unspoken word in another's speech; he added the qualifier himself out of sheer reflex. "But?"

"But . . . there's something a little off-putting about him. One of the unwritten rules of magic is *never scare the audience.* You might think that's strange, what with escape artists risking death and women getting sawed in half, but all of that stuff is designed to thrill, not scare."

"I'm not sure I understand the difference."

"When you're thrilled, you have a sense of adventure, that you're plunging into the unknown, that anything's possible. But it's like a roller coaster—you feel like it's dangerous, even though you know that it's not. Ultimately, you have to trust the magician—he's like the track the roller coaster's on. Batin . . . well, sometimes you get the impression his track's a little shaky."

"Are you saying he's unstable?"

"No, no, that's not it. . . . Look, it's hard to explain. It's just that—sometimes I get the impression he *wants* to scare people. Really shake them up. It's almost like he has this personal antagonism toward his audience."

"I see. . . . Have you ever seen him behave in a violent manner?"

"Oh, no, no. Never. The man's a consummate professional, I'll give him that. It's just . . . well, it's like he's always on. His stage persona, his off-stage persona, they're the same thing. Very polite, very professional, very calm. There's this thing about really good magicians when they're working, they have this sort of focused intensity. Like they're aware of every detail around them. He projects that, all the time—if anything, he's *too* stable, you know? A real control freak."

Horatio nodded. "Intensity and control. I think I understand . . ."

After he hung up, Horatio sat at his desk for a while and thought. It was possible to fake fingerprints, but every case he was familiar with had to do with either planting the fakes at a scene or using them to fool biometric ID devices.

The procedure wasn't even that difficult. You started by lifting a print from a surface—preferably glass or glossy paper—using standard graphite powder or fuming it with superglue. You then photographed it with a digital camera and used a laser printer to print it onto the kind of transparency slide used for overhead projectors. The toner formed a relief image, which would then be coated with a mixture of wood glue and glycerin. Once that dried, it could be peeled off and attached to actual fingertips with theatrical glue.

The thing was, there was a world of difference between fooling a machine and fooling a human being. Horatio had talked to the booking officer who finally took Pathan's prints, a cop named Elliot Chan, and he swore there was nothing unusual about them; there was just no way Pathan could have slipped a false set of prints past the hands-on process of having his fingers pressed into ink and then rolled onto paper by an experienced officer.

Not unless he was very, very good.

Horatio was in the lab with the fingerprint card in front of him. He had examined it minutely under high magnification, looking for any telltale discrepancies around the edges of the prints. He had also run a sample through the mass spec/gas chromatograph, in the hopes of turning up traces of glycerin or an adhesive.

So far, he'd had absolutely no luck. If the prints were fake, they were perfect, completely indistinguishable from the real thing. Horatio found that hard to believe; what made more sense was simply that he was looking at the wrong piece of evidence.

He went back to the print lifted from the magazine. It pained him to do so, because Calleigh was the one who'd done the work in the first place, and she was never less than scrupulously accurate. Still, if the prints from the booking weren't faked, the one from the magazine must have been.

He ran the same tests all over again—and got exactly the same results.

Both prints were real.

Alexx found Delko in the lab, going over explosives data. "Eric? I just received the report on the stomach contents of John Doe."

He looked up. "Yeah? Anything interesting?"

"Sad, more like. Roast turkey, rice, smoked oysters, apricots, cashews, banana, kale, pumpkin seeds, manioc, prunes, bacon, sausage—"

"That's quite a meal—"

"—olives, hard-boiled egg, onions, garlic, tomatoes, and chili peppers."

Delko took the report from her outstretched hand and studied it. "Okay, a real feast. A little hard on the digestion, maybe, but why sad?"

"Don't you get it, Eric? This was a Christmas dinner, his very last one. Wherever he ate it, he was probably surrounded by people who loved him. And from where we found the food in the digestive system, he probably ate only a few hours before he died."

"Well, that could help us identify him. You know, some of those items sound familiar, too . . . can you send me the stomach contents? I'd like to run a few additional tests."

"Sure. You think you know where he ate?"

"Not yet—but I may be able to figure out who cooked the meal . . ."

"How's the big Santa hunt going?" Calleigh asked Wolfe when he returned to the lab.

He pulled on his lab coat before answering. "Well, Reindeer Girl admitted getting her stocking stuffed, but says Santa was still alive when she left."

"You believe her?"

"I don't know. It's consistent with what we found, but I still don't have a COD. Waiting on Alexx for the post."

"Well, here's a little something to consider while you're waiting. I identified that fiber you couldn't match."

"Really?" Wolfe came over to where Calleigh was perched on a stool beside the comparison microscope.

"Take a look for yourself."

He peered into the eyepiece. "Yeah, that's a match . . . what is it?"

"It's a polypropylene blend. Specifically, the kind used to make indoor/outdoor carpeting."

"Wait a minute. I found that fiber trapped in the vic's pubic hair—but there wasn't any indoor-outdoor carpeting in the area the body was found."

"Which suggests," Calleigh said, "that Santa got naughty in a different location."

"Well, witnesses did say he was doing a lot of flirting. And I haven't checked with Valera yet about the DNA from the sexual traces I recovered. Hang on a second."

Wolfe pulled out his cell phone and punched in a number. "Valera? It's Wolfe. Just wondering about the Santa case. . . . You did? Great. Uh-huh. Really. Okay, I'll be over to pick up the results in a few. Bye."

"You know," Calleigh said thoughtfully, "with

the open design of the new lab, all the glass louvers and everything? I could actually watch Maxine answer the phone and talk to you."

"So?"

"So you could have just walked over there in the time it took to dial the phone."

Wolfe shrugged. "I heard one of the receptionists is running wild with a piece of mistletoe. I'm not going out there if I can help it. . . . Anyway, Valera told me she found DNA from *two* women in the sample I gave her. One matched Valerie Blitzen."

"Ah. So who was the other one—and where?"

"I don't know, but I think I know how we can find out. Valerie Blitzen said that the Santas always plan a food stop on their route."

Calleigh nodded. "And a route can be retraced."

"Exactly. Where they ate might even be the source of that fiber." He paused. "Wait. That sounds like a commercial for oat bran."

"Is that an improvement over Santa puns?"

"*Anything*'s an improvement over Santa puns."

Delko had once dated a woman from Rio de Janeiro, and she had invited him over to her parents' house for a traditional Brazilian Easter feast. The main course had been a roast turkey, marinated in lime juice and *cachaça* rum and stuffed with a dense mix of fruits, nuts, meats, and rice. One of the side dishes had been kale, and another had been rice mixed with pumpkin seeds.

"We call turkey *el ave de los ricos*," she'd told him. "The bird of the rich."

"Well, this is certainly rich," he'd admitted.

Not to mention hot. He'd had a great time that evening, particularly enjoying the food, and had gone so far as to do some research on the dishes afterward. It was difficult to obtain the peppers used outside of Brazil, but you could order them online— and he had. He'd retrieved some of his supply from home, and now he presented one to Maxine Valera.

"This is a pepper," Valera said.

"Very perceptive," Delko replied. "Specifically, it's a malagueta pepper, from Brazil. Very hot, too."

"How hot?"

"Thirty to fifty thousand on the Scoville scale. Don't touch your eyes after handling it."

"Thanks for the tip. If you already know what it is, why do you need me?"

"To see if any of these samples match its DNA." He presented her with three vials. "From a vic's stomach. The contents were pretty degraded, but I'm pretty sure one of these little red bits is from a pepper, too."

Valera took the vials. "Don't tell me this is what killed him."

Delko grinned. "They're not *that* hot, Maxine."

He followed up by running down a few Brazilian recipes. Sure enough, he found a stuffing recipe that listed almost all the foods found in John Doe's stomach.

He checked the yellow pages. Around twenty Brazilian restaurants were listed in Miami-Dade County, and John Doe could have eaten at any of them . . . or at none. But if his last meal had been at a large family dinner, surely somebody would have filed a missing person's report by now, and nobody who had disappeared in the last week fit John Doe's description—what there was of it, anyway.

Assume he ate at a restaurant. A big meal like this is usually a family feast—not that many places are going to be serving it, even over the holidays. Only some of the larger, upscale places.

He made some phone calls. A few of the restaurants offered a big roast turkey meal over the holidays, but only served it on Christmas Eve itself—the traditional time in Brazilian culture. None of them had it on their menu a week ago, and Delko was starting to think he'd hit a dead end when one of the places called him back.

"Miami-Dade Crime Lab, CSI Delko speaking."

"Yes, hello. My name is Maria Arrisca. I understand you called asking about our *ceia de natal*?" The woman's voice was warm, with a hint of a Portuguese accent.

"That's right. You're calling from which restaurant?"

"Apimentado's. You talked to one of my waitresses."

"Yes. She told me you don't put it on the menu until Christmas Eve."

"Not usually, no. We stay open late that night and serve it after midnight mass. Usually, we get many single men who are away from home and miss their families. For them, it is a way of not being so alone on Christmas. The reason I called you is because of one such man."

Delko sat up straighter. "You remember someone in particular?"

"Oh, yes. He came to see me about ten days ago. He very much wanted a *ceia de natal*, with all the trimmings. When I asked him how many people the dinner was for, he told me it was just for himself. I told him it would be much less expensive to simply come for the Christmas Eve meal, but he told me he would be unable to attend on that night. He was willing to pay and told me to give whatever he did not eat to those less fortunate."

"When did he have this meal?"

"Three days ago. He left a most generous tip, as well."

Delko sighed. "I'm guessing he paid in cash, right?"

"Oh, no, he used a credit card. Would you like to see the receipt?"

The page with the fingerprint had carefully been excised from its source; now, Horatio retrieved the rest of the magazine from the evidence box.

If I can't figure out how *he did it . . . maybe I can figure out why.*

The pictorial in question was of a young woman named Jazeera. She had an impressive physique, dusky skin, dark eyes, and a shy smile—although her shyness apparently didn't extend to keeping her clothes on. There was no last name listed, of course.

A slightly less revealing picture of her also graced the cover. While she was, in fact, wearing a single item of clothing, it managed to cover her in a strategic way.

The item in question was a black silk scarf wrapped to cover her head, ears, and throat. The caption below the picture read, *Beneath the burka! Our Arabian beauty shows you what you're missing!*

She was wearing a *hijab*, a Muslim head scarf. Although the article inside made no mention of her actually being Islamic, the cover photo certainly implied that she was.

It was starting to make sense. Horatio thumbed through the magazine until he found the publisher's information, then made a few more calls.

"Thanks for giving me a hand, Frank," Wolfe said.

"No problem," Tripp said. "You really think we'll find something along Santa's backtrail?"

"If the route you obtained is accurate, I'm sure of it."

Tripp and Wolfe were a few blocks away from the skating rink where the body had been found. They were walking down the sidewalk slowly,

Wolfe on the inside, Tripp on the outside. Both held flashlights and used them to scan the immediate area.

"Well, the Claus I talked to said they always establish a few key points beforehand," Tripp said. "An initial meeting spot, an end point, and a few highlights along the way. It tends to get a little chaotic though; apparently it's not easy riding herd on a hundred and fifty Santas."

"Santi," Wolfe said absently.

"Huh?"

"That's how they refer to themselves in the plural. *Santi*. Like the plural of *sarcophagus* is *sarcophagi*."

"Whatever. Anyway, I talked to a few of them and managed to put together a reasonably detailed list of where they went, including detours."

"Well, it's been less than twenty-four hours. Witnesses' memories should still be fresh."

"Somehow, I don't think we have to worry about whether or not people will *remember* seeing our suspects . . ."

What surprised Wolfe, though, was the range of reactions they got when they questioned people along the route. Santa had rampaged through hotels, bars, shops, two strip clubs, and a bowling alley; for the most part, he seemed to have been met with open arms. Every now and then, though, someone took exception. One waitress complained that Santa had made her spill a tray of drinks; a salesclerk at an upscale shoe boutique seemed visibly angry that the female Santas had been flashing passersby. "It's just—*horrible*," the woman sniffed. "What about the *children*?"

"Yeah, we don't want children exposed to breasts," Wolfe muttered to Tripp. "Not *real* ones, anyway . . ."

"What?" the woman said.

"Nothing," Tripp said. "Thank you for your time."

Wolfe expected a rebuke from Tripp after they'd left the store—but got a grin instead.

"Kid," Tripp said, "you are gonna get both of us in trouble."

"Sorry," Wolfe said, grinning back. "But c'mon—she had enough silicone in her to regrout my shower."

"Let's just focus on the job at hand, all right?"

The third hotel they hit was a little more downscale than the others—Santa had apparently been attracted by the garish display in the lobby, which included reindeer, plastic snowmen, elves, and a full-blown nativity scene featuring a stuffed donkey and three wise men carrying surfboards.

Wolfe looked around while Tripp talked to the front-desk clerk. The nativity scene had some straw scattered around, but no indoor/outdoor carpet.

Then he spotted the sign.

"—well, they were *boisterous*," the man at the front desk said. He was in his twenties, black, and wore a navy blue blazer and black tie. "But good-natured, you know? They weren't out to cause any trouble, they were just having a good time. They danced around our little display there, sang a Christmas carol—well, sort of a Christmas carol—and then they were out the door. They didn't break or steal anything."

"Excuse me," Wolfe said. "That sign says you have a miniature golf course on the premises?"

The clerk nodded. "Yes, it's on the roof of the first floor. Nine holes. It's mainly for the kids, but any of our guests can use it."

"Did any of the Santas go up there?"

The clerk frowned. "Not that I saw, but I guess it was possible. Access is through that stairwell right there." He pointed to the other side of the lobby. "It's not locked. I suppose one of them could have slipped up there while the lobby was full."

"Mind if I take a look?" Wolfe asked.

"Sure, go ahead."

"You have an inspiration?" Tripp asked, following Wolfe into the stairwell.

"Maybe," Wolfe said. "Worth checking out, anyway."

Most of the hotel's rooms were in a twenty-story tower, but the main floor was more spread out; some enterprising manager had decided to take the large, flat space of the first-floor roof and turn it into a recreational area. The mini-golf course consisted of short putting greens, sometimes angled at the end, with various obstacles to make the game more interesting: small, arching bridges, tunnels made of PVC pipe, even a stereotypical model of a windmill.

And lots and lots of green indoor/outdoor carpeting.

Wolfe knelt down, pulled a few strands out, and peered at it. He nodded in satisfaction. "I'll have to get this back to the lab, but I'm pretty sure it'll match."

Tripp glanced around, then up at the tower. "So this is it? Pretty exposed—especially if you're dressed all in red."

"Most of it, yeah." Wolfe walked over to the windmill. "This is the only structure with enough height to give any privacy from the hotel room windows . . ."

He shone his flashlight at the sheltered side. There, on the ground, was a small blob of white.

"Used condom," Tripp said. "Looks pretty fresh, too. Think the DNA will match our vic?"

"Unless this is a popular make-out spot for horny teenagers, it should." Wolfe knelt down and peered into the narrow wooden slot at the base of the windmill where the ball was supposed to go. Reaching inside, he felt around and pulled out a crumpled ball of red fabric with bits of white fur trim sticking out.

"And this," Wolfe said with a satisfied smile, "should match the fibers I found on his body."

"So somebody else was jingling Santa's bells."

"And since whoever wore this suit left it here, they didn't rejoin the other Santas. Why?"

"Maybe they had a fight," Tripp suggested. "Alcohol and sex can be a pretty volatile mix."

"That's a possibility. But why hide the suit? I can see leaving it behind if she stormed off, but this was stashed where it wouldn't be seen."

"Sounds like Mrs. Claus didn't want anyone to connect her to Santa," Tripp said.

Wolfe put his hands against the windmill and pushed. It rocked slightly, obviously not attached to its base. "Give me a hand, will you, Frank?"

Together, they tipped the windmill over on its side. A variety of detritus had accumulated on the floor inside, including three dusty golf balls, a candy wrapper—and a small metal flask.

"Looks like Santa," Wolfe said, "has left us another present . . ."

The magazine's name was *Exotic Skin*, and it was published right in Miami. Their offices were in a squat, white building off Flagler, with only a small sign over the door that read PRIAPIX PUBLISHING. Horatio pushed the glass door open and went inside.

The receptionist was both a stereotype and a self-contained story all in one; she had the same bosomy, narrow-waisted, long-legged body that the magazine's pictorials deified—but her face was defined by a large, purplish birthmark that began in her blond hairline and spread over one eye, most of her nose, crept around her mouth, and then ended halfway down her neck. Her desk was made of clear Plexiglas; obviously, her employers wished to emphasize her best assets, which the white miniskirt and belly-baring, matching top she wore definitely did.

She looked up from her computer when he entered and gave him a dazzling smile. "Hi! What can I do for you?"

He pulled aside his jacket, revealing his badge, and smiled back. "I'm Lieutenant Horatio Caine, Miami-Dade Crime Lab. I was wondering if I could speak to someone about one of your models."

The badge didn't faze her in the least. "Just a second—I'll see if Johnny's available." She picked up a phone. "Johnny? There's a police lieutenant here named Horatio Caine. He wants a few words about one of our models. . . . No, he didn't say which one. Yes. Okay." She put down the phone and said, "Go right in."

"Thank you."

The man in the inner office was seated behind a much less transparent desk, and got up and walked around it to extend his hand when Horatio entered. He was in his early thirties, dressed in a lime green bowling shirt and a pair of cargo shorts with sandals. His hair was long, unkempt, and brown, his nose prominent and freckled, and his teeth so white they didn't look real.

"Hi!" he said, shaking Horatio's hand. "I'm

Johnny Fieldstone, the publisher. This isn't bad news, I hope."

He motioned Horatio to a chair and resumed his own.

"Nothing like that." Horatio leaned forward, hands clasped together, his forearms resting on his thighs. "At least, I hope not. The thing is, there was a violent incident in which the focal point seemed to be an issue of your magazine. More specifically, the woman on that issue's cover."

Fieldstone frowned. "Which issue?"

"This one." Horatio pulled out a photocopy of the cover and handed it over.

Fieldstone glanced at it and sighed. "Oh, yeah. I should have known." He handed the copy back. "That was our foray into the Middle East. Not exactly our most popular move."

"Oh? Not a big seller?"

"Oh, it brought in plenty of cash—but that wasn't all. We get hate mail all the time, but this generated three times as much. Some of it even surprised me."

"How so?"

Fieldstone picked up a pen from his desk and toyed with it between two fingers. "The offended Muslims, that I expected. Hell, the whole point of the issue was to generate some controversy—I figured that for every outraged Muslim who proposed a boycott, five more would buy the issue. Forbidden fruit, right? What I didn't expect was all the angry letters I got from self-proclaimed patriots."

"People took exception to her supposed nationality?"

"Big-time. Like it was somehow un-American to find a woman of Arabic descent attractive." He shook his head. "Though I admit, I've got a blind spot on this particular subject. I find women of every kind attractive."

"Forgive me for saying so, but the range of your magazine's output—ethnic variations notwithstanding—would seem to contradict that."

Far from being offended, Fieldstone chuckled. "Oh, *Exotic Skin* isn't the only thing we publish. It's just the highest-profile—what makes it into the corner stores. Some of Priapix's other titles are devoted to women over forty, large women, women who aren't professional models. You'd be amazed how many women find the idea of thousands of strangers drooling over their naked image empowering."

"But not all of them do."

"No, we get plenty of criticism from antiporn crusaders, both left- and right-wingers—even when our cover girl *isn't* Arab-American."

"Would it be possible to talk to the young lady herself? I'd like to eliminate any possibility this might be personal, for her own safety."

"I don't see why not. We're usually very careful about guarding our models' identities, but that's for their own security. Obviously, that's not a problem here." He picked up his phone and pressed a button. "Sharlane? Sweetheart, could you pull up the files on our cover girl for the December issue? Lieutenant Caine needs her contact information. No, she isn't in any trouble, it's just a precaution. Okay, thanks."

He put the phone down. "They'll be ready for you in a minute."

Horatio got to his feet. "Thank you. Would it also be possible to take a look at some of the hate mail you've received?"

"Sorry, but I don't keep that stuff around. The email gets erased, the rest gets thrown out. It's just too negative, you know?"

"Well, if you could hang on to anything that shows up in the next little while, I'd appreciate it."

"Sure, I can do that."

The door opened and Sharlane strode in. She walked up to Horatio and held out a sheet of paper. "I printed it out for you."

"Thank you very much."

She turned to Fieldstone. "I don't want to interrupt, but Sherry called. Soccer practice was canceled and she needs a ride home after school."

"Okay, I'll do it. Can you maybe grab some takeout on your way home?"

"Thai okay?"

"Sounds great."

She flashed a smile just for him and went back

to her desk. The look on Fieldstone's face lingered even as the door closed.

Horatio glanced down at the man's hand and wasn't surprised to see the gold band there. "I wouldn't have pegged you as the domestic type, Mister Fieldstone," he said with a smile of his own.

"Hey, even Hugh Hefner got married. There's a world of difference between pretty and beautiful, Lieutenant—and I've never had any trouble seeing the difference."

The manager of Apimentado's was a slender, pixieish woman named Maria Arrisca. She strode up to Delko with a large, beaming smile on her face. "Yes? A table for how many?"

"I'm Eric Delko—the CSI you talked to on the phone?"

"Oh? I didn't expect you to be so *young*." The smile on Arrisca's face took any sting out of the words. "Well, I'm glad to be of assistance. Come, come."

She led him to a table and sat him down, then insisted on bringing him some strong Brazilian coffee before they discussed anything else. Delko, familiar with the social niceties ingrained in Latin American culture, accepted a cup graciously. The restaurant was decorated with an abundance of tropical greenery, so much so that it was like sitting in a rain forest. Carved wooden toucans with colorful bills hung from perches; posters advertising Carnivale or samba dancing decorated the walls. A sultry female voice sang in Portuguese from hidden speakers, joined in the chorus by her audience singing along.

Once protocol had been taken care of, Arrisca joined him across the table and proferred a piece of paper. "Here is the credit card receipt," she said. "Was he involved in something unsavory? Was it perhaps"—she lowered her voice and leaned forward—"drugs?"

"I honestly don't know," Delko said, taking the receipt. "So far, in fact, I know practically nothing about"—he glanced down—"Hector Villanova." *If that is your real name, and not an alias.* "Which is why anything you can tell me about him would certainly help."

"I will do my best." She gave him a brief description that seemed to match that of the man who'd bought the boat: Hispanic, middle-aged, fairly well-dressed but nondescript. "I can also tell you that he came alone, that he was from São Paulo, and that he was married. He was very appreciative of all the food." Her smile widened. "He told me our turkey reminded him of his mother's."

"How did you know he was married? Did he talk about his personal life?"

"He was wearing a wedding ring, so it was obvious. But even though he was friendly, he did not want to talk about himself—he would politely change the subject when I tried. I did not wish him to be uncomfortable, so I took the hint."

Delko nodded and took a sip of his coffee. It was excellent, rich and dark. "But you say he was friendly?"

"Oh, yes. It was like he was celebrating something, though he wouldn't say what. I will confess, it has preyed on my mind ever since; I cannot resist a mystery."

Delko grinned. "I know what you mean—they're kind of addictive. I'm just happy I get paid to solve them."

"So—may I ask why you are chasing this man? Has he gone missing, or perhaps committed a crime?" She leaned forward, her eyes bright and intent.

Delko hesitated. "I'm sorry. We recovered a body in the Everglades yesterday. We don't have a positive ID yet, but I'm pretty sure it's Mister Villanova."

She leaned back, her eyes going wide. "*Merda.* What a shame. He seemed like such a nice man—but, then again, who is to say? A man who smiles can still hide many dark things in his heart."

"Very true. He didn't give any clues to what his business here in Miami was?"

She shook her head. "No, nothing."

"Well, if he was from Brazil, I should be able to track down a passport photo. Is it all right if I bring it by later so you can confirm it's the same man?"

"Of course." She sighed. "Poor Mister Villanova. So close to Christmas, too; it will be very sad news for his wife."

Maybe, Delko thought. *But then again, maybe not . . .*

7

LUNCHTIME FOUND WOLFE in the break room, eating an egg-salad sandwich. Alexx walked in with a file folder in her hand and sat down across from him. "Just finished the autopsy on Santa," she said, then stopped herself with a frown. "Boy, there's a cheery holiday greeting for you."

"I know, I know," Wolfe said. "I don't think I'll ever be able to watch another Christmas special without certain disturbing images coming to mind. Anyway, what stopped his clock?"

"A stroke. Brought on by acute hypertension."

"High blood pressure," Wolfe said, nodding. "Preexisting condition?"

"I don't think so. What was really interesting wasn't the COD, though—it was the time of death. According to his liver temperature, around eleven p.m."

Wolfe stopped with his sandwich halfway to his

mouth. "What? Alexx, I watched the ME's wagon take the body away myself—just after ten."

"I know. And he was lying in a snowdrift, right?"

"Right. Which should have sped up the body's cooling rate."

"Exactly. But when I added that to my calculations, I came up with a time that was obviously wrong, because his liver temp was too high. He was experiencing hyperpyrexia—his body might have been as hot as a hundred and six degrees when he died."

Wolfe frowned. "The woman he had sex with said steam was coming off his body. But—he was in an ice rink for a while beforehand, and then lying mostly naked in a pile of snow. That should have cooled him off, at least a little."

"Yes, it should have. So I checked the tox screen. It showed traces of two antidepressants: imipramine and phenelzine. One's a monoamine oxidase inhibitor; the other reacts with MAOIs. The range of symptoms produced by an MAOI overdose include vomiting, increased libido, hypertension, and hyperpyrexia—but the amounts I found weren't high enough for that."

"If the drugs didn't bring on the stroke, then what did?"

"His diet. Doctors are very careful about prescribing MAO inhibitors, because of the way they react with other substances. MAO breaks down monoamines like epinephrine, norepinephrine, dopamine—and one called tyramine. Tyramine is present in high concentrations in certain kinds of foods, especially foods produced by an aging process."

"Like what?"

"Like what I found in his stomach. Beer, pickled herring, pepperoni, sauerkraut, aged cheese— sometimes the effect is even called the cheese syndrome. A large intake of tyramine is thought to displace noradrenaline from neuronal storage vesicles, causing vasoconstriction and increasing systolic blood pressure."

"Enough to cause a stroke?"

"Definitely. No doctor would prescribe these two drugs together—and if she did, she'd forbid her patient from ingesting any of these items, including alcohol. MAO inhibitors interact with central nervous system depressants, increasing their effect."

Wolfe eyed his half-eaten sandwich, then put it down. "So either our Santa was badly misinformed, extremely stupid—"

"—or murdered," Alexx said.

When he learned John Doe's name, Delko thought the hard part was over. He tracked down the man's passport information through INS, found out he'd only been in the country two months, and got not only a picture but the address of the motel he'd been staying at. Maria Arrisca confirmed that yes, that was the man who'd come to the restaurant, and the motel manager agreed to let him look around Villanova's room; the man had paid for the next month in advance, and his things were still there.

But once he'd spent a few minutes poking around room 214, he was forced to change his mind.

The room held nothing.

No clothes, no suitcase, no toiletries. The bed was made, the garbage empty. He called the front desk to make sure they'd given him the right room, and the manager swore up and down they had.

There was no evidence that Villanova—or anyone—had lived there. The room was as empty as an amnesiac's memory.

Someone had erased any trace of Villanova's presence.

Room 214 was on the second floor. Delko went back downstairs and knocked on the door to the manager's office again. The manager, a corpulent woman with straggly white hair and a long-suffering expression, opened it and sighed, "What now?"

"I'm sorry to bother you, but has anyone been in room 214 in the past week?"

"No. Mister Villanova liked his privacy. He'd let me come in to clean once a week, but that was it. I haven't been in there yet this week."

"How about visitors?"

The woman shook her head. "If he ever had any

visitors, I never saw them. No women, no friends, no nothing."

"How about you? Did you ever talk to him?"

"Only when he paid his rent. He never said much."

"So you have no idea what he did for a living?"

The woman gave him a suspicious glare. "No. And don't try to tell me he was involved in drugs—I don't let that go on around here. You think I want the DEA kicking in my doors and confiscating my business? He didn't have people knocking on his door at all hours, he paid using a credit card, and he didn't drive a flashy car. What kind of drug dealer does *that* sound like?"

"A very unusual one," Delko admitted. "Look, I'm just trying to get some sense of who this guy was. So far, I'm drawing a blank."

"Then you got a good sense of who he was," the manager said, and closed the door.

The model's real name was Zenira Tariq. Horatio tracked her down through her modeling agency, who told him she was on a shoot at Haulover Beach. Horatio drove over to talk to her.

Haulover Beach was a popular gay spot, with its clothing-optional section on the north end. Horatio felt more than a little conspicuous trekking through the sand in his suit and dress shoes; the irony of being uncomfortable because he was the only one wearing clothes brought a wry smile to his face.

The section of the beach being used for the shoot

was blocked off by yellow caution tape and guarded by a man with an improbable blond Afro, gold-framed sunglasses, and a walkie-talkie. He was dressed in baggy shorts that came to his knees, sandals, and a short-sleeved Hawaiian shirt covered in electric-blue flamingos. He held up his hand imperiously as Horatio approached—Horatio almost expected him to say, *Halt! Who goes there?*

What he said, though, was "Hey. Sorry, man. Closed for a private function."

"Not to me, it isn't," Horatio said calmly. He displayed his badge discreetly; the man raised his eyebrows and waved him in.

A hundred feet farther on, Zenira Tariq lay posed on a large, bright pink towel. The color of the towel contrasted sharply with the darkness of her skin, a rich brown that reminded Horatio of hazelnuts and chocolate. She wore nothing but a pair of oversize sunglasses with white plastic frames, and was balancing a large, pink-and-white-striped beach ball on the soles of her feet.

The scene's eroticism was significantly eroded by the half-dozen men and women clustered to one side with light diffusers, cameras, makeup kits, and sundry bags of equipment. The general attitude they projected was as clinical as if they were taking pictures of furniture.

"That's good. Lilly, lose the glare off her left breast. Too much oil."

"Move her legs apart, just slightly."

"I need a different filter—this one's too blue."

He walked up to the person taking the photos, a man with a scruffy black beard and enormous, muscled arms. The camera looked like a toy in his oversize hands.

"Excuse me." Horatio showed his badge. "Lieutenant Horatio Caine, Miami-Dade Crime Lab. I need a few moments of your model's time."

The photographer glared at him from beneath bushy eyebrows. "Can it wait? I've got clouds coming up and I'm paying every one of these parasites by the second."

Horatio took off his sunglasses. "Then I'll make sure I don't keep her long," he said levelly.

The bearded man threw his hands up and said, "God*damm*it! Okay, everybody, take five—and not one bloody eyeblink longer, either." He threw Horatio a murderous look and turned away, fiddling with his camera and muttering under his breath.

Horatio approached the model, who had dropped the beach ball and sat up. She stared at him curiously, leaning back on her hands with her legs straight out in front of her.

"Zenira Tariq? I'm Horatio Caine, Miami-Dade police. I'd like to ask you a few questions."

"About what?" She had no trace of an accent, except possibly a touch of Southern California.

"I was wondering if you'd gotten any negative mail or phone calls concerning your recent appearance in *Exotic Skin* magazine."

Her eyebrows were long, dark, and plucked to form two subtle, inverted V-shapes; when she frowned, Horatio was reminded of twin ravens banking toward each other. "Maybe the magazine got some, but not me. I'm careful about who I give my digits to, you know?"

"What about personally? Is there anyone you know who took exception—a boyfriend or a relative, maybe?"

"I don't have a boyfriend, I have a girlfriend—and she's cool with what I do. My mom isn't crazy about it, but I don't get along too well with her, anyway. My dad died when I was a little kid. Why?"

Horatio paused. He didn't want to worry her for no reason, but she deserved a warning. "An employee was assaulted in a store that carried that particular issue—in fact, it seems your picture is what triggered the attack."

"What do you mean? What were they fighting over?"

"That's what I'm trying to figure out," Horatio said. "Do you know a man named Abdus Sattar Pathan?"

"No, I've never heard of him."

"Have you heard from any organizations or individuals that might have a religious or political reason to be upset?"

Now she started to look worried. "What, you mean like some kind of terrorist group? I don't *know* anyone like that. I'm not even Muslim."

"Even so, you seem to have offended someone—

though so far, there's no evidence that person is Islamic. They could very well be on the other end of the political spectrum."

"Like some kind of right-wing fundamentalist crazies? Oh, boy." She sat up straighter, bringing her knees up and hugging them. "This person who was attacked—is he all right?"

"Yes, he's fine. He suffered a mild concussion, but he's already out of the hospital."

She shook her head. "I don't know what to tell you, Lieutenant. It's not like I have any control over what they shoot, you know? They tell me where to show up, what to wear, how to pose, what kind of look they want on my face. Stilettos and fishnets or a veil and a toe ring—it doesn't make a lot of difference to me, you know? It's not like I was *trying* to be controversial."

"You could always walk away," Horatio said.

"Walking away doesn't pay the rent," she said softly. "And honestly—this pays the rent and then some. And I'd rather be lying on my back on a beach than some motel room that charges by the hour. You know?"

Horatio didn't answer. Instead, he took a card from his pocket and handed it to her. "If you receive any threats, or if you feel someone is watching you—give me a call."

"People watching me? Yeah, like I'd even notice. . . . One question, though?"

"Yes?"

She held up the card with a mischievous grin. "Where do you expect me to *put* this?"

Horatio slipped on his sunglasses with a smile of his own. "Some things, Ms. Tariq," he said, "you have to figure out on your own . . ."

"You're kidding me," Tripp said. He and Wolfe were in a PD-issue Crown Vic, with Tripp at the wheel. "Our guy was killed by *deli food*?"

"Potentiating with the antidepressants and the alcohol in his system, yeah," Wolfe said. "But that's not the clincher. When I processed the flask we found under the windmill, I found a print that matches our vic on the outside—and traces of phenelzine and alcohol on the inside."

"And since phenelzine isn't exactly a party drug, someone must have slipped it to him."

"Looks that way. But I didn't find any sign of imipramine in the flask—which means it must have been given to him by some other means."

Tripp pulled over and parked at the curb. "Well, I've been doing a little investigating of my own. Been talking to cabdrivers that dropped Santas off at the initial meeting point—think I've backtrailed our vic to his residence."

They got out of the car in front of an apartment building that had seen better days. Its avocado-green exterior had faded in places and darkened in others, giving the impression the entire structure was long past its expiry date.

Tripp checked the list of names beside the front door, found the manager's suite, and buzzed it.

"Yes?" A woman's voice, high and wavery, sounding elderly and not quite sure of its footing.

"Miami-Dade PD," Tripp said. "Can you come to the front, please? I've got a few questions for you."

"What? I can't just let you in . . . how do I know you're the police?"

"That's why I want you to come to the door, ma'am," Tripp said patiently. "So I can show you my ID. This won't take long."

"Well, I'm watching my show . . . can you come back?"

"Please, ma'am. It's important."

"Oh, all right . . ."

Abruptly, the door buzzed. Tripp shrugged and pulled it open. Wolfe followed him in, carrying his CSI kit at his side.

"Great security here," Wolfe said. "Guess she didn't want to miss any important plot points on her favorite soap."

"Hey, it's probably the high point of her day. You want to be a public servant in Miami, you better get used to dealing with senior citizens. If we're lucky, her memory won't be too bad."

They found the suite listed as the manager's just off the front hall and knocked on the door. They could hear the sounds of daytime television inside, canned laughter from some old sitcom.

When the door opened, the woman who stood there was almost exactly as Wolfe had pictured her: little-old-lady eyeglasses, gray hair in a bun, a tatty yellow sweater over a faded flower-print dress, and fuzzy pink bedroom slippers.

What he hadn't foreseen, though, was the large-caliber handgun she currently had pointed at both of them.

Hector Villanova's stated reason for coming to America, according to INS, was purely a pleasure trip. He had made very little impact during his stay, it seemed; his credit card records were as frustratingly opaque as the man himself. He'd spent money on groceries, the occasional restaurant meal, some clothes, and a bus pass.

A bus pass, Delko thought. *How many hardened international criminals buy a bus pass?*

He sighed and leaned back in his chair, staring at the monitor in front of him. Villanova could have been leading a secret life, of course, paying cash for all sorts of illicit activities—but if so, what were they? What had he done to wind up in a swamp with his head blown off, and who was responsible?

Delko had gone back to the motel room with his kit and gone over every surface carefully. He'd gotten a few latent prints and found some hair on a pillow—the DNA matched the body currently occupying one of Alexx's storage bays, but he had nothing to compare the prints to. He thought he knew how to get around that, but it meant making a call he wasn't looking forward to.

Still, it was part of his job. He picked up the phone and punched up the number on the screen.

"*Olá,*" he said. "*Solana Villanova, se faz favor.*"

Wolfe froze. Tripp sighed.

"Don't think I won't use this," the woman said. Her voice had the same high, querulous tone they'd heard over the intercom, but the hand holding the gun seemed firm enough.

"For pete's sake, lady," Tripp growled. "We're with the police. If you'll put that bazooka down long enough for me to show you my badge—"

"Oh, I don't think so," the woman said nervously. "I know the law. I can shoot people now, you know. Are you with the Mafia?"

Wolfe rolled his eyes. In 2005, Florida had enacted a law that allowed people to use lethal force to protect themselves in their home or car without fear of legal reprisals. "Terrific," he muttered. "Abreast of current events but not on speaking terms with reality."

"Look, just let me show you . . ." Tripp tried again.

"Not so fast!"

Tripp froze, his hand reaching for his pocket. The moment stretched out.

"Okay, go ahead," the woman said at last. "But don't move so *fast* this time."

Tripp started reaching again.

"Slower!" she shrieked.

Tripp's hand edged toward his lapel at a glacial pace. Wolfe had the sudden absurd feeling they were all trapped in the slow-motion part of some bad action movie.

The badge finally made its appearance a few decades later. The woman peered at it. "I can't see without my glasses."

"You're *wearing* your glasses," Wolfe said.

She peered at him suspiciously. "How do you know these are *mine*?" she snapped.

Wolfe had to admit she had a point.

"Grandma?" rose a voice behind her. "Grandma, who are you talking to?"

A woman appeared behind their captor. When she saw what was going on, she groaned. "Oh, Grandma. Not *again*."

"Darlene? These boys say they're the police. Do you know them?"

The woman, a busty redhead in her thirties wearing a white track suit, reached out and took the gun out of her grandmother's hands. "No, Grandma. I don't know any police. But that badge looks pretty real to me." She gave Wolfe and Tripp an apologetic look. "The gun isn't loaded."

"Don't tell them that! We may as well just give them the good silver!"

"Ma'am, are you the manager?" Tripp asked.

"Yes, I'm Darlene Florence. What can I do for you?"

The grandmother threw her hands up in despair. "Surrendering already? I'll go and get my purse so you don't tear the house apart looking for it . . ." She turned and shuffled away.

Tripp produced a picture of the deceased Santa. "Do you know this man?"

She looked at the picture and gasped. "Yes, that's Mister Patrick. Kingsley Patrick, in 419. He looks—"

"Yes, ma'am, I'm afraid so. Did he live alone?"

"Yes, it's just a small studio apartment. What happened to him?"

"That's what we're trying to find out," Wolfe answered. "We're going to need you to let us into his apartment."

"I'll get my keys."

"Will your grandmother be all right by herself?" Wolfe asked.

"Oh, she'll be fine." Darlene opened a closet and put the gun on a shelf. "There's no bullets for the gun, anyway—but I'd rather have her pointing this at people than waving a fireplace poker around. She gave a UPS guy nine stitches once."

"Let's hear it for the golden years," Wolfe said under his breath.

"Come on in!" Grandma Florence called out. "We've got jewelry! I'll get you a *sack*!"

8

MUSLIMS, HORATIO KNEW, took instruction in their appearance and day-to-day conduct from both the Quran and a collection of traditional teachings known as hadith. The hadith stated that a Muslim woman's clothing must cover her entire body—with the exception of the face and the hands—and that her attire should not be formfitting, sheer, or so eye-catching as to attract undue attention or reveal the shape of her body.

Zenira Tariq obviously had a very different opinion on the subject.

Acting on that opinion in Florida earned her a paycheck; acting on it in some countries would get her a jail sentence or even death. However, the benefits of being a celebrity in America—a small *c* celebrity, granted—were contradictory. Zenira's publisher established a buffer of privacy between her and the obsessed or dangerous, while simultaneously providing those same obsessives with extremely intimate images of her.

But the magazine didn't grant any such protection to the people who sold it.

Horatio had checked into the background of the shopkeeper. Talwinder Jhohal claimed he had never met Abdus Sattar Pathan before—but then, Jhohal also claimed he had no memory of the attack.

What Horatio had dug up was less than promising. Talwinder Jhohal was married, had four children, and had owned and run the same business for the last decade. He had never been arrested, had no known connections to any criminal organization, and had been an American citizen for over twenty years, having emigrated from his native India. His store had been robbed three times in seventeen years, but this was the first time anyone had been hurt.

He could be a poster boy for the American dream, Horatio thought. *Right up to the point where he was attacked by someone less tolerant than himself.*

At least, that had been Horatio's theory. It seemed to hold true; the Islamic angle provided a motive that explained the emotional and impulsive nature of the attack, plus it tied in with the background of the victim and the assailant. Horatio had even gone so far as to check into the derivation of Pathan's name, knowing that Muslim names were chosen to reflect specific traits of their faith. *Abdus Sattar* meant "slave to the one who conceals faults"; Pathan's stage name, *Batin,* meant "unseen."

The unseen and the concealed, Horatio thought. *Both appropriate for one who specializes in sleight of hand.* There was just one problem . . .

Pathan wasn't a Muslim.

"Are you *kiddin'?*" one talent booker had said to Horatio. Even over the phone, the incredulity in his voice was overwhelming. "As far as Muslims go, magicians are right up there with Satan. You want to see a Muslim get mad, forget about strippers and showgirls—try suggestin' a magic act. You'd get a better reaction tryin' ta book Black Sabbath at the Vatican. . . . B'lieve me, the Brilliant Batin could no more be a Muslim than Kermit the Frog could be Jewish." There was a short pause. "I'd tell ya *why* Kermit the Frog couldn't be Jewish, but my wife says I can't tell that joke no more."

After he hung up, Horatio did some research. What he found was intriguing.

"Three persons will not enter paradise: the habitual drunkard, one who believes in magic, and one who breaks the blood relations," Horatio said aloud.

Calleigh looked up from the paperwork she was doing. "Excuse me?" she said neutrally.

Horatio suddenly realized what he'd just said. "I'm sorry," he said. "It's a hadith, a traditional Muslim teaching. Magic that didn't come from Allah or through the pious actions of saints or prophets is referred to as Istidraaj. Those who practiced it were regarded much the same way witches were by the Old Testament."

Calleigh's tone softened. "Oh. Doesn't sound as if they were very popular."

"No, but they were probably good at making things disappear. As is our friend Mister Pathan. His current accomplishment seems to be making his lawyer vanish."

"You can't contact him?"

"I can't find any evidence he actually exists. The Florida bar has never heard of him, and so far neither has anyone else."

Calleigh frowned and got up from her seat. She came over to where Horatio was seated in front of one of the lab's computers. "Well, *someone* showed up to talk to Pathan while he was in custody."

"Someone named Francis Buccinelli, according to the checkpoint at Miami-Dade booking," Horatio said. "He showed a driver's licence as ID, but I can't find him listed in the state database, either."

"So the ID must have been fake. Falsely identifying yourself to a police officer is a crime—"

"—but not one we can go after Pathan for. Whoever Buccinelli really is, he must have smuggled in what Pathan used to fake his fingerprints."

"Which we still can't prove."

"No. But if we find Buccinelli, we can charge him—which may get him to roll over on Pathan."

Horatio hit a key, calling up security footage from the front desk of the Miami-Dade Pre-Trial Detention Center. It showed a dark-skinned man in a three-piece suit, with long, curly black hair, heavy-framed eyeglasses, a prominent mole on his cheek, and a short, neatly trimmed black beard.

"Sounds like a plan," Calleigh said. "So where do we start looking?"

"I've already contacted the booking agents who've worked with him. Now I think it's time I talk to some of his peers . . ."

The apartment that Darlene Florence let Wolfe and Tripp into wasn't exactly luxurious. It seemed Santa Shaky had derived his name from his financial status—and possibly his grasp of basic hygiene.

The only furniture seemed to be a foldout couch, a small table with two chairs, a dresser, and a floor lamp. It was hard to tell, though, because only the floor lamp and the table were easily identifiable; the rest were buried under mounds of clothing, so much so that it took Wolfe a second to realize there was anything under them at all.

"Either the guy was a real clotheshorse," Tripp said, walking into the room, "or he was running some kind of business out of here."

"He was an actor," Darlene offered from the doorway. "That's what he told me, anyway. He said he'd been in some commercials, but I didn't recognize him."

Wolfe entered and picked up the topmost item draped over one of the chairs, a silvery jumpsuit on a hanger. There was a plastic fishbowl helmet resting on the table that plainly went with it, next to a low-end computer. "Looks like he kept some of his wardrobe," he said. "Either that, or he was planning an expedition to Jupiter."

"You need me here?" Darlene said. "I should probably get back to Grandma."

"No, we're fine," Wolfe said. "Go look after your grandmother." *Before she wanders down to the laundry room and takes someone else hostage.*

When the door closed, Tripp and Wolfe went to work.

Tripp looked through the apartment for anything obvious: documents, weapons, drugs, or any other sort of contraband. Wolfe concentrated on the more subtle aspects of a search, looking for biological and chemical evidence: bloodstains, sexual fluids, traces of anything that seemed unusual or out of place.

Wolfe moved the piles of clothing off the fold-out sofa and shone an ALS on the rumpled sheets underneath. "Don't see any evidence of sexual activity. If Santa was getting any, it wasn't here."

Tripp, looking through the medicine cabinet in the tiny bathroom off the kitchen, said, "No antidepressants here. Lot of hair-care products, though."

"Yeah, I think Mister Patrick had a certain

amount of ego—which would go hand in hand with his being an actor."

"So you think he really was an actor—that wasn't just a line?"

Wolfe pointed to a small bookcase on the other side of the bed. "Old scripts, books on Method acting—I'd say he was telling the truth. Doesn't look like he made it past the struggling-artist point, though."

"No shortage of those," Tripp said. "Question is, why would someone want to kill him?"

"Don't know. But the answer might be here." Wolfe tapped a few keys on the computer, which immediately brightened to life. "All right, I'm going to try to get into his email . . . no good. I was hoping he'd have it set up to automatically remember his password. I'll have to get this to the lab, see if one of our techs can pull anything out."

Tripp was looking around thoughtfully. Abruptly, he walked over to the door and examined the lock. "Wolfe, come here and take a look at this."

Wolfe did. "Strange dent just above the lock. You think it might have been tampered with?"

"I don't know," Tripp said. "I get the feeling the place has been tossed. Nothing obvious, just a few things that seem out of place. Couple of dresser drawers ajar, door to the medicine cabinet was open. Guy might have just been sloppy, but something isn't quite right."

Wolfe looked around. "Well, if someone did break in, what did they take?"

"I don't know." Tripp crossed his arms and frowned. "I guess the real question is: what's *not* here?"

"Sure, I know Abdus," the man behind the counter said. He was thin, in his twenties, with a bristle of brown crew-cut over his scalp. "He comes in here to buy supplies."

Horatio glanced around the magic shop. Pegboards of cheap magic kits hung along one wall, while small tables covered in black velvet cloth spotlighted the more expensive props.

"I understand you know him on a personal level, as well," Horatio said. "One of the talent bookers I talked to mentioned that you and he were friends."

Matt Fresling, the man behind the counter, scratched at the stubble on the back of his head. "Well, a little, I guess."

"More than a little. You and he sometimes fill in for each other when one of you can't make a performance, correct?"

Fresling shrugged. "Sometimes, yeah. But it's strictly business, you know? I mean, I've never even been over to the guy's house."

"Uh-huh. So you two don't socialize?"

"Well . . . we've gone out for a few drinks after a show, just to talk shop. But Abdus is pretty uptight—sticks with bottled water. He's a very focused guy."

"So it would seem," Horatio said. "Did you two ever discuss anything other than business?"

"Talked about his family a little. I gotta say, I didn't believe him at first."

"How's that?"

"The whole growing-up-incredibly-rich thing. I mean, if my family had that kind of money, there's no way I'd be working three shows a night on a cruise ship, competing for attention with the midnight buffet."

"I hadn't realized he came from money."

"Oh, yeah. His old man's some kind of Arabian oil tycoon. I guess he and Abdus don't get along that well."

"Tell me," Horatio said, "did Abdus ever mention a man named Francis Buccinelli?" He watched Fresling's reaction carefully, but if the name meant anything to him, he kept it hidden.

"No, I don't think so," he said. "But like I said, we don't hang out together that much."

"Thank you for your time," Horatio said.

Less than twenty-four hours after Eric Delko talked to Solana Villanova on the phone, she walked into the reception area of the Miami-Dade Crime Lab. She asked for directions at the front desk and thanked the receptionist.

Then she headed straight for the morgue.

Alexx looked up from washing her hands as the woman strode in. "Yes? Can I help you?"

The woman gazed at Alexx evenly before answering. She was in her late thirties, with sharp cheekbones and a cleft in her chin. She wore a simple black dress and low-slung, black pumps. "Yes," she said, her voice crisp and controlled. "I believe there must have been some sort of mistake, which I am here to correct."

"I see," Alexx said carefully. "I'm Doctor Woods. And you are?"

"Solana . . . Villanova. I understand you have someone here you think is my husband."

Delko had talked to Alexx, told her what he'd discovered. He'd also told her how Solana Villanova had reacted to the news.

"Mrs. Villanova, there really wasn't any point to you traveling all this distance," Alexx said. "There's no way to visually identify your husband from the remains—"

"That's because it's not my husband," the woman snapped. "Let me see this body."

Alexx studied the woman for a second. "All right," she said calmly. She walked over to the wall with its rows of dull silver drawers, grabbed the appropriate handle, and pulled. The woman walked briskly over, showing no emotion at the sight of the torso covered in a sheet.

"This is all we recovered." Alexx pulled the sheet back, revealing the body.

The woman looked down, and her face—already expressionless—seemed to get even blanker. "This is not Hector. This is—how can you say this is anything? It could be anyone."

"I guess you're right. This is just a John Doe, then. We'll dispose of it in the usual way."

"What? That seems . . ."

"What do you care?" Alexx said. "This isn't your husband, right? It's not the man whose last meal was *ceia de natal*, even though he had a problem with his cholesterol. It's not the man who used to be a heavy smoker but gave it up about a year ago. It's not the man with a compression fracture in his lower spine that happened in his twenties. Right?"

Solana's face was still expressionless, but it had paled visibly. "How . . . how can you tell these things?"

"That's my job," Alexx said, her voice softening. "The people that pass through my hands have stories to tell, and I'm the last one they're going to tell them to. I do my best to listen."

The woman looked down at the body, and Alexx could see the change in her eyes; one second it was just a cold, inanimate thing lying in front of her, and suddenly it was something else. The mask she had fixed so securely in place cracked, and the grief she was trying to hide trembled beneath the surface.

"The man you talked to on the phone, Eric Delko?" Alexx said. "He asked you to bring in something of your husband's. Something we could get a DNA sample from?"

"Yes. Yes, of course." The woman fumbled for her purse and withdrew a small, flat package. "This is a hat he used to wear. I found it in an old box that—that he forgot to take with him."

"I'll make sure it gets to the right place, Mrs. Villanova."

"It's Miss," she said, handing over the package without taking her eyes off the body. "I mean—we were divorced. I don't go by the name Villanova anymore, but I thought it would complicate things, so I just . . . I just . . ."

And then the mask shattered and her eyes overflowed and she was sobbing, arms wrapped around herself as if she were trying to hold herself together. Alexx didn't shut the drawer; instead, she came around the other side and put her hand on the woman's shoulder.

"It's okay, honey," Alexx said softly. "It's all right. We're going to take care of him."

The once Solana Villanova didn't answer, but then, Alexx hadn't expected her to.

Alexx wasn't the one Solana needed to talk to.

Pathan wasn't a common name in Miami; there was, in fact, only one other Pathan that Horatio could track down . . . and the address that it was attached to raised his eyebrows.

Fisher Island wasn't so much a suburb of Miami

as a separate kingdom. Accessible only by boat or aircraft—or maybe private submarine—it was 216 acres of diamond-studded, gold-plated luxury that boasted two deepwater marinas, a championship golf course, and its own polo field. Celebrities and CEOs maintained homes that started at two million and climbed into the stratosphere from there. Those who couldn't afford to live there could still take the ferry across and visit the acclaimed Spa Internazionale, to be pampered with mud baths, hot wraps and massages.

The spa wasn't Horatio's destination, though. He drove his Hummer off the ferry and down quiet, empty streets; a peacock, his rainbowed tail spread like a corporate advertisement, stared at him from its perch on top of a fire hydrant. Horatio passed more golf carts than cars, and noted that at least two of the drivers had their own talk shows.

Fisher Island had been constructed in 1905, the result of dredging a marine passage to Biscayne Bay. A black businessman named Dana Dorsey bought the island, planning on turning it into a resort for rich African-Americans, but wound up selling it in 1919 to Carl Fisher, who gave the place its name. Fisher, in turn, got rid of the island, but didn't sell it; he swapped it instead, trading it to William Vanderbilt for his yacht. Vanderbilt upgraded the place, installing tennis courts, a pool, a golf course, a mansion, and a library. The key passed through a number of hands after that, getting another face-lift in 1979 that added upscale condominiums and restaurants.

Despite its luxurious trappings, the island wasn't large; within minutes, Horatio was presenting his ID to a video camera set into a concrete post. A moment after that, the large, ornate iron gates beside it swung open.

At the end of a long driveway stood a truly opulent mansion, built in a style that would do an emperor proud. The roof was a gleaming glass pyramid, with minaret-style towers rising from its four corners. Wings branched off from two sides of the pyramid, paralleling the seafront the building faced.

The entrance was framed by six large marble columns, more Egyptian than Greek, and a door that looked as if it had been stolen from a pharaoh's tomb; it appeared to be made of solid stone, with an intricate hieroglyphic frieze carved into its surface.

The man who opened it as Horatio walked up the front steps was dark-skinned, with a thick black mustache. Other than the spotless white turban on his head, he was dressed in traditional English butler's livery, right down to the white gloves.

"Please come this way, sir," the butler said, his accent somewhere between Calcutta and Oxford.

Horatio followed him into a foyer large enough to hold a basketball game and lit by a chandelier that resembled a frozen explosion in a diamond warehouse, then into an adjoining room through a set of large glass doors. It was a study, of the kind often depicted in Sherlock Holmes novels: tall bookshelves full of leatherbound volumes, a stone fireplace, a large desk with a wingback chair behind it. Those with too much money, Horatio had noticed, often substituted an obsessive attention to detail for taste. It was as if, rather than evaluate any one object for its own worth, they simply pointed at a page in a catalog and said, "Make it look like this. *Exactly* like this."

The butler told him to wait. He took a seat on an antique divan upholstered in dark green velvet and looked around the room curiously. A large, brass-mounted globe dominated one corner, while a thick book propped up on an angled stand stood in another.

The man who entered the room a few moments later was tall, broad-chested, with a fringe of iron-gray hair around a brown, smooth skull. He wore a white linen suit, brocaded gold slippers, and a red silk tie. His beard, mustache, and eyebrows were a scattershot of black and gray, his features strong and angular. Khasib Pathan had passed down many things to his son: his jutting nose, his chin, his sharp black eyes.

But not, Horatio thought, *his beliefs.*

He rose when Khasib walked in the room. "Mister Pathan. Thank you for seeing me."

Khasib nodded. The smile he gave Horatio was

polite, but guarded. "Lieutenant Caine, correct? I'm not sure what this is all about—it concerns Abdus in some way?"

"Yes. I don't wish to alarm you, Mister Pathan, but it seems your son was involved in a physical altercation that resulted in his being arrested and another man spending the night in the hospital."

Khasib's reaction was only a slight frown. "I see. What sort of criminal charges is he facing?"

Horatio paused. "Well, sir, at the moment he isn't being charged with anything. There have been some technical problems with both the evidence and the witness."

Khasib nodded. "Ah. And it would be reasonable, I suppose, for the person responsible for freeing my son to seek out his grateful father." His tone was mild, with just a touch of amusement.

Horatio smiled. "I'm sorry, but you misunderstand. Nobody in my department tampered with the evidence, nor am I here looking for a payoff."

It was Khasib's turn to hesitate, but when he spoke again the amusement in his voice had deepened. "Well, it's a good thing you aren't, because you would be sadly disappointed. What *are* you here for, then?"

"A little understanding. The attack was sudden and violent, but triggered by something trivial—a revealing photo of a woman in a magazine. Your son has no connection to this woman that I can find. Does this make any sense to you?"

Khasib shook his head. "You presume a great deal, Lieutenant. To come to a man's house, to accuse his son of crimes while admitting he has no proof . . . what makes you think I won't take offense?"

"In my line of work, Mister Pathan," Horatio said, "I frequently have to take that risk." What he didn't add was that sometimes a lot more was revealed in anger than in friendship. Horatio was often asked to leave . . . and just as often, he came back. Usually with a warrant in his hand.

"I certainly could play the offended father," Khasib said coolly. "But I value honesty in my dealings—especially with those in authority—and so I will not. My son Abdus and I do not see eye to eye on many things. In truth, he is largely a mystery to me. While I have attempted to instill in him the wisdom of Muhammad's teachings, he does not see the truth and glory of Allah."

"So you have no idea why a nude photo of an Arabic woman, one he doesn't know, would make him angry?"

Khasib shook his head, his dark eyes never leaving Horatio's. "I do not. He has never shown any reverence for the traditions of the hadith, including those that dictate dress or behavior. If this . . . *woman* . . . was in some way connected to what he calls his trade, his behavior might be explainable."

"You mean his career as a magician?"

"Yes. It has consumed him, his entire life. I think perhaps one of the reasons he chose it was because of my protests. Islamic teachings are very specific concerning the subject of *al-qamrah*; it is the seventh apostasy, like *as-sarf* and *al-'atf,* and whoever practices it or is pleased with it has disbelieved," Rasulullah said. " 'The prayer of everyone is accepted in the night of fifteenth Shaban but not the prayer of the magician and tax collector.' "

Horatio glanced around the room. "Well, I can see why you might have a problem with the tax collector . . ."

"But not with a harmless hobby? With card tricks and pulling rabbits from hats?" Khasib scowled and crossed his arms, and for a second Horatio could see how intimidating his displeasure might be to a young boy. "I realize that to those who do not believe, the traditions and practices of the faithful sometimes seem foolish. I am not an unsophisticated man, Lieutenant; but the essence of faith is trusting that there is a higher power who knows and understands far more than you ever could. I trust in that wisdom, and in the wisdom of all the great Islamic scholars who have interpreted it throughout the ages. That wisdom, sadly, was not enough for my son."

"When was the last time you talked to Abdus?"

"I see him rarely—once every six months, perhaps. We last spoke a few weeks ago, I believe. It was concerning plans for a party for one of my wives."

Horatio's eyebrows went up, but he said nothing.

"I am a citizen of Saudi Arabia, not the United States. Polygamy is common there; the Quran says that a man may have as many as four wives, as long as he is able to properly look after them." Khasib smiled. "As you can see, that is not beyond my means."

"Obviously not," Horatio said. "May I ask which of your wives is Abdus's mother?"

Before Khasib could reply, the butler reappeared at the doorway to the room. "Excuse me, sir. Your son Abdus is on the telephone. He says it is most urgent."

Khasib cocked a quizzical eyebrow at Horatio. "Well," he said. "Most unusual timing, wouldn't you say?"

"Maybe he's calling to ask for the name of a good lawyer," Horatio said, but Khasib's only reaction was to stride to the desk, pick up the receiver, and push a button. "Hello? Yes, I—what?"

Khasib's demeanor changed abruptly. A look of shock and alarm erased any trace of parental irritation. "Where are you?" he demanded, almost shouting. "Where? No! No! Let me talk to my son!"

"Sir? Is everything all right?" Horatio snapped. Every cop instinct he had was roaring.

Khasib held the receiver in front of him, staring at it as if it were some sort of foreign object he couldn't identify. "It was Abdus," he said, his voice somewhere between confusion and fear. "He said . . . he said that he's been kidnapped. That they are going to kill him . . ."

9

THE HAT—A BASEBALL CAP EMBLAZONED with the name of some South American soccer team—that Solana Villanova had given Alexx found its way to Delko. He managed to pull a few epithelials from the sweatband, and even a hair with the root intact, meaning he could DNA-type it. The samples went to the DNA lab.

He was planning on talking to Solana Villanova herself—but his entire day changed with one phone call from Horatio.

"Delko. What's up, H?"

"Eric, I need you and Calleigh to meet me at this address." Eric grabbed a pen and jotted it down. "I'll join you there as soon as I can."

"Sure," Delko replied, "but I'm supposed to do an interview with this woman in about twenty minutes—"

"The Villanova case?"

"Yeah. She flew in from Brazil."

"I'm sorry, Eric, but she'll have to wait. We've got a kidnapping—and the clock is ticking."

"I'll be right there." Delko hated pushing a case—any case—to the back burner, but in a kidnapping time was crucial. He'd have to talk to Solana Villanova later.

He tracked down Calleigh in the gun lab, signed out a department Hummer, and flipped a coin to see who drove. Calleigh won.

"So," she said as Eric buckled his seat belt and she started the engine, "our reluctant magician has pulled his own vanishing act, huh?"

"This guy's really a magician? Live doves up his sleeve, the whole bit?"

"Well, I don't know about any doves," Calleigh said, pulling out of the staff parking lot, "but he's definitely got something up his sleeve. You heard about the fingerprint?"

"Yeah. You think it might have been—"

"Ex*cuse* me," Calleigh snapped—not at Delko, but at a car that was being a little slow to get out of her way. "Trying to make a lane change here . . . Actually, I don't know what to think. Horatio checked my work, and he says there was no evidence the print was planted. Our best guess is that the guy doctored his own prints while in custody—but so far, we're not sure how he did it. We figure his lawyer's involved, but the guy used fake credentials. Horatio's trying to track him down."

"I gotta say—this Pathan getting snatched right after the whole fingerprint thing? Something's off."

"You mean the kidnapping might be phony? Fool me once, shame on you, fool me twice, shame on me?"

"That's how it looks to me. What do you think?"

"*I* think we should wait until we see the crime scene. There's definitely something odd going on, but we shouldn't be making any judgments ahead of time."

"Can't argue with you there—"

"Would you *please* mind moving over? Thank you *so* much," Calleigh said, apparently to the driver of a small black truck.

"You know they can't hear you, right?" Delko asked with a grin.

"I know, I know." Calleigh smiled. "But I was raised to be polite. They may not be able to hear me, but it makes me feel better. Honking a horn just seems so—well, *rude.*"

"Let's hear it for Southern hospitality," Delko said. "Or should that be Southern horsepower?"

"Whatever gets people out of my way," Calleigh murmured. "Pardon me, the posted speed limit *is* more than fifteen miles an hour. . . . Why, thank *you*, too."

Delko smiled and shook his head.

*　　*　　*

Under Title 18 of the United States Code, Sections 1201, 1204, and 1073, the Federal Bureau of Investigation had jurisdiction over kidnappings. Horatio had no choice but to notify the Miami field office of the FBI as soon as he learned of the crime . . . but that didn't mean he was happy about it.

Horatio had a history with the *federales,* and it wasn't exactly a friendly one. Though the friction between the Bureau and local law enforcement was so firmly entrenched it had almost become a cliché, Horatio had nothing against the FBI itself. The job came first, and who slapped the cuffs on was much less important than who wound up wearing them. The FBI had access to manpower, equipment, and resources that Horatio's department did not, and he was all for cooperation if it helped take a criminal off the street.

The key word was *cooperation.*

In Horatio's experience, the Bureau used the word strictly as a euphemism for "give us everything we want and we won't come down on you like a ton of dead fish." It was a euphemism Horatio himself was familiar with, but he tended to use it on suspects; certain representatives of the Bureau, though, seemed to use it on just about everyone they met.

Representatives like Special Agent Dennis Sackheim.

Sackheim strode into Khasib Pathan's study like a general entering the parade ground: back straight, eyes sweeping from side to side, three other agents—two men and a woman—in step right behind him. When he saw Horatio sitting there, the look on his face didn't change at all—but then, it had been as blank and unforgiving as a brick wall to start off with.

"Lieutenant Caine," Sackheim said.

"Agent Sackheim," Horatio replied. He didn't get up, and Sackheim didn't introduce any of his fellow agents.

Horatio had dealt with Sackheim before. The FBI man and he had clashed over several cases, and Horatio's opinion of Sackheim was that he cared more about solving the case than he did about the people involved. *Not the best person to be handling a kidnapping,* he thought.

Khasib stood at the window, staring out over the ocean with an unreadable expression on his face. Horatio had already talked extensively to him, but now Khasib would have to answer the same questions all over again.

"Mister Pathan, I'm going to put a tap and trace on the phone line." Sackheim nodded at the female agent, and she went straight to the phone. "I'll be handling the investigation; it's vital that you share any and all information you have concerning your son. Friends, romantic affiliations, business associates . . ."

Horatio stood. "Why don't you give him a moment, Dennis? I'd like to speak to you, if I may?"

Sackheim turned his blank gaze on Horatio for a moment. Horatio looked back mildly.

"All right," Sackheim said. "Excuse us, Mister Pathan."

Sackheim turned and walked out into the foyer, taking the two male agents with him.

"Mister Pathan?" Horatio said. "I promise you—you'll see your son again."

Khasib's voice held only a hint of a tremor. "I know . . . I know that you will do everything you can, Lieutenant. Thank you."

Horatio followed Sackheim into the foyer, closing the study door behind him. The two other agents had disappeared, well-trained hounds taken off their leash. Horatio had no doubt they were already interrogating the staff.

"What's the problem, Caine?" Sackheim said.

"No problem," Horatio said, putting his hands on his hips. "But I thought you might appreciate a heads-up about your vic."

"I'm listening."

Gracious as ever . . . "Abdus Sattar Pathan is not exactly an innocent." Horatio gave Sackheim a condensed version of the events that had brought Horatio to the Fisher Island mansion.

"So you screwed up a piece of evidence," Sackheim said. "Wish I could say I was surprised. I'm going to need to look at everything you've collected, anyway."

"My people," Horatio said, "did *not* screw up.

And we'd be happy to share what we have so far, *Dennis*—but I expect to be kept in the loop as far as the ongoing investigation is concerned."

"Look, Caine, this is federal now. My game, my rules. You can't even print a man in custody properly, and you want us to partner up?" The look Sackheim gave him was openly skeptical. "Do you even know who you're dealing with here? Khasib Pathan is the head of a Saudi family with more oil than blood in their veins, and he has some powerful friends who are very aware of that—if I wind up sharing jurisdiction with anyone, it'll be the State Department or Homeland Security. You couldn't even hang on to your guy when he was in a jail cell—so unless you feel like suiting up to play scapegoat, I suggest you stay out of my way."

Horatio met his eyes. "Suggestion noted. And I have one of my own, Agent Sackheim."

"Really."

"Really. I suggest you don't forget you're looking for a human being. Because if you lose sight of that, it's not the State Department or Homeland Security who's going to be standing over his grave . . . it'll be his family."

Horatio slipped on his sunglasses and walked out the front door.

The primary crime scene was the spot where Abdus Sattar Pathan had been abducted. Unfortu-

nately, Horatio didn't know where that was . . . so
he told his team to start with the man's home.

Pathan lived in Sweetwater, just west of
Miami. Although Pathan's Arabic heritage might
have drawn him to a suburb like Opa-locka, with
its faux Middle Eastern architecture and streets
like Shaharazad Boulevard, Sweetwater had apparently proven irresistible to the showman in
Pathan. Founded in 1941, the community's initial
residents were primarily Russian circus midgets
who were looking for a warm place to retire; they
had their homes custom-built to their size, giving
Sweetwater the nickname of the "Midget City."

Pathan's home was built neither for the diminu-
tive or the rich—despite his family's money, he
seemed to be living a decidedly middle-class lifestyle. The house was a two-story, squarish ranch-
style with an attached garage, the yard small but
well-maintained. A car was parked in the driveway,
a late-nineties, gold-colored Camry; Calleigh pulled
in behind it.

"Don't see H's vehicle," Delko said as they got
out. "Guess we beat him here."

Calleigh handed Eric's kit to him and grabbed
her own. "No reason to wait, I guess."

"Not if we want to see anything before the
Feebs get here."

Calleigh frowned. "You know, I've never liked
that term. Can't you just call them the Bureau?"

"Hey, every cop I know calls them that," Delko

said, smiling. "I think they're used to it by now."

"Well, I'm not. And anyway . . ."

She stopped halfway up the walk. Delko, a step behind her, stopped too.

"Door's ajar," she said, her voice all business. She put her CSI kit down and drew her gun. Delko did the same—he knew better than to question Calleigh's instincts.

They approached the front carefully.

"I've got a bloody handprint on the edge of the door," Calleigh said.

"I see it," Delko said grimly.

"Miami-Dade police!" Calleigh called out. "Is there anyone in the house?"

No response. Calleigh pushed the door open.

The large room just inside had obviously seen a fight; chairs were overturned, the coffee table lay in splinters, a lamp with a crushed shade threw fractured shadows across the wall.

And then there was the blood.

It was splashed in a great arc around the room, across furniture, the floor, the walls. From the color and consistency, both CSIs knew it was fresh.

"Looks like arterial spray," Delko said quietly.

"It does," Calleigh said. "Maybe enough to be fatal. Let's see if our donor is still on the premises."

They moved quickly and efficiently through the building, checking the bedrooms, the kitchen, the bathroom.

"Nobody home," Calleigh said, holstering her gun. "But I think it's safe to say we've found our primary crime scene."

"I'll let H know," Delko said, pulling out his cell phone.

"I'll start processing," Calleigh said. "Before the—*Bureau* gets here."

Delko grinned.

Blood-pattern recognition was a hybrid science; a proper understanding of it required a working knowledge of biology, trigonometry, and physics. Being handy with a camera didn't hurt, either. By the time Horatio arrived, Delko had documented the crime scene extensively with photographs, and Calleigh had processed the handprint on the doorframe and taken samples of blood droplets.

"Wherever Mister Pathan goes, violence seems to follow," Horatio murmured, surveying the wreckage of the room. "Not to mention blood . . ."

"I was just going to search the rest of the house," Calleigh said. "Unless you'd like to wait for Special Agent Sackheim?"

Horatio gave her a smile without any humor in it. "You know, he seemed kind of busy the last time I talked to him. We should probably just go ahead on our own . . ."

Horatio could usually tell a great deal about someone from observing where and how he lived; usually, a place occupied by only one resident tended to showcase that person's personality in a variety of ways. Considering Pathan's background, Horatio hadn't been sure what to expect—but it certainly wasn't what he found.

Pathan's occupation, for instance, was hardly evident. No posters of famous magicians, no pictures of him onstage or posing with other performers, none of the trappings of an entertainer's lifestyle at all. The house was decorated in a bland, middle-American style, with off-white drapes, a big-screen TV, a bookshelf stocked with bestselling paperbacks. The bedroom featured a double bed, a medium-size closet, a dresser with a mirror, and a portable stereo on a nightstand. Any vices Abdus Sattar Pathan had, he kept well-hidden—Horatio found no drugs, no alcohol, no porn or sex toys or women's underwear. Pathan's one nod to chemical indulgence was a top-of-the-line espresso machine in the kitchen, where the contents of the fridge seemed to indicate he ate out a lot. His bathroom showed a run-of-the-mill assortment of antacids, painkillers, and personal-hygiene products: dental rinse, mouthwash, toothpicks. Horatio collected DNA samples from a hairbrush and some dental floss in a wastebasket. If the blood in the living room was Pathan's, he'd soon know.

"Horatio," Calleigh called out. "Take a look at this."

He followed the sound of her voice out to the connected garage. It had been converted into a workshop, and here at last was evidence of Pathan's trade. A large metal bookshelf on one wall was stocked with books pertaining to stage magic, while two long tables loaded with a variety of tools both esoteric and mundane ran the length of two others. At least half the workshop was crammed with props from his act: an upright coffin with holes cut into it for the face and hands; a set of large, inter-linked steel hoops; a trunk decorated with Day-Glo stars and moons. Smaller props were hung from hooks on a Peg-Board or stacked neatly on shelves bolted to the wall.

"Looks as if he likes to keep his work separate from the rest of his life," Calleigh said, echoing Horatio's thoughts.

"Yes," Horatio said thoughtfully. "Compart-mentalized. Everything nice and neat and in its proper place. Everything except Mister Batin him-self . . ."

"I thought his name was Pathan?"

"The Brilliant Batin is his stage name. And this would be his domain . . . where he goes to con-struct his illusions."

Calleigh picked up on Horatio's line of reason-ing immediately. "You think the kidnapping was staged?"

"I don't know. But Mister Pathan wouldn't be the first estranged offspring of a rich parent to fake his own kidnapping. What I can't understand is how the initial assault ties in, or how he pulled off the fingerprint switch. But if he *is* trying to fool us, this is the place he used to make his preparations."

"Kind of an anti-CSI lab," Calleigh said. "Finding ways to hide the truth instead of uncover it."

"In which case," Horatio replied, "it's our skills against his . . . but where he has to make do with a home workshop, we have the full resources of the Miami-Dade Crime Lab."

"And your assistants don't have to dress like showgirls," Calleigh said. "Which is probably just as well. I mean, *I'd* look great in fishnets and a top hat, but I really don't want to see Ryan wearing anything featuring sequins . . ."

"You realize," Sackheim said, "that every piece of evidence you've collected is going to wind up in my hands, anyway."

Horatio looked at the FBI agent and smiled benevolently from behind his desk. He clasped his hands together in front of him and said, "Are you sure about that?"

Sackheim glared at him. "Are you implying you would impede the progress of a federal investigation?"

"Of course not. But given your lack of respect for my department's abilities, you probably doubt we'll be able to *find* anything. Right?"

Sackheim thought about this and turned his glower down a few notches with a visible effort of will. "I didn't mean to impugn the competence of your staff. I'm sure that whatever you discover will prove valuable."

"That," Horatio said, "almost sounded like an apology." He paused, met Sackheim's eyes, then added softly, *"Almost . . ."*

Sackheim looked away, apparently finding a framed certificate on Horatio's wall of sudden interest. "I'm sorry if I offended you or your team. Now, can we stop this posturing and concentrate on the job at hand?"

"I never stopped," Horatio said. "Any word from the kidnappers?"

"Not yet. We have all the standard procedures in place. Our first priority, despite what you may think, is the safe return of the victim."

"Good. My team is analyzing everything we took from the crime scene now . . . as soon as we learn anything, we'll let you know."

"You realize the lab at Quantico is better staffed and better equipped—"

"—and it's in Virginia," Horatio pointed out. "Shuttling material back there increases the chance of contamination or breaking the chain of evidence, and loses us valuable time as well. I think it's in the best interest of all concerned if we do the work here . . . and you might be surprised at the equipment we have access to. I can arrange a tour, if you'd like . . ."

"That won't be necessary," Sackheim said.

                    *   *   *

Calleigh was studying enlarged photos of the blood spatter from the Pathan house on the light table, her face illuminated by lurid red splotches of color, when Horatio walked up and said, "Hey. Got a minute?"

"Sure, H. What do you need?"

"I just got off the phone with Alexx. It seems that the widow of that John Doe has been waiting patiently to be interviewed, and she's getting a little distraught. The poor woman flew all the way in from Brazil, and she'd really like to get this over with."

Calleigh frowned. "I thought that was Delko's case."

"It is, but he seems to have hit a wall on the investigation. I'm thinking maybe a fresh set of eyes might see something new."

"So I'm your go-to?" Calleigh said, smiling. "That's sweet, but I don't know how Eric will take it."

"You let me worry about that. For now, he's too busy on the Pathan case to care about a stalled investigation. What I need you to do is go down to interview room two and talk to Mrs. Solana Villanova." He took a folder out from under his arm and handed it to her. "This is everything Eric came up with—unfortunately, it isn't much."

Calleigh flipped the folder open, scanned

through the contents. "Hmm. I can see why he'd be frustrated. The guy's life is pretty much a blank."

"Which I'm counting on you," Horatio said, "to fill in."

Horatio left her there, studying the file's meager contents. Like all of them, Calleigh loved a good puzzle—hopefully, it would absorb enough of her attention that she wouldn't notice Horatio had just pulled her off a high-profile investigation to work on a much less urgent case. But butting heads with the FBI was a dangerous job—and right now, the confusing fingerprint results in the assault case placed Calleigh right in the crosshairs. Sackheim could use those results as an excuse to question the validity of her work and maybe even leverage the entire case away, damaging her career irreparably in the process.

There was no way Horatio was going to let that happen.

"Miss Villanova?" Calleigh said, walking into the room. "Or do you prefer Garcia?"

The woman on the other side of the interview table looked exhausted, her eyes red and puffy and her posture slumped. "Call me Solana, please."

Caleigh hesitated. "I'm sorry, Solana. The DNA results came back—the body is your ex-husband's."

Solana nodded, but no tears came. Calleigh

could see from the look in her eyes that the woman had already realized the truth in her heart; hearing the words was just a formality.

"You know, we don't have to do this right now," Calleigh said, taking a seat. "If you'd like to go back to your hotel, get a little sleep, that'd be fine."

"No, I just came from there. I can't sleep. Please, I want to—to get this done."

"All right." Calleigh opened the folder she'd brought with her, glancing at the notes she'd made. "I apologize if these questions seem too personal," she said. "But any information you can give us will help us understand what happened."

"I understand."

"First of all—is there anyone you know of who would want to hurt your ex-husband?"

"I don't believe so, no. He was a good man. A little reserved perhaps, but—but he had a good heart. He always meant well."

"And what did he do for a living?"

"He is—he was a plumber. He had his own business in São Paulo. It never did very well—he wasn't very ambitious. I—I used to try to push him to try a little harder."

"What about life insurance? Did he have any?"

"Not that I know of."

"How long were you two married?"

"Seven years. We divorced about six months

ago." She paused, her lower lip quivering, and dug in her purse for a tissue. Calleigh waited until she'd wiped her eyes and blown her nose.

"I'm sorry," Solana said. "Please continue."

"I apologize for asking, but—why did you and your husband divorce?"

Solana gave a long, trembling sigh. "I was the one who left. Hector did not want me to go. But I . . . I was not happy. Hector was content with his lot in life, but I wanted more. In the end, we agreed it was best to go our separate ways."

"So it was amicable?"

She gave Calleigh a sad smile. "I suppose that is as good a word as any. It was, at first—he was hurt, very hurt, but he did his best to make things easy for me. We did not see each other often, but whenever we did, we were polite . . . until just before he left for America." She shook her head. "The last time I saw him, it was not pleasant. I can't even remember what started the argument, but I've never seen him act that way before. Loud, angry, saying things I couldn't believe. He was like a different person."

"What sort of things?"

"Hurtful things. Insulting, accusing. He kept saying he didn't need me, that he was going to America to do great things. At the time, it sounded like he never wanted to see me again; now, I wonder . . ."

"You think he might have gotten involved in

something he normally wouldn't? Trying to show some ambition, maybe?"

The miserable look on Solana's face showed that she had been considering the same thing. "Perhaps," she whispered. "If so, may God have mercy on my soul. I never meant for this. Not for anything like this."

"If Hector *was* going to do something illegal, do you have any idea what it might be? Did he have any friends or associates that he might have gone to?"

"No. Hector didn't know anyone like that. He was a *plumber.*"

"How about here in the States? Did he know anyone here?"

"He had one friend, yes, someone he went to school with. Marco Boraba. I think he is in Miami, but I never knew him well. When I heard that Hector was . . . when I heard, I tried to reach Marco. I could not find him."

"I see. And what does Mister Boraba do?"

"I don't know. I think Hector mentioned something about importing or exporting, but I'm not sure. He never talked about him like he was some sort of criminal, though."

"Well," Calleigh said, "sometimes we don't know people as well as we think."

"No," Solana said softly. "No, we do not."

"Eric," Horatio said, shrugging into a lab coat. "What do we have?"

Delko eyed his boss curiously. It wasn't that Horatio never got his hands dirty with labwork, but he usually let the rest of the team handle the routine stuff; he was more likely to be found in the field or the interview room, collecting testimony or uncovering new evidence.

"A lot, actually," he answered. "First of all, the blood. It matches the DNA of the samples from the bathroom, and epithelials I collected in the bedroom, the kitchen, and the living room. The blood definitely came from someone who'd been living in that house for a while."

"How about the blood itself?"

"The first thing I did was have it analyzed for any trace of anticoagulants or preserving agents. Nada. This stuff hadn't been stored previously— it was fresh."

"And the stain pattern?"

Delko turned to a light panel on the wall, where several photos were clipped like X-rays, illuminated from behind. They depicted the bloodstains on Pathan's wall, a pattern that resembled a crude painting of crimson tadpoles swimming upward. "Looks genuine. Projected blood from arterial spurting, probably a neck wound—you can see the impact points clearly." Delko pointed to the heads of the tadpoles. When an artery was opened, every beat of the victim's heart forced a stream of blood out through the wound; the rise and fall of blood pressure was visible as a distinctive rounded pattern

on the target surface—the initial splash—followed
by a downward-trailing tail.

"What about castoff?" Often, blood droplets on
a weapon like a knife would be flung onto another surface by the violent motion of the
weapon during an attack.

"Didn't find any, but that's not really a surprise."

"No," Horatio said. "This was a slashing attack,
not a stabbing one. One strike to the throat, which
opened the artery but didn't collect enough blood
to cause castoff."

"Which means the blade was thin, very sharp,
and used quickly."

"Yes," Horatio said, studying the photos.
"Which makes very little sense. This reads more
like an assassination attempt than a kidnapping.
In an abduction, your captive is your greatest
asset; you want him quiet, under control, and un-
damaged. Bleeding heavily and fighting back is
hardly optimal . . ."

"Maybe something went wrong. If the kidnappers were amateurs, they might have thought
showing Pathan a blade would be enough to get
him to go along."

"Possible, but unlikely. After all, obtaining a
gun in Miami is hardly difficult—and offers a
much better guarantee of cooperation."

"True," Delko conceded. "So maybe kidnapping
was never the objective."

"Maybe not. It could have been added as an afterthought to muddy the waters, buy the killers some time. Or maybe Pathan used his father's money to bargain for his life, change the attacker's mind."

"Either way, we don't know if he's dead or alive."

"No, we don't. The only thing we know for certain," Horatio said, "is that the FBI is going to be watching everything we do very, very closely . . ."

10

"ALL RIGHT, HERE I AM," Tripp told Wolfe. "I got your message, but it didn't make much sense to me. Exactly what did you find, and *what* was it wrapped in?"

"Not 'wrapped in,'" Wolfe said. "*Rapped in.* Here—let me show you."

He motioned Tripp deeper into the lab, where Wolfe had a variety of components laid out on a table. "I took apart the lock on our dead Santa's door and brought it here. First, I examined the outer surface. The most obvious sign a lock has been picked is small scratches around the keyhole, made by the pick or the tension wrench. The problem is that these can also be made innocently, by somebody missing the hole and hitting the plate with the key. However, I didn't find any—just that little indentation you noticed."

"Uh-huh. What'd you find once you took it apart?"

"Nothing. Again, this isn't conclusive—a skilled lockpicker can manipulate the pins and tumblers of a standard lock without leaving internal scratches, either. At least, not to the naked eye. Under the microscope, it's another matter."

"So you found microscopic scratches?"

"No."

Tripp studied the grin on Wolfe's face and sighed. "Okay, science boy," he growled, "I give up. Was the lock picked or not?"

"Not picked. Bumped."

"Excuse me?"

"It's also called *rapping,* and it's existed long enough to stake an honest claim to the term," Wolfe said. "Well, maybe *honest* isn't the right word. . . . Anyway, the technique's been around for at least five decades. Here, let me show you."

Wolfe had mounted three locks on three wooden frames, miniature doors held upright and clamped to the table. "These are the same model of lock as the one on Kingsley Patrick's apartment. The way a regular lock works is with a set of pins and two cylinders. The keyway runs through the inner cylinder of the lock. As the key goes in, the grooves cut into it move stacks of two or more pins through holes drilled into both inner and outer cylinders. Tiny springs push the pins back into position as the key goes further inside and the height of the grooves changes along the length of the key. When it's fully inserted, the end of the last groove—what's called the shoulder—rests against the inner cylinder, and all the gaps between the pins inside the lock are aligned. At that point, the inner cylinder can turn and the lock will open."

"Right." Tripp's tone had shifted from impatience to resignation; Wolfe guessed he'd become used to hearing long-winded explanations from CSIs.

"Anyway," Wolfe continued, "most lockpicking tools let you manipulate individual pins. Since the pin stacks are never perfectly aligned, some pins get stuck between the two cylinders, meaning they're lined up before any of the others. When the lock is turned slightly, the pins that jam first— the outer ones—stay on the outside of the inner cylinder. That lets you place the rest of the pins, and the lock should *open sesame*.

"Or . . . you could use one of these." Wolfe picked up a small, white tool from the table. It was made of a strip of lightweight, flexible metal around a foot long, with a squared-off, weighted end the size of a shot glass. "It's called a Tomahawk," Wolfe said. "Made by a guy named Kurt Zühlke. It was created specifically for the bumping technique, but you don't need a tool this specialized—I've been told a butter knife, held by the blade, would work the same way."

"How's it work?"

"Well, you also need one of these." Wolfe held

up a key. "This is a bump key, sometimes called a 999. It's an ordinary key that's been recut so all the grooves are at their maximum depth. There are two different techniques for using it, but both rely on one simple principle: Newton's third law of motion."

"For every action there's an equal and opposite reaction?"

Wolfe looked surprised. "Right. Guess you paid attention in physics class."

"Yeah, I can chew gum and walk at the same time, too. Get on with it."

"Okay, okay. Tools like lockpick guns or vibrating picks transfer energy to the pins via Newton's third law, moving them into the correct position for a split second—in order to open it, you have to turn the lock before the internal springs push the pins back into place.

"Both bumping methods utilize the same principle. The pull-back technique consists of inserting the bump key, then pulling back one pin's worth. After that, you rap the key with the tool, and turn it an instant later. It's tricky to do—took me a dozen tries before I could get the lock to open."

"And the second?"

"It's called the minimal-movement method. When you insert a normal key into a lock, the pins make contact with the key's deepest groove at the point where the shoulder touches the inner cylinder. A bump key has a very small amount of metal shaved off both the tip and the shoulder—about a quarter of a millimeter. This lets the bump key go deeper into the lock and push against the internal springs, which will then push it back out just enough to have the pins rest on its deepest groove."

Wolfe demonstrated, inserting the key into one of the locks. He hit the projecting end sharply with the Tomahawk tool, then grabbed and turned the key quickly. The lock popped open.

"Terrific," Tripp rumbled. "But I'm not here to be impressed by your break-and-enter skills, am I?"

"No. What I wanted to show you was this." Wolfe pointed to the spot above the keyhole on the lock he'd just opened. "See that dimple in the metal? It was caused by the shoulder of the key hitting the lock plate. It's almost exactly like the one on the lock plate from Patrick's apartment."

"Almost?"

"You stamp two pieces of metal together like that, you get a tool mark, and the more distinctive the tool the more distinctive the mark. Bump keys are highly individual because they're made by personally filing them down to the right tolerance; if we can find the bump key used to break into Patrick's apartment, I can match it to the mark on the lock."

"Good work, kid," Tripp said, clapping Wolfe on the shoulder. "Now all we have to do is figure out why they broke in and what they took."

"Hopefully Patrick's computer will give us something. Jenson's working on it. In the meantime, I've also been taking a closer look at the Santa suit we found inside the mini-golf windmill. The fibers from it were a match for some of the fibers I found on the vic, but I also found an interesting stain on the cuff of the jacket."

"Biological?"

"No, chemical—an electrolyte, to be exact. Lead, lead peroxide, and sulfuric acid. Or, in other words, battery acid."

Tripp frowned. "Think it came from the windmill?"

"No, I checked—the thing does have a motor, but it runs on AC."

"Car battery?"

"Maybe. That's the most common use for a lead-acid battery, but it's not the only one. Electrical backup systems use them, as well as other kinds of vehicles like golf carts. Their low energy-to-weight ratio means they're mainly used in situations where it doesn't matter how heavy they are—like in forklifts, where they're actually used as a counterweight."

"So this Santa could have been in a warehouse," Tripp said. "Well, I've got some news of my own. I think I know another spot where our female Santa might have made an appearance: Rosemary's Deli on Fourth."

"The vic did have deli food in his stomach, but—

how do you know that's where it came from?"

"That's where they stopped to eat. Valerie Blitzen mentioned a deli, so I checked on the list of places Santa was scheduled to hit. Not only is the deli listed, but the approximate time Santa was supposed to show up."

"We only found one of the antidepressants in the flask," Wolfe said. "She had to have slipped him the other one somewhere. Maybe she did it at the deli?"

"Could be. This chemical that certain foods are full of—tyrosine?"

"Tyramine."

"It works even better if it's side by side with one of those chemicals Patrick was dosed with, right?"

"Right. Alcohol amplifies the effects, too."

"So to get the best effect, you'd try to give your target both at once."

"Like booze and phenelzine," Wolfe admitted. "So, imipramine and—what? Aged cheddar?"

"Won't know until we see for ourselves, will we?" Tripp said. "C'mon, Wolfe—time to get out of the lab. I'm in the mood for a little pastrami on rye . . ."

Calleigh Duquesne had a BA in physics from Tulane University, and she had worked as a beat cop in New Orleans. She lacked neither street smarts or higher education, and a childhood spent with two alcoholic parents had given her a personal radar finely tuned to the moods of others. She had chosen a field where keen perception was as important as intellect, and she had excelled in it.

She'd figured out why Horatio had taken her off the Pathan case before the words were out of his mouth.

She didn't resent it, though—if anything, she was touched. Horatio was fiercely protective of his team, and Calleigh knew he would try to place himself between her and any possible repercussions from an error. Not that she'd let him, of course; she took responsibility for her own actions, and that included any mistakes she might make.

But she could see the wisdom in taking a step back, too—and even if she didn't, she trusted Horatio's instincts. If he thought she should work on another case, she would, and she'd give that case as much of her attention as any other—which is to say, all of it.

After talking to Solana, Calleigh set out to find Hector's friend Marco Boraba. He wasn't listed in the Miami phone book, but she punched up his driver's license and got an address in Coconut Grove. When she called the number listed, she got a recording, a Spanish-accented voice giving her another number to try if her call was urgent. When she tried that, a man answered with "Hello, Wildside Menagerie, this is Roberto. How can I help you?"

"Hi, my name is Calleigh Duquesne. I'm trying to get hold of Marco Boraba?"

"Mister Boraba is out for lunch right now," Roberto said. "He'll be back in an hour, maybe an hour and a half. Do you want to leave a message?"

"Does he have a cell phone number? I really need to speak with him."

"I'm sorry, but Mister Boraba doesn't like me giving that out. I can take your number and get him to call you, though."

Calleigh frowned. "You know what? I'll just come down and talk to him personally. Thank you."

She hung up. She knew she should probably have left her number, but sometimes it was better to not give a suspect any warning. Of course, she had no idea if Marco Boraba actually was a suspect—but then, ideas seemed to be in short supply in this case.

Besides, this way she could go down early and check out Mister Boraba's workplace. Wildside Menagerie, from the noises she had heard in the background, was some sort of pet store—either that, or the employees like to watch the Discovery Channel with the sound turned up way too loud.

Before she left, though, she had a little research to do. Forewarned was forearmed—and Calleigh always felt more comfortable when she was armed.

Rosemary's Mediterranean Delicatessen was the kind of place that made your mouth water as soon as you stepped inside. Glass cases full of fresh ravioli, fettuccine, tortellini; thick coils of smoked sausage hanging from the ceiling; shelves stocked with canned *dolmades,* olives, clams, and shrimp; big glass jars stuffed with pickled artichokes, peppers, mushrooms, and eggplant. The dairy case held plastic vats full of feta cheese in brine, bags of creamy Alfredo sauce, and wheels of Edam, Gorgonzola, Parmesan, and mozzarella.

The place was large, too, more like a small supermarket than a deli, with a seating area that abutted a sidewalk patio. Despite that, it didn't really look as if it could accommodate 150 Santas, though Wolfe supposed that the overflow could always hang around outside.

"Something's been bugging me," Tripp said as they looked around. "What are the odds that the place the Santas picked to chow down just happens to specialize in the kind of food our killer needed?"

"I was wondering about that, too," Wolfe said. "It suggests she was involved with planning the route itself. Who did you say you got the map from?"

"Woman named Monica Steinwitz. I think maybe we should go have a little talk with her next."

Tripp strode up to the front counter. "'Scuse me."

The man behind it looked up from the large meat slicer he was operating. He was fairly large himself, with the kind of bulging features that seemed to cry out, *I'm not fat—I'm just supposed to be three feet taller.* His hair was short, black, and curly, and that included his fleshy forearms and the inch or so of pudgy chest visible above the top of his full-length apron.

"Yeah?" The man continued to shave paper-thin slices from a large ham. "What can I get for you?"

Tripp showed him his badge. "Got a few questions about the Santas that were in here. Only take a minute."

The meatcutter shut off his machine and walked over. "I heard one of 'em dropped dead, over by the rink. But, yeah, they were in here. Before that, I guess."

"Any idea why they picked this place?" Tripp asked. "No offense, but it doesn't seem all that Christmassy."

The meatcutter shrugged. "Beats me. All I know is, I gotta phone call 'bout a week ago, some woman sayin' she's organizin' this big party. I ask if she wants it catered, and she says, no, they'll come to me. Then she tells me everybody's gonna be dressed as Santa, and they're gonna be hungry. I says I don't care if they're dressed like the Easter Bunny, long as they don't expect table service or anything deep-fried. We ain't licensed for that."

"Run into any problems?" Tripp asked.

"Nah, they were okay. They were pretty wasted and kinda loud, but nothin' we couldn't handle.

You want outta control, you should see what we get during spring break—I had a couple frat boys throwin' pickled squid at each other, one time. Wouldn'a minded so much, but they hadn't paid for it yet."

"What was the name of the woman you talked to?" Wolfe asked.

The man frowned, his meaty forehead corrugating like an accordian. "I think it was . . . Claudia. Yeah, that was it. Didn't get a last name, though."

"How about the food?" Wolfe asked. "Any problems with that?"

"Just the fact that we ran outta beer. I woulda known they were such boozers, I woulda stocked up. And they were a little confused about the bill, too."

"How's that?" Tripp asked.

"Well, they all paid separate, right? But just before they all left, this woman comes up to me and asks about the charity donation. 'What charity donation?' I say. 'You know, ten percent of what we spend goes to the burn unit or the Red Cross or something'—I don't remember, exactly. I tell her I'm sorry, but my money goes in my pocket—you wanna give to charity, great, but don't go donatin' *my* cash. Turns out there was some kinda mix-up with this Claudia woman, the one who set it up."

"Did you ever meet with this Claudia?" Wolfe asked.

"Nah, we just talked onna phone."

Wolfe eyed an immense jar of pickled arti-chokes. "Has the garbage been picked up since they were here?"

"Nah, they pick up tomorrow. Why?"

"Because," Wolfe said, "I'm going to have to confiscate it. And all the open containers here that the Santas might have eaten out of."

"You're kiddin' me," the man said incredulously. "What, you think *my* food had somethin' to do with that Santa who kicked off? You're crazy! The health inspector was just in here, gave me the thumbs-up—I run a clean place!"

"I'm sure you do, sir," Tripp said, "but some folks—even ones in Santa suits—play *dirty.*"

Wildside Menagerie was in Coconut Grove, not far from the famed CocoWalk open-air mall. Like many neighborhoods in Miami, Coconut Grove had its own unique character and history. The Grove was the oldest settlement in the state, its first residents two families of lighthouse keepers that arrived at Cape Florida on the edge of Biscayne Bay in 1834. By 1873, its residents included black sailors from the Bahamas, Conchs from Key West, and a cluster of sophisticates from New England—artists and intel-lectuals who came to the Grove when winters in the North proved to be too much. The Bay View House was the region's first hotel, and when it opened, it attracted both members of refined society and black

Bahamians looking for employment. Both groups stayed, establishing an eclectic community that by the twenties boasted a school, library, chapel, and yacht club—and in 1925, was annexed by Miami. Even more artists made the place their home after the Second World War, and throughout the fifties and sixties its reputation grew. Real estate prices drove many of the galleries out of business in the eighties and nineties, and today it was better known for its shopping than its art.

Calleigh liked driving through the Grove; everything seemed all mixed together, middle-class houses next to modern architectural experiments, pricey mansions side by side with tiny bungalows. The starving artists might not be able to afford gallery space in the Grove anymore, but they were still around, and they'd definitely left their mark.

As she'd thought, Wildside Menagerie was a pet store—but not just *any* pet store. It specialized in the exotic, in the hard-to-find and expensive. Its website had claimed it carried or had access to over fifty breeds of dogs, sixty kinds of exotic birds, and a large variety of lizards, rodents, spiders, snakes, scorpions, insects, and frogs. About the only thing they didn't seem to carry was ants, for which Calleigh was grateful. Just looking at ants made her itch.

She double-parked on the street—one of the perks of driving a Miami-Dade CSI Hummer was being able to stop wherever you needed to—got out, and walked up to the front door. There were two large display windows on either side of it, one featuring a three-foot iguana sprawled on a piece of driftwood, the other a dozen puppies in a plastic-bottomed enclosure. The iguana regarded her with one disinterested eye; the puppies did puppyish things, wrestling and chewing and sleeping and generally just being cute as all get-out. Calleigh took a moment to smile at them and tap on the glass; she was a firm believer that every moment spent with a puppy or kitten was subtracted from your own aging process. She realized that this belief meant that anyone who worked in a pet store was effectively immortal, but she also believed certain ideas should never be examined too closely. Being a scientist didn't mean you couldn't embrace the occasional irrational thought; after all, it wasn't irrational beliefs that got you in trouble. It was irrational behavior.

Inside, the noise of the place was considerable— puppies barking, birds screeching or whistling or singing, even the chatter of a monkey. It wasn't deafening, but it did give Calleigh the sudden feeling she wasn't in the middle of a city anymore. The smell of the place was considerably less than wild, though; more than anything, it smelled of disinfectant. *I suppose that's better than animal feces,* she thought.

A young man in a short-sleeved, yellow shirt with a WILDSIDE MENAGERIE logo stitched on the breast approached her. He had bushy sideburns, thick, black-framed glasses, and a nametag that read ALLEN. "Hi," he said. "Need any help?"

"I do," she said pleasantly. "But I think I'll just look around for a bit, first."

"Sure. Just let me know if I can find anything for you."

She strolled the length of the store. It seemed more to her like a boutique than a pet store; the layout, the lighting, the price tags, everything seemed as upscale as any designer clothing shop in South Beach. She saw gourmet dog food, cat jewelry, even interactive robot toys that claimed to simulate the movements of a mouse.

At the back of the store was the aviary, an entire room walled off with wire mesh. Inside were dozens of species that ranged from tiny, black-and-white songbirds to brilliantly colored parrots as long as her arm.

Calleigh took her time, looking around and getting the feel of the place. She kept an eye out for anyone who might be Marco Boraba, as well as anything unusual or odd.

After twenty minutes or so all she had noticed was how many people under the age of twenty-five had come in shopping for small dogs. Where Calleigh had grown up in Louisiana, anything smaller than a bloodhound was hard to find; these days, the only kind of canine anyone seemed interested in had to be no larger than a house cat.

She eavesdropped on one extremely blond and tanned teenage girl who'd been grilling a salesclerk for the last few minutes: "Now, are you sure this breed doesn't get any bigger? I just bought this Prada bag, and I do *not* want him outgrowing it."

Of course, she thought to herself. *The latest trend, the accessory dog. Soon to be followed by a parrot that can answer your cell phone and a trained bear to park your car.*

She shook her head and picked up something that looked like a long-handled ladle made of bright blue plastic.

"*Atlatl,*" a voice said behind her.

She turned. The man who had spoken was tall, well-built, with the kind of high widow's peak of curly black hair that often seemed to crop up on middle-aged Latino men. He wore a black linen suit with a crisp white shirt and a bolo tie, two braided leather strands joined at his throat by a silver-and-turquoise eagle. One of his eyes, she noticed, was slightly bloodshot and puffy.

"Pardon me?" she said.

"It's what the Aztecs called it," the man said. "This particular version is designed to throw tennis balls for dogs, but its traditional uses are much more serious. It is one of the oldest weapons known to man, predating the bow and arrow by thousands of years. If I may?" He held out his hand. Calleigh hesitated, then gave it to him.

"The word *atlatl* comes from the Nahuatl words

for 'water' and 'thrower,' " he said. "This is because they were used primarily for hunting waterfowl. Of course, they were not throwing tennis balls at them." He chuckled, and Calleigh smiled politely. "The *atlatl* was used to throw the *yaomitl,* a kind of spear or long dart. The butt of the dart rested here," he said, pointing to the round end of the ladle, "with the shaft held parallel to the *atlatl* itself. Other than that, it was used in exactly the same way, with an overhand or sideways throwing motion." He demonstrated, moving his arm in a slow, exaggerated sweep. "It's like adding another joint to your arm. It can increase the amount of throwing power up to two hundred times, letting you launch a five-ounce dart at a hundred miles an hour. The current world distance record for an *atlatl* dart is just under eight hundred and fifty feet."

"Impressive," Calleigh said. "And here I thought it was a soupspoon. Silly me."

Allen walked up and stopped. He had that look on his face that people got when they have something to say, but don't want to interrupt. His eyes flickered nervously from Calleigh to the man holding the dog *atlatl* and back.

"Yes?" Calleigh said.

"Uh, Mister Boraba?" Allen said. "There's a phone call for you."

"Take a message," Boraba said. "I'm busy talking to this young woman right now."

"Okay," Allen said, and hurried away.

"Mister Boraba," Calleigh said. "I'm Calleigh Duquesne, Miami-Dade Crime Lab. I was wondering if you had a few moments to speak with me about Hector Villanova."

"Hector? He is not in any trouble, I hope?"

"I'm afraid I have some bad news, Mister Boraba. Mister Villanova's body was recovered a few days ago in the Everglades."

Calleigh studied the man's reaction carefully. He had seemed cordial and at ease at first, but a guarded quality had entered his eyes when Calleigh had told him who she was; that was only to be expected. What she saw when he learned of his friend's death, though, was—relief? Just a flash of it, perhaps, followed by an immediate rush of grief.

"Are—are you sure?"

"I'm afraid so," she said gently. "However, the circumstances of his death are somewhat mysterious. Anything you could tell me about Hector and his activities in Miami would be appreciated."

"I'll tell you what I can, but I'm afraid Hector and I did not see each other very much. He tended to keep to himself—or, at least he did when he was in Miami. I saw him more often in São Paulo than I ever did here."

"The two of you weren't close? Or did you have a falling out?"

He sighed. "We were friends. Good friends, once. In recent times less so, but there was no falling out, no argument. You know how it is with friends from school, yes? When you are young, you are bound as much by your differences as your similarities; you seek the new, in people as well as experiences. You are all fellow travelers, eager but nervous. You make friends as much out of fear of being alone as any common interests. Then, as time goes by, you discover who you are, what you like and dislike, what your goals and limitations are. And somehow, your friends drift away, like boats on many different currents."

"Not always," she said. "Some friendships last a lifetime. You two kept in touch, right?"

He nodded. "Yes. We were very different, though; Hector, at heart, wanted the safe, the familiar. A wife, a family, a house. I was always the adventurer." He tapped the *atlatl* against his open palm absently, staring past Calleigh into the distance. "That is why we were friends, I suppose."

"Well, he must have had some adventure in his soul," Calleigh said. "He came to Miami to take advantage of a business opportunity, after all."

"Did he? I was under the impression it was simply a vacation."

"He was here for two months. That's a pretty long vacation."

"That depends on what you are taking a vacation from. I only spoke to him once or twice, but I could tell he was still in a great deal of pain. His wife left him, you know."

"I know. She says Hector claimed he was coming to Miami to make a lot of money—and on the last night he was seen alive, he appeared to be celebrating. You wouldn't have any idea why, would you?"

Boraba frowned. "No, I have no idea. How—what was the manner of his death?"

"He was killed by an explosive device." Normally Calleigh wouldn't give out that much information about an ongoing case, but she wanted to see Boraba's reaction.

He shook his head, seeming more puzzled than shocked. "A bomb? Who would want to kill Hector with a bomb? It makes no sense."

"Not so far. But sooner or later, Mister Boraba, it will."

Calleigh turned into the lab's parking lot at the same time Wolfe and Tripp were getting out of Tripp's car. She pulled up and rolled down the window of the Hummer.

"Hey, Calleigh," Wolfe said.

"Hey, guys," Calleigh said. "Anybody seen Horatio?"

"I think he's in his office," Wolfe said. "He mentioned something about that FBI agent coming by just before I left. Didn't sound too happy about it, either."

"Any news about Pathan?"

"Not that I've heard," Wolfe said. "I don't think

the kidnappers have been in touch yet. Why are you asking me, anyway? I thought you and Delko were working that."

"I've been . . . reassigned," Calleigh said. "H needs my help on another case."

"What, the John Doe from the swamp? Yeah, like he's going anywhere." Wolfe shook his head. "I don't know. I hate to second-guess Horatio, but you'd think he'd want his best people on a kidnapping."

"Horatio knows what he's doing," Calleigh said coolly. "He also knows when to keep his mouth shut." She rolled up her window and drove on.

Wolfe stared after her with a frown on his face. "What? What did I say?" he asked Tripp. "I could have sworn I just paid her a compliment."

Tripp shook his head. "Wolfe, you may be a helluva CSI, but you have a lot to learn about office politics. Not to mention stepping on other people's toes."

Horatio followed his nose down the hall and into the main lab. "Mister Wolfe," he said. "It smells like a Greek restaurant in here. Is this case-related, or is the lab branching out into other areas?"

Wolfe gave him a rueful smile. "Well, it beats decomp—but, yeah, the aroma is a little strong. I'm testing samples from a delicatessen; I think this is how our dead Santa wound up with two antidepressants in his bloodstream."

"I see. Any leads on suspects?"

"Frank's bringing in one of the organizers of the event. The deli stop was planned in advance, but it's unclear if the killer was involved or just taking advantage of the situation—calls made to the business were from a pay phone in downtown Miami, could have been anyone. And we still have no idea why the vic was murdered."

"The holidays can be a very stressful time," Horatio said. "Family conflicts come to the fore, finances are strained . . . all factors that can trigger a murder. Have you looked into his relatives?"

"Only one we've been able to discover is a sister, but she lives out of state and hasn't talked to her brother in years. Frank says her story checks out."

Horatio nodded. "How about money? Insurance policy?"

"No. Patrick was an actor—he didn't even have health insurance, let alone life. So far, the only reason anyone might have to kill him was a couple of bad commercials he made. I found his demo tape and played it—his big moment in the limelight seems to be an ad for a supermarket chain he did five years ago. Since then, he's been in a few local plays and done some voice acting. Barely paying the bills, as near as I can tell."

"Well, the entertainment industry is built on overnight success stories," Horatio said. "And for every actor who suddenly hits the jackpot, there's a long line of people behind him who didn't make the grade."

"So if Patrick suddenly got his big break, whoever he beat out might have felt cheated," Wolfe said thoughtfully. "Nobody likes second place."

"But removing Patrick," Horatio said, "would put them back in first."

"Jenson's decrypting Patrick's hard drive right now. Hopefully, that'll tell us what his current project was."

"Don't forget to check in with his agent," Horatio said. "And you might want to reinterview a few of the other Santas as well. If he'd just gotten a big part, Santacon may have been his way of celebrating. In that case, it's doubtful he could have resisted talking about it."

"None of the Santas I interviewed mentioned anything like that, but they were all pretty intoxicated. I'll do some reinterviews, see if I can jog a few memories."

"Do that," Horatio said. "And Mister Wolfe?"

"Yes?"

"Good work . . ."

11

"HEY, NATALIA," CALLEIGH SAID. "You've got access to more than just human DNA databases, right?"

Natalia Boa Vista set down the tray of samples she was carrying beside the autoclave. "Sure. The Justice Project is primarily about using DNA to re-examine old cases, but we exchange data with all sorts of other agencies, including ATF, Fish and Wildlife, and APHIS."

Calleigh looked puzzled. "AFIS? I thought that was a fingerprint database."

Natalia smiled. "Not AFIS, APHIS—the U.S. Department of Agriculture's Animal and Plant Health Inspection Service. They oversee the importation of flora and fauna into the country."

"That's exactly the kind of resource I need. I've got a suspect who might be involved in animal smuggling, and I may need to match a sample against prohibited species."

"Well, there's no shortage of those—of the three hundred and thirty species of parrot, two hundred and twenty-eight are regulated. Forty-five of those are on a list banning all trade, and the rest require export permits from their country of origin."

Calleigh's eyebrows went up. "You seem to know a lot about it."

Natalia shrugged. "I knew a guy who was a parrothead. Not a Jimmy Buffett fan, a tropical-bird nut. When I found out how big the black market in animals and animal parts is, I took a professional interest—according to some estimates, the only other criminal enterprise that makes more money is the drug trade."

"Even more than arms dealing? Maybe I went into the wrong branch of forensics."

"Well, you're in the right place, anyway—the U.S. is the biggest market for wildlife and wildlife products. A law was passed in 1992 restricting the import of psittacine species, but by that point, we were bringing in a hundred and fifty thousand birds a year. And that was just through legal channels—there was an underground even then, and it's gotten a lot bigger since. Birds are usually 'laundered' by bringing them in through Mexico, where it's easier to get export documents."

"How about Brazil?"

"Home of the Amazon rain forest? Let me put it this way—what cocaine is to Colombia, exotic species are to Brazil. The illegal wildlife trade there generates somewhere between six and twenty billion dollars a year, involving the theft and smuggling of up to thirty-eight million birds and animals. They're trapped in the forest, then routed through big cities like Rio or Brasília."

"Or São Paulo?"

"Sure. Then they're smuggled out of the country to customers in Europe, the Far East, or here. In Asia, they seem to favor using animal parts for aphrodisiacs; in Italy, it's all about gourmet cuisine. *Spiedo uccelli* is still considered a delicacy."

"Am I going to regret asking what that is?"

"Depends on how you feel about robins, thrushes, and finches. It means 'songbird on a spit.'"

"If you can't find the bluebird of happiness, settle for having barbecue?"

Natalia laughed. "Something like that. Here in the States, we seem more interested in keeping them as pets—and apparently, we're willing to pay for it. A bird like a Lear's macaw—of which there are only about two hundred in existence—will go for upwards of sixty thousand dollars."

Calleigh whistled. "I hope it talks. For that much money, it should dance and sing, too."

"Actually, a captured bird like that will be lucky if it can still breathe. They use large nets to catch them in flight or coat branches in glue. Only one in four smuggled birds lives through the process—sometimes as little as one in ten. Often, they're drugged and crammed into tiny spaces, or even taped to people's bodies. And even if they don't die from being crushed or dehydrated or just sheer stress, they often carry diseases that can kill them and infect other birds."

Calleigh looked thoughtful. "Which diseases?"

"I'm not sure—parrot fever is the only one I can remember. According to my friend, it can be transmitted from bird to human, but it's rarely fatal."

"Do you remember anything about the symptoms?"

Natalia studied Calleigh for a second and frowned. "Why? You don't think you're—"

"No, no. I'm just collecting data."

"Well, I've about exhausted what I know about the subject."

"That's okay," Calleigh said with a smile. "I think I know just the person to go to next."

Monica Steinwitz was obviously not happy to be sitting across an interview table from a CSI and a police detective. She'd pushed her chair back and sat with both her arms and legs crossed, a scowl on her face. She had a long, angular face, made more so by her dark hair pulled back in a tight braid. She was dressed in jeans and a baggy sweatshirt that had a large cartoon pig wearing sunglasses on it. Wolfe didn't think she'd chosen the shirt by accident.

"You're one of the organizers of Santacon,"

Wolfe said for the third time. "We know it and we can prove it. So why don't you just admit it?"

"Am I being charged with something?" Steinwitz asked sharply. "Because I have a lawyer who will just *love* both of you."

"No, you're not being charged," Tripp said.

"Not yet, anyway," Wolfe said flatly.

Tripp gave him a warning glance, then continued, "We'd just like to ask you a few more questions about your group."

"It's not *my* group," she snapped. "There *is* no formal organization. There are no leaders, no membership lists, no grand plan—just some people who exchange messages on the Internet. And none of what we discuss is illegal."

"Right," Wolfe said. "So who planned your Santa route, elves?"

Tripp sighed. "Look, you've got the wrong idea. We are not interested in prosecuting Santacon for illegal activities. But we have reason to believe that your group was used to help plan a crime, and the quicker we find the person responsible, the sooner we'll leave you alone."

She didn't seem convinced. "If a Santa committed a crime, they did it on their own. Anyone can join the group, anyone can put on a suit and rampage."

"But not everyone can tell the Santas where to go to eat," Wolfe said. "You did that. Which means that right now, you're our number one suspect."

She glared at him, but Wolfe met her eyes with a hard look of his own. After a few seconds she looked away. "It wasn't my idea to use the deli. It was somebody calling themselves Amelia Claus. And no, I don't know her real name; I never even met her in person. She told me she could get the deli to pony up ten percent of whatever Santa spent to go to charity, plus deli food is fast and we could get back on the street sooner."

"Did that turn out to be true?" Tripp said.

"No," Steinwitz admitted. "The food was quick enough, but when I asked the owner about the charity donation, he didn't know what I was talking about. I was going to ask Amelia about it, but she never showed."

Not under that name, anyway, Wolfe thought. "We're going to have to take a look at any and all correspondence you had with this woman," he said.

"You're going to need a warrant," she said coldly.

"Then we'll get one," Wolfe said.

"All birds, from canaries to eagles, can be carriers of parrot fever," Alexx said. "When a psittacine species—like parakeets, parrots, or cockatoos—carry it, it's called psittacosis. If it shows up in another avian species, it's referred to as ornithosis. They're both caused by the same bacterium, *Chlamydia psittaci.*" She reached up and opened a cubbyhole door, revealing boxes of latex gloves. She counted them silently, tapping a neatly manicured fingernail against each one, then wrote a number on the clipboard she held.

"I can come back later if you're busy," Calleigh said, glancing around the autopsy room. There was no body currently on the table.

"No, no, I can talk at the same time." Alexx pulled out a box of gloves that was already opened and frowned. "Hmm."

"What about symptoms?"

"Usually presents as the common flu: chills, fever, headache, muscle soreness, a dry cough. Hepatitis, endocarditis, and neurologic complications can show up, too. It's usually not life-threatening, but a severe case can progress through to fatal pneumonia." Alexx took the open box of gloves over to a digital scale, took one out, and laid it on the metal tray. "And then there's exotic Newcastle disease. Nasty little bug, but it mainly affects poultry. The incubation period is from three to twenty-eight days, but carriers sometimes have no symptoms at all and can spread the virus for up to a year from their feces, feathers, blood—even their exhalations. Outside the host body, it can live for a long time in all sorts of environments: in lake water or damp soil, on insects or rodents. It's resistant to many disinfectants, laughs at anything under fifty-six degrees C when it comes to sterilization, and can survive indefinitely when frozen. When it does kick in, its mortality rate is close to a hundred percent."

Alexx weighed the glove, made a notation, then replaced it on the scale with a full box.

"You said *mainly*," Calleigh said. "So it can be caught by humans, too?"

"Oh, sure. Symptoms are usually malaise and some conjunctivitus—that's about it. It's a real killer when it comes to birds, but it's not a threat to people." Alexx weighed the full box, took it off the scale, and made another notation.

"Don't you have an intern or something that could do that for you?" Calleigh asked.

Alexx rolled her eyes. "Sure, if I didn't care about the results. I like to know what I have on hand, and I like to know *exactly* where it is. Anyone but me does the inventory, there's no telling what they might miss. I like to keep my hand on the rudder, girl."

"Can't argue with you there. Not when I can tell you exactly how many boxes of ammunition I have stored in the ballistics lab, and which kinds. But even I don't *weigh* them."

"When you deal with as many biologicals as I do, you get used to weighing all sorts of things," Alexx said. "I'm just trying to figure out how many gloves are left in this box . . ."

"Well, I'm trying to figure out if Hector Villanova might have been involved in bird smuggling. Is it possible he was infected with psittacosis or END?"

Alexx glanced at Calleigh sharply. "It's possible," she conceded. "Highly unlikely in the case of psittacosis, though; ninety percent of cases present with respiratory symptoms, and the X-ray I took of his chest was clear. A simple blood test would tell us, though, one way or the other."

"Great. I mean, I don't want to interrupt your inventory—"

Alexx gave her a look.

"Right," Calleigh said. "Just kidding."

Alexx put down the box of gloves. "Calleigh? No disrespect meant, but—I thought Delko was handling the Villanova case."

"He was," Calleigh sighed. "But it got kicked to me. Delko's working the Pathan kidnapping."

"But—"

"It's a long story, Alexx—I'd rather not get into it, okay?"

"Okay, honey. I know you'll do a great job." Alexx paused. "And I know a live victim matters more than a dead one. But Hector—and the people that loved him—they deserve some justice, too. Don't forget that."

"I won't, Alexx. I'll talk to you later, okay?"

"Sure."

After Calleigh left, Alexx glanced over at the wall of steel drawers, where Hector Villanova's remains still rested. "Sorry, baby," she murmured. "Even the dead have to wait in line, sometimes . . ."

One of the perks of working for the AV department of the Miami-Dade Crime Lab was not having to wear a lab coat. Tyler Jenson usually took full advantage of this, favoring short-sleeved shirts in eye-catching patterns, but today he was wearing a drab beige sweater. His usually cheerful face was pale and his nose was red. He sneezed just as Wolfe walked in the door.

"Gesundheit," Wolfe said.

"Thank you," Jenson said. "Man, I get sick every year, just before Christmas. I swear, most of my memories of the holidays are linked to the taste of cough syrup."

"I thought I saw Delko blowing his nose, earlier. But did you give it to him or did he give it to you?"

"Who knows?" Jenson said. "A cold is like a fruitcake—it gets passed around so much nobody remembers who had it in the first place. You're here about the Patrick computer, right?"

"Right. Any luck?"

"Sure. The guy wasn't exactly a hacker—his password turned out to be *Hamlet*. I just ran a dictionary program through the log-in page. Anybody that uses a single word like that isn't serious about security."

"Well, he wasn't James Bond—though he might have wanted to play him," Wolfe said. "What did you find?"

Jenson held up a disc. "Here. I downloaded all his files onto this. Besides his email, there's some scripts, some very pedestrian pornography, and what looks like an attempt at a novel."

Wolfe hesitated, then took the disc gingerly by one corner. "You know, the number one way germs are spread is through lack of hand-washing."

Jenson smiled and inhaled loudly through his nose, producing a noise like an elephant gargling. "Misery loves company," he said. "You better go— I think I'm about to contaminate the entire room. Again."

Wolfe left.

It didn't take him long to scan the files. The scripts were all two or more years old and amateurish; he checked online, but none of them seemed to be in production, either. The novel was about a struggling actor in Miami, was only two chapters long, and was mostly devoted to long descriptions of casual sex punctuated by the angst of the misunderstood artist.

The emails were more interesting, but only in a voyeuristic sort of way—Kingsley Patrick's life, despite the sheen of glamour being an actor was supposed to supply, was mostly a series of part-time jobs, part-time relationships, and party-time whenever he could afford it. If he'd gotten a big break recently, he wasn't talking about it online. He didn't even have an agent—he'd been searching for new representation since he'd fired his old one nine months ago.

And then Wolfe found the emails from Amelia C. She'd contacted him. She claimed to know his work from television and was a fan; while Wolfe thought that doubtful, Patrick seemed to have bought it. The emails were flirty in tone, and gradually led up to an invitation to join the Santas in their annual rampage.

So she lured him to Santacon, Wolfe thought, *and presumably to the mini-golf course and the deli. But why? Was she a crazed fan, an ex-girlfriend, or something else entirely?*

"Ms. Blitzen," Wolfe said. "Feeling better?"

"I am, thanks," Valerie Blitzen said. She was dressed a little more provocatively than last time, in a tight-fitting top and a short skirt. Her complexion didn't seem as pale, but it was hard to tell—she was wearing makeup.

"You're going to tell me I'm under arrest, aren't you?" she said nervously. "Oh, God. I killed that guy by having sex with him, didn't I?"

Wolfe chuckled. "No, you didn't. You're in the clear as far as sexual homicide goes—the cause of death was something else. I just wanted to talk to you once you'd had a chance to recover yourself; sometimes, after a little reflection, certain things that were hazy clear up a bit."

She closed her eyes and let out a huge sigh. "Oh. Oh, man. That is such a big relief."

"I know you were kind of . . . distracted, but you spent more time with the victim than anyone else. Did he mention his own plans for Christmas, or Christmas Eve?"

She thought about it. "Uh . . . now that I think about it, he might have. I have this vague memory of him asking me if I wanted to go to a really big Christmas Eve party. He said it was in some swanky hotel, but he could get both of us in. I asked him if he worked there or something, and he just laughed."

"Do you remember the name of the hotel?"

"No. I don't think he told me what it was. Anyway, I told him I already had plans—Christmas Eve, you know? I'm going to spend it with family."

"Right. You mentioned that the victim had also been flirting with other Santas—do you remember any particular one standing out? Maybe one that was hanging around him a lot and then abruptly left?"

She shook her head. "Not really, no. I hadn't really noticed the guy at all until he started hitting on me—and by then I sort of had tunnel vision, you know?"

Wolfe thanked her for coming in and told her to contact him if she remembered anything else. She promised to do so, and he watched her leave with the gloomy realization that he was running out of leads.

He shook his head, trying to regain his focus. *C'mon, Ryan*, he thought. *You've still got the mysterious Amelia Claus's email to track down. Time to go bug Jenson again.*

This time, though, he'd bring some latex gloves with him.

And some tissues.

"What's the good word, Wolfe?" Tripp looked at the deli samples spread around the lab and grinned. "Lunch, maybe?"

"The good word," Wolfe said, "is herring. Pickled herring, to be exact."

He pointed to a large jar filled with silvery, barrel-shaped rollmops. "I tested the brine they're soaking in, and it came back positive for a very small amount of imipramine. I think she dosed one or two of the pieces and the drug leached into the surrounding liquid."

"How could she know he'd get the right ones?"

"Maybe she brought them over to his table herself—Santas are generous, remember? Imipramine is soluble in alcohol and water, so she might have just had a vial of the stuff in liquid form and dumped it over the top. A small amount would just diffuse throughout the jar and probably wouldn't be harmful to anyone else."

"But whoever got the first helping would get a lot more," Tripp said grimly. "And with all the confusion, no one would notice one of the Santas adding a little extra holiday cheer to a jar."

"I dusted the lid and the glass for prints, but didn't get anything," Wolfe said. "Not much of a surprise; a lot of the Santas wear gloves as part of their outfit. I expected to at least get some of the employees' prints, but they must wipe everything down on a regular basis."

"So he was telling the truth about running a clean place. I'll keep that in mind the next time I get a craving for Greek salad," Tripp said. "Where does that leave us?"

"Looking for Amelia Claus. I've got Jenson trying to locate her IP address from Patrick's computer."

"Good. The warrant for Monica Steinwitz's computer records just came through," Tripp said, pulling a folded piece of paper from his pocket. "Between hers and Patrick's, maybe we can find this woman."

"Let's go," Wolfe said, shrugging out of his lab coat.

Monica Steinwitz lived over a warehouse on Northwest Twenty-third Street. The warehouse itself was a gallery space, bare concrete floors underfoot and thick, squared-off ducts of gray galvanized tin overhead. The main room was two stories tall, big and echoey with the smell of oil-based paint sharp and heavy in the air. The banks of fluorescent tubes that had once provided lighting were just empty shells now, their function now performed by tiny halogen spots suspended by fishing line and angled to highlight the walls.

Tripp studied the sculpture just to the right of

the entryway, one fist propped under his chin, the other holding his elbow. The sculpture was a large piece of clear Lucite in the form of a teardrop; captured inside was a crumpled and charred metal container, the rectangular, gallon-sized kind used for white gas. Flecks of rust and ash were suspended around it, their edges as intricate and detailed as snowflakes.

"*Fuel Fossil,*" Wolfe said, reading the label on the base. "I get it. Lucite is a form of plastic, which is derived from petroleum, which in turn is made from dinosaurs—it's where we get the term *fossil fuel.*"

"Yeah, that much is obvious," Tripp said. "I was just trying to decide if it reminded me more of Jeff Koons's stuff or Brian Jungen's."

Wolfe stared at him. He blinked.

Tripp scowled. "What, I'm not allowed to know about anything other than football and beer? Miami has a lot of great art."

"Yeah, but—you're from Texas."

Tripp snorted. "So? Guess you've never been to Austin, huh?"

"Well—"

"C'mon. Let's go grab Ms. Steinwitz's computer before she turns it into a planter or something."

The curator directed them up a flight of wooden stairs; Steinwitz's apartment had apparently been converted from the warehouse's office space. Loud music could be heard from inside—something that sounded like a Russian military band staging a frontal assault on a techno dance club. Tripp paused on the landing and pounded loudly on the dented metal of the door.

"Miami-Dade police!" he shouted. "Please open the—"

The music abruptly shut off. A bolt slid back and the door opened, revealing Monica Steinwitz in a pair of flannel pajama pants, an oversize T-shirt covered with paint stains, and bare feet. "All right, all right. What do you want *now*?"

Tripp held up the warrant. "Your computer, Ms. Steinwitz."

She glowered at him. "Well, I guess I can't stop you. But if you damage a single cable, I'll see you in court."

"You may, anyway," Wolfe said as he walked in. "Depending on what we find . . ."

Steinwitz's place was large, but crowded; art in various mediums and stages of completion covered tables, counters, walls, and floors. A dominant theme seemed to be figures with exaggerated pro-portions, either skeletal, grossly inflated, or some combination of the two.

The computer sat on a desk in a cubbyhole space beneath a bed on an elevated platform. Wolfe made sure it was unplugged, then started disconnecting cables.

"I can't believe you'd invade my privacy like this," Steinwitz fumed. "I told you, I've never met this Amelia in person and I don't have any idea who she is. All my computer is going to give you is her email address, and she could have an anonymous account set up anywhere."

"Let us worry about that," Tripp said.

Wolfe straightened up, almost hitting his head on the underside of the bed. "Uh, I hate to impose further, but I had a lot of coffee today—you think I could use your bathroom?"

She glared at him. "You know what? No, you can't. I don't have to give you access to anything other than what's specified in the warrant, and my bathroom is *not* on the list."

She stomped over to the kitchen sink—her apartment, other than the bathroom, was just one big room—and turned on the water. "I hope this doesn't *bother* you," she said acidly.

"Wolfe?" Tripp asked.

"Uh, I'll be fine. Actually, I guess it wasn't as urgent as I thought. We'll be out of your way shortly."

He went back to work.

And smiled.

Calleigh found Marco Boraba at home. He lived in one of the stylish, art deco apartment buildings Miami Beach was well-known for, but when he came to the door he didn't look as if he was in any shape to appreciate his surroundings. Both his eyes were red and swollen, and his posture and expression suggested that he wanted nothing more than to go back to bed. He was dressed as impeccably as he had been last time, though, in a dark gray suit with a purple silk tie.

"Miss Duquesne," he said. "A pleasure to see you again. Have you found out what happened to Hector?"

"That's what I'd like to talk to you about. May I come in?"

"Certainly."

He ushered her inside and into a living area decorated in colorful South American wall hangings and rugs, counterpointed by a couch and several low-slung chairs upholstered in spotless white leather. Boraba lowered himself carefully into one of the chairs, and Calleigh perched on an end of the couch.

"You seem to be moving a little slowly today, Mister Boraba. Not feeling well?"

"Just a touch of the flu. It's the season for it, I suppose." He rubbed the corner of one bloodshot eye wearily.

"It's the season for many things, actually. For instance, the hatching season for wild birds starts in early January and goes through until mid-May. Busiest time of year for the illegal bird trade."

The look on his face didn't change, but he blinked several times before answering. "Is it? I didn't know that."

"I want to thank you for the background you gave me on that dog toy. You had no way of knowing, but I have a certain affinity for weapons. I've never investigated a murder by *atlatl*, but, hey, maybe someday. In the meantime, the one I bought from your store will have to stay in the evidence locker."

"Evidence? Of what?" He rubbed his other eye, somewhat nervously.

"That's the problem with conjunctivitis, isn't it? I remember getting pinkeye as a kid—rubbing your eyes only makes it worse, but you just can't stop. Which, inevitably, transfers the virus from your eyes to your hands to whatever you touch. I took that toy back to the lab hoping to get lucky with a fingerprint, but after talking to a friend, I swabbed and tested it for velogenic neurotropic NDV. It came back positive. You have Exotic Newcastle disease, Mister Boraba."

He met her eyes and sighed. "I know."

"END is a notifiable disease as defined by USDA regulations," Calleigh said. "Punishable by fines of up to twenty thousand dollars per violation and a five-year jail sentence. The Department of Agriculture spends a million dollars a year eradicating outbreaks of END—they take it very seriously."

A phone chimed. "That's probably the Wildside Menagerie," Calleigh said. "Right about now, they're being shut down and the premises searched. I'm afraid your entire stock of birds is going to have to be destroyed, Mister Boraba—Newcastle is just too dangerous to take chances. An outbreak in Southern

California in the early seventies resulted in the destruction of twelve million laying hens and cost fifty-six million dollars; nobody wants that to happen again."

"I understand." Boraba's voice was subdued. "What should I tell my staff?"

"Tell them to cooperate. That would be best for everyone."

Boraba picked up the phone. "Yes. Yes, I know. Someone is here now. No, just—show them where the birds are. Yes. No, don't worry about that. Yes, I'll take care of that." He hung up.

"So I have been caught," Boraba said. "And I suppose the story about Hector was just to make me let my guard down, eh? He is alive and well and probably wonders what this is all about?"

"No, Mister Boraba. Hector Villanova didn't tell us anything."

He nodded. "No, of course not. What could he tell? He didn't know anything. All he knew was that his old friend Marco was making money, and he was a divorced plumber far from home. Poor Hector—he never had any ambition. But look what ambition got me, hey? Perhaps Hector was the smarter of us, after all—better a free plumber than a caged millionaire."

"I'm sorry, Mister Boraba, but I told you the truth. Hector Villanova is dead. I thought at first you might be involved, but you just got back into the country after several weeks in Mexico—and

Hector Villanova's blood showed no traces of psittacosis or Newcastle. He had no idea what you were up to, did he?"

"No. No, he—he wasn't like that. The idea of Hector as a criminal? If you knew him, you wouldn't think that for a second. He was a good man."

Marco Boraba gave her a sad, red-eyed smile. "A much better man," he said softly, "than me."

"You know, that's the third time you've washed your hands in the last hour," Wolfe pointed out. "I'm all for hygiene—especially after visiting Jenson in the AV lab—but as someone who knows something about obsessive-compulsive disorder, I gotta say you're starting to worry me."

Calleigh shot him a dirty look as she dried her hands. "All right, all right. I guess I'm overreacting a little—I just don't want to wind up in quarantine. Marco Boraba is going to spend the holidays all alone, probably eating hospital food. No, thank you."

"Yeah, the holidays. When people gorge themselves with all sorts of rich foods . . . but some people are more about the unstuffing than the stuffing."

Calleigh came over to where Wolfe was working. "In what sense? Are you talking about a computer file?"

"That's Jenson's department. His filthy, disease-ridden department . . . sorry. No, I'm talking about food—and the quickest way to serve it with an eviction notice."

"Okay, you've lost me. How does this tie in with your dead Kris Kringle case?"

"One of the Santas is an artist. When Tripp and I served her with a warrant to confiscate her computer, I noticed that a lot of her art dealt with exaggerated body images, either very thin or very fat. And I remembered that one of the drugs used to poison the vic, phenelzine, is also used in the treatment of certain psychiatric disorders—including bulimia."

"Splurge and purge? Did you check her medicine cabinet?"

"Tried, but the warrant only covered the computer and she wouldn't let me in the bathroom."

"Makes sense. Bulimics are secretive, and most of them have a highly developed sense of radar when it comes to other people invading their privacy. One of my roommates in college was bulimic, but I never knew until I found her stash of laxatives—she used to unwrap candy bars and substitute chocolate Ex-Lax. I probably never would have found out if my sweet tooth hadn't gotten the better of me."

"Well, that's one argument against raiding somebody else's fridge. . . . Anyway, I'm hoping Jenson can pull something probative off her hard drive. Unless I can get a warrant, there's no way to prove she has access to phenelzine."

"You're still doing better than I am. Boraba was my only lead in the Villanova case—now I'm back to square one. I haven't got any further than Delko did."

"Really? The lab's top two investigators, both stumped? That's . . ."

"Irritating? Frustrating? Depressing?"

"Not really the direction I was headed," Wolfe said with a grin. "Actually, it's nice to know you guys aren't infallible."

"Oh? You think you could do any better?"

He raised his eyebrows. "Is that a challenge?"

"Depends. If it'll get my case jump-started, then yes. Otherwise, consider it idle workplace banter."

"Okay, I accept. Consider it an early Christmas present."

"For who? Me, or your ego?"

"Depends on whether or not I get anywhere, I guess. . . but there is one condition."

"So this is a gift exchange? What did you have in mind?"

"*You* have to deal with Jenson."

Calleigh sighed. "I just can't get away from germs, can I? All right, I'll do it. But if I come down with something, I'm going to be sneezing in *your* direction."

"The Pathan case," Sackheim told Horatio, "has taken a somewhat . . . unusual turn."

Horatio leaned back in his office chair and regarded the FBI agent curiously. Delko, his arms crossed, stood beside Horatio's desk with an impassive look on his face. Sackheim had asked to speak to Horatio alone; Horatio had smiled, shaken his head, and told Sackheim to just say what was on his mind.

"Unusual in what way?" Horatio asked.

"We've heard from the kidnappers. This disc was delivered two hours ago." He held up a CD, the prismatic surface catching the late-afternoon sun slanting through the window. "My own people have been over it—zero for prints or trace, of course. The only thing on it is a text file."

"With a list of demands, I assume."

"There's only one. The kidnappers insist on dealing with a particular person as intermediary, and that person only." Sackheim dropped the disc on Horatio's desk with a clatter. "You."

12

"THE THING ABOUT KINGSLEY PATRICK that you have to remember," the bald woman said thoughtfully, "is that he was a *schmuck*."

"What makes you say that?" Tripp shifted in the leather chair and rested his notebook on one knee, his pen in the other hand. The small office smelled of extremely good coffee, and he found himself wishing he'd said yes to her offer of a cup.

"I was his agent, I should know. I mean, I may not be the best agent in the world—or even the state—but I got him paying gigs. You want to know why he quit me? I wasn't getting him the parts he wanted. I tried to tell him, look, you're the one that gets or doesn't get the part; me, I just set up meetings and do lunch. A lot of lunch."

Stella Ragosa reminded Tripp of a squirrel—

small, energetic, with prominent front teeth that were spotlessly white. Her completely hairless head somehow increased the effect, though Tripp wasn't sure how. Maybe it was the way her ears stuck out.

"Cancer," Ragosa said.

"Excuse me?"

"The hair, or lack thereof. People always stare, I'm used to it. Shaved it after the chemo, but I hate hats. Always have. Tried wigs, but they itch."

"I'm, uh—"

"Sorry for my loss? Don't worry about it. The cancer was back in '86, I beat it to death with drugs and attitude—*that,* I got plenty of—and it's never been back. I kept the look because it starts conversations and gets me remembered. My husband thinks it's sexy, but he's an even *bigger* schmuck. Of course, I married him, so what does that make me?"

Tripp didn't even try to answer that. "Was Patrick ever involved in any criminal activities?"

"Just his acting, that was criminal enough. No, I'm sorry, that was a cheap shot. I shouldn't speak ill of the dead." She sighed theatrically, which was apparently the way she did everything. "He wasn't that bad an actor. His ego was bigger than his talent, but God knows *that's* not a rarity in this business. But anything illegal? He wouldn't turn down a little coke if it was being handed out, but that was about it. At least, that's all I know about; since he left my agency, we weren't exactly in touch. I think he called once to get his head shots back, that was about it."

"All right, Ms. Ragosa. Thank you for your time."

"My pleasure, Detective. You ever want to go into acting, give me a call." She looked him up and down frankly as he stood. "Put you in a cowboy hat, you could sell anything from barbecue sauce to Range Rovers."

"Thanks," Tripp said, "but I'll leave that kind of thing to the professionals."

Jenson had pulled a list of contacts from Kingsley's email and given it to Wolfe. While Tripp talked to Kingsley's associates, Wolfe was trying to link Monica Steinwitz to a source of phenelzine.

Or that's what he was supposed to be doing—but since Jenson was doing the actual work on Steinwitz's computer, Wolfe was free to spend a little time on the Villanova case. He went over Delko's and Calleigh's notes carefully, then pulled the physical evidence from the evidence locker. There wasn't much: the chain the body had been wrapped in, a few fragments that had survived the explosion, the samples Delko had collected from Villanova's hotel room. The boat was still in the lab's garage, downstairs; Wolfe took a trip in the elevator to look at it.

Delko had it up on two blue plastic sawhorses. Wolfe walked around it, noting the jagged hole that had sunk her, the empty oarlocks, the long pole beside her. He tried to envision the sequence of events.

Hector Villanova has just had a big Christmas dinner, for which he paid extra cash to have early, because he's not going to be around on Christmas Eve. He's celebrating something—a big business deal, probably. Maybe one that involves traveling on Christmas Eve, even though he's not booked on any flights or cruises or trains—at least, not under his own name.

But something goes wrong. Someone takes him for a boat ride to the middle of nowhere. Hector must have been rowing, probably with a gun aimed at him; once they got into the swamp, they ditched the oars and switched to the pole. Maybe the killer had already attached the bomb and used it to control Hector.

Wolfe shook his head. *No. Couldn't have done that unless the bomb was remote-activated, and it used a simple fuse, the light-and-run kind. So where did the killer run to? Delko found only one footprint in the immediate area, on a log.*

He went back upstairs and dug through the stack of photos Delko had taken. The footprint matched Hector Villanova's shoe size, and from the tooth fragment Delko had found in the tree trunk it seemed obvious that Villanova had been standing on that spot when the bomb went off. The killer must have stayed in the boat.

It must have been a long fuse. Delko found traces of

duct tape—maybe Villanova's eyes were taped shut so he couldn't see what was coming.

And afterward, the killer had wrapped the body in chains, used drain cleaner to dissolve Villanova's hands—

No, that's not right. If Villanova was standing on the log, his body would have toppled into the water after the detonation. So the killer would have wrapped the chains around him first.

That worked—except it left Villanova at the bottom of the swamp with his hands intact.

So the body hadn't fallen into the swamp after the bomb went off. It had stayed out of the water long enough for the killer to remove Villanova's hands—and even with a strong chemical agent like lye, that would have taken a while. And then . . .

"Then the killer sinks the boat he arrived in and makes his way out of the swamp without leaving behind any tracks," Wolfe muttered. "Which means he waded or swam his way to more solid ground, far enough away from the crime scene to be undetected. And either walked out of the Everglades on his own, at night, or was picked up by someone nearby."

He didn't like either scenario. Two boats seemed complicated and unnecessary, and the killer would have to be extremely confident and knowledgeble of the 'Glades to risk gators, snakes, and quicksand—especially at night.

He studied the photos of the crime scene closely. It made even less sense; if Villanova had been standing on the log the footprint had been found on, he would almost certainly have toppled into the water when the bomb detonated, unless he'd been secured somehow.

Wolfe had a sudden inspiration. He checked the photos again, then went over the chain carefully, link by link. Delko walked in when he was almost finished.

"Is that the chain from the Villanova case?" Delko asked.

"Yeah." Wolfe told Delko about what he'd figured out. "So I thought, maybe the chain wrapped around Villanova went up, into a tree. That would keep the body from falling into the water when the explosives detonated."

"Good theory," Delko said. "But I was there—there weren't any overhanging branches long enough or strong enough to support the body's weight."

"I couldn't tell for sure from the pictures. But the chain would have had to run through the blast zone, so I checked it for charring or blast damage. No luck."

"What are you doing working on this, anyway? I thought H had Calleigh assigned."

"Just thought I'd do her a favor, that's all."

Delko grinned. "Sure. What's she doing for you?"

"Dealing with Jenson. Apparently AV techs are allowed to work while carrying communicable diseases. Speaking of which—didn't I see you suppressing a sneeze today?"

"Me? Nah, I'm healthy as a racehorse. Just a little allergic reaction to something in the air."

"Right . . . anyway, there's something definitely off about the whole Villanova scenario. I just haven't quite figured out what yet."

"Well, good luck. I'm going to have my hands full with the Pathan kidnapping."

"Yeah? You mean the Feebs are actually letting you play with their ball?"

"They don't have a choice. The kidnappers finally got in touch, and they say Horatio is the only one they'll deal with."

Wolfe's eyes widened. "Really? That's kind of *weird*, isn't it?"

"You can say that again. I thought Sackheim's head was gonna explode."

"Well, every cloud has a silver lining, I guess . . ."

"Hi, Tyler," Calleigh said brightly. "You don't look so bad."

Jenson raised his eyebrows and smiled back. "Gee, that's the nicest thing anyone's said to me all day. Which means everyone hates me. Which, considering my dazzling personality, I'm at a complete loss to understand."

"Well, from the way Ryan was carrying on, it sounded like you were at death's door. You don't even look like you're in the neighborhood."

"Wow, you Southern gals really know how to charm a guy. Keep that up and I may swoon."

"Oh, please," Calleigh said. "It takes *years* to learn how to swoon properly, not to mention a highly specialized wardrobe. You might be able to pull off a case of the vapors, but swooning is definitely out of your league."

"Very well, madam, I stand corrected. Except I'm sitting. How can I help?"

"You know, you seem a little manic for someone who's supposed to be sick."

"Cold medication. You know how they come labeled *drowsy* and *nondrowsy*?

"I'm guessing you took the nondrowsy one."

"I took several. *Nondrowsy* is my new favorite euphemism. As in, 'I'm so nondrowsy I think I'll go for a little walk at three a.m. Or a jog. Or, what the hell, a flat-out run for a few miles, see if I can get stopped by Miami PD. 'Excuse me, son, have you been drinking?' 'Why, no, Officer, I just took a little non. I feel a little nonny.' Actually, to tell the truth, I'm completely and totally *nonned*."

"Uh-huh. You sound like me the time I accidentally inhaled cocaine dust. Tell me you're not drinking coffee, too."

"No need, no need. Now. What were we talking about, again?"

"Ryan sent me. He wants to know if you've cracked the Steinwitz computer yet."

Jenson pointed at the monitor in front of him. "Yep. Just scanning the data now, in fact. Anything in particular you're looking for?"

She leaned over his shoulder, studying the screen. "Ryan said he was initially interested in the emails from a woman calling herself Amelia Claus, but anything to do with a drug called phenelzine could be important, too."

"I'll do a search, see if anything comes up." Jenson hit a few keys, studied the results, then tapped on a few more. "Hmm. Looks like you got lucky. *Phenelzine* shows up in a couple of different files."

"Can you isolate all those files in one folder for me?"

"Done and . . . done. So why am I getting a visit from Bullet Girl instead of the Wolfman?"

She cocked an eyebrow. "The Wolfman?"

"Okay, nobody actually calls him that, I just made it up. Still."

"I'm doing him a favor, that's all."

"Really? I thought you tore a strip off him earlier."

She frowned at him. "Where'd you hear that?"

"When you lose your temper in the parking lot, people are going to notice."

She crossed her arms. "I did *not* lose my temper. It was just a difference of professional opinion."

"The squealing tires afterward is what I heard

about. That's the kind of detail office gossips love, you know."

"Like you, you mean?" She glared at him.

"Hmm. Apparently the package should have read *nonthinking* as well as *nondrowsy*. And warned me against operating heavy machinery—like my mouth."

Her glare softened a little. "Just put those files on a disc for me, okay? I know the *Wolfman* wants to see them as soon as possible. And Jenson?"

"What?"

"The next time you're sick? Stick to aspirin."

"You mind telling me," Tripp said, his hands on his hips, "what a rowboat with a hole in it has to do with our case?"

Wolfe had flipped the boat upside down on the blue sawhorses and was squatting underneath it, looking up with a flashlight in his hand.

"It doesn't," Wolfe said. "While you were talking to Kingsley's known associates, I thought I'd do Calleigh a favor."

"Well, that's awfully generous of you, but I'm all done talking to Kingsley's friends. None of them knew about anything he might have been into that he shouldn't. I thought you were gonna see what you could pull from his computer?"

"Jenson's working on it. In the meantime, I thought I'd take a look in the SS *Minnow* here . . . and I think I just found something interesting."

He went into a crouch, his head disappearing inside the boat.

"What'd you find?"

"It's what I didn't find that's interesting," Wolfe said, his voice echoing hollowly. "The vic's hands were burnt off with household drain cleaner, a powerful corrosive. The active ingredient is sodium hydroxide, or lye—and lye reacts with water and aluminum. If the killer had spilt any at all in the boat, which seems likely, I'd be able to tell. I haven't found any traces, and Delko didn't find any tracks around the pool where the body was discovered—so where were the hands removed?"

"Don't ask me," Tripp said gruffly. "Hell, this isn't even my case. Or yours, *compadre*."

Wolfe extricated himself from underneath the boat and straightened up. "I know, I know. I'll check in with Calleigh, see if that computer data is ready."

"Calleigh? I thought Jenson was working on it."

"Does it matter?"

"Not as long as you preserve the chain of evidence. There's a couple judges get real sticky about that kinda thing, and those are the ones I always seem to draw."

Wolfe headed for the elevator, Tripp right behind him. "Don't worry, Calleigh and I are pros," Wolfe said.

"I know—but even pros make mistakes. Look at Calleigh and those fingerprints."

Wolfe frowned. "What? You mean in the original Pathan case?"

"Yeah. Your boy got cut loose because of a fingerprint, right? Word is, Horatio isn't too happy about that."

The elevator door opened and they stepped on. "You're saying that's why she was taken off the case? No wonder she got mad at me when I brought it up."

"Yeah, well, I wouldn't worry about it too much. She'll get over it, and Horatio takes care of his own. He'd take a bullet for anyone on his team, and that includes friendly fire. She'll be all right."

"I'm sure she will. If there's one thing I know about Calleigh Duquesne—"

The doors slid open, revealing Calleigh standing there. "Yes?" Calleigh said. "What exactly is it you know, Mister Wolfe?"

"—it's that she has really, really good hearing," Wolfe said. "Hi."

She gave him a smile that made him swallow involuntarily. He wondered if she'd learned that from Horatio, or if it was the other way around.

"I have the information you were waiting for," she said, handing him the disc. "Apparently, there *are* some files that mention phenelzine. Any luck on your end?"

He told her what he'd found—or rather, hadn't found. "I don't know what it means yet," he finished. "But at least it's something."

"Thanks, I'll follow up on it." She turned around and walked away.

"You think she'll let me live?" Wolfe asked.

"Too soon to tell," Tripp said. "But I wouldn't make any firm plans for the new year."

As it turned out, the phenelzine wasn't the big news. Jenson had managed to trace the email back to its source through the ISP, a local Internet company that gave up the address without a whisper of complaint.

"Probably don't want us getting a warrant and looking at their files too closely," Tripp said. "Which is fine, because the warrant we want is for this place right here."

"Looks like it's in the warehouse district," Wolfe said, studying the address on the screen. "Not too far from Ms. Steinwitz's loft, as a matter of fact."

"You want to try for a doubleheader? Might be able to get a judge to sign off on two warrants at the same time."

"Let me read through these files, first."

"All right. I'm gonna go grab a coffee in the break room."

"Fine," Wolfe said absently, his attention already focused elsewhere.

Steinwitz, it seemed, had done a fair amount

of research on phenelzine, but that didn't mean
she was necessarily taking it. She'd bookmarked
sites that featured information about the drug, including one that detailed the adverse reactions
possible when it was combined with other antidepressants.

There was only way to find out if she'd done
more than look. Wolfe headed for the break
room.

He found Tripp sitting alone at a table, blowing on a mug of coffee and looking pensive.
"What do you think?" he asked before Wolfe
could say a word.

"I think we ask a judge for a peek inside Monica Steinwitz's medicine cabinet," Wolfe said.

"I'll get the paperwork started." Tripp set down
his cup and stood up. "Lousy coffee, anyway . . ."

"Ms. Steinwitz?" Wolfe said, meeting the woman's
hostile stare with a pleasant smile. "I was in the
neighborhood and I was wondering if you'd recon-
sider my request to use your bathroom."

"What is this, a joke?"

"Kind of." He handed her the warrant. "But I'll
let you read the punch line yourself."

She stepped back from the doorway and Wolfe
brushed past her as she was reading the docu-
ment.

"Ms. Steinwitz?" Tripp said. "I'm going to have
to ask you to wait out in the hall, please."

"You—you—" She seemed to be at a loss for words, but from the rising color on her face, Wolfe could tell that wouldn't last long. He headed straight for the bathroom, leaving Tripp to deal with its owner.

It didn't take long to examine. The warrant covered more than just the bathroom, though, and Wolfe followed up with a search of the entire apartment.

It wasn't really necessary; he was just being thorough.

"Got it," he told Tripp, holding up a bottle of pills.

"What does that have to do with anything?" she demanded. "I have a prescription for that!"

"You're going to have to come with us, Ms. Steinwitz," Tripp said. "We've got a few more questions to ask."

"This is *unbelievable*," she spat.

"That's not how I would put it," Wolfe said. "Unappetizing, maybe . . ."

Monica Steinwitz left in the backseat of a patrol car. She'd be waiting for them—probably with her lawyer—when they were done, but Wolfe and Tripp had another job to do first.

Their next stop was a storefront three blocks over. It sat between a parking lot and a liquor store, and from the tattered awning over the door it had once been a pawnshop. The grimy front window was papered over on the inside with yellowing newspapers, the sill littered with the corpses of flies and moths.

"Looks abandoned to me," Tripp said.

"Well, someone's been here recently." Wolfe pointed to one corner of the papered-over window that seemed a little whiter than the others. "The date on that newspaper is only two weeks ago. The rest are all three years old or more."

"The original probably fell down."

"And someone replaced it. Someone who wanted this place sealed off from prying eyes."

"Well then," Tripp said. "What do you say we take a look at what they're keeping under wraps."

He pounded on the front door. "Miami-Dade police!" he called out. "Open up!"

No response.

Tripp pulled his gun, and Wolfe did the same. "Guess I should knock a little louder," Tripp said. He reared back and kicked the door once, just above the knob, and it flew open in a shower of splinters.

They moved inside cautiously. Tripp called out again, but his voice just echoed through the empty, dusty room. A quick search found an empty storeroom in the back and a bathroom with the fixtures ripped out.

Tripp holstered his gun. "Nobody home."

"Yeah, but someone was here not too long ago," Wolfe said. "The floor's been swept, and I can smell Pine-Sol." The only furniture in the room was an eight-foot-long wooden table with folding legs. Wolfe walked over and examined it, then looked underneath. "Power outlet and telephone jack. They could have set up a computer here."

"Registered owner of the property lives in Hong Kong," Tripp said. "Haven't been able to get in touch with him, but I'm betting he doesn't know anything about this. Back door has a little dimple above the lock—just like the one at Kingsley Patrick's apartment."

"Well, they were getting power and Internet access. I'll see what I can dig up on that end." Wolfe bent over and peered closely at the tabletop. "I can see some grains of white powder here."

"Cocaine?"

Wolfe nodded thoughtfully. "I believe so. And from the size of the granules and the distinctive clumping pattern, I can tell you they were processed from coca plants three to four feet high, grown on the south . . . no, the southwest side of a mountain."

"Really? You can tell that?"

Wolfe sighed. "Of *course* not, Frank—it's a few grains of a white powder. What, you think I have microscopic vision or something?'

Tripp shook his head. "Well, sometimes that's what it seems like. Usually when I ask one of you CSIs what something is, I get a description that sounds like it came out of an encyclopedia."

"And I'll do my best to supply you with one. But not until *after* I've gotten a sample of this back to the lab."

"All right," Horatio said. "How do you want to do this?"

Sackheim stared at Horatio from an expensive upholstered chair. The FBI had set up a temporary command post in Khasib Pathan's mansion, on the grounds it was where the kidnappers were most likely to make contact. Horatio suspected the Bureau just liked the plush surroundings and the excellent coffee and pastries Pathan's cook was supplying.

"We'll wait for them to get in touch. You'll be wired with a GPS transponder and headset, which you will use to stay in constant contact. Other than that, we follow their instructions. Mister Pathan wants his son back and is willing to pay whatever ransom is demanded."

"And what if the kidnappers don't ask for money?"

"We'll deal with that as the situation warrants."

Which was FBI-speak for *we don't know but we're not going to admit it.* Horatio didn't push him—if the kidnappers demanded something they couldn't give, such as the release of political prisoners, then they would have a very dicey situation. Most likely, it would mean that Abdus

Pathan was already dead, and the kidnappers just
wanted to make a point.

"If I'm going to do this," Horatio said, "then
you keep me in the loop. I don't want any sur-
prises while I'm out there."

"Of course." Sackheim gave him the thinnest
of smiles. "We take care of our men in the field."

A phone chimed. It was Khasib's house line,
the same one the kidnappers had called before.
Horatio picked it up calmly. "Yes?"

He listened intently, knowing others tapped
into the line were doing the same. The caller said
only one thing, then hung up.

Horatio glanced at Sackheim.

"It's on," Horatio said.

13

THE SINGLE SENTENCE THE KIDNAPPER had spoken, filtered through a voice-changer, was to direct Horatio to a website. Sackheim's unit had it up and running before Horatio had put the phone down.

"It's a geocaching site," the clean-cut young man with the laptop said. Horatio knew about geocaching; it was a hobby that combined orienteering skills with treasure hunting. People hid caches in locations that ranged from remote to urban, then posted Global Positioning System coordinates on a website. Treasure seekers used handheld GPS units to track down the caches, then reported their successes on the website. Caches could contain anything from large amounts of money to inconsequential trinkets you were supposed to move to another cache.

"Do a search for *Caine*," Horatio said. The young man hesitated.

"Do as he says, Caldwell," Sackheim said.

"Yes, sir. There's a new cache that's just been posted under the name Caine. Downtown Miami, it looks like."

"Then we'd better get a move on," Horatio said. "Before some other cacher beats us to the punch."

"We can get you outfitted in a few minutes," Sackheim said.

The door opened, and Delko walked in. Sackheim frowned at the same instant Horatio smiled.

"Good," Horatio said. "That'll give me just enough time to get Eric up to speed. He'll be monitoring me in the field."

"We've got that covered—" Sackheim began.

"I'm sure you do," Horatio said, cutting him off. "Nonetheless, I know Mister Delko's assistance will prove invaluable . . . right, Eric?"

"Hey, I'm a team player, H," Delko said, staring at Sackheim impassively. "Ask anyone."

"Fine," Sackheim said.

As Wolfe expected, Monica Steinwitz had demanded legal representation before she'd give a statement. Her lawyer sat beside her now in the interview room, a squat, frowning black woman with rows of intricately beaded braids lining her scalp.

Wolfe and Tripp sat on the other side of the table, Tripp doing his best to outscowl the two women. Wolfe took one look at the ongoing competition and decided he might get better results with a lighter approach.

"Hi, I'm CSI Ryan Wolfe," he said to the attorney.

"I'm Ms. Scapello," the woman said coldly. "And I'd like to know why my client is being held."

"Your client was found in possession of a drug used to murder a man," Tripp said.

Scapello turned her icy gaze on Tripp. "Then why hasn't she been charged?"

"We'd like to give her the chance to explain herself first," Wolfe interjected.

"Explain what?" Monica Steinwitz snapped. "I told you, I have a prescription for that drug."

"That doesn't mean you didn't use it to poison someone," Tripp said.

"Well, I *didn't*."

"Look, we found emails from the woman who called herself Amelia Claus on your computer, and they seem to support your story," Wolfe said. "But you could have planted those. What we need from you is a DNA sample—the person who slipped our vic the phenelzine also had sex with him."

"Is *that* all?" Steinwitz demanded. "No problem. Bring it on."

Wolfe stood and unwrapped a swab. "Say *ah*."

If there was one building that symbolized Miami's downtown core more than any other, it would have to be the Freedom Tower. Built in 1925, the sixteen-story building housed the *Miami News & Metropolis* for the next three decades, the light shining over Miami Bay from the apex of the Mediterranean Revival–style tower symbolizing the light of truth. In 1955 the newspaper moved, leaving the building empty until it was taken over by the U.S. General Services Administration in 1962. The light from its tower now signified not truth, but freedom; the building was Miami's answer to Ellis Island, processing the thousands of Cuban refugees fleeing Castro's regime.

But in the seventies, like the newspaper before it, the government abandoned the building. Over the following decades it changed ownership many times, but never regained its former glory; at one point it was a squat for the homeless and the criminal, filled with rotting garbage and discarded syringes. A face-lift in '87 by an overseas developer failed to attract commercial success and was discovered to be merely cosmetic when the building was evaluated in 1997; the structure's concrete was riddled with chlorides from Miami's salty air, and its steel supports were rusting. A major overhaul was begun, with the objective of turning the place into a Cuban-American museum, but as with many of Florida's grand projects, it proved elusive. After eight years it had yet to open, and the building was sold again. This time, the owners planned to build a sixty-two-story high-rise on the property, demolishing part of the building but keeping the tower intact, enfolded like a tiny needle between two enormous, curving wings. This plan was met with less than enthusiastic approval by the community—until, in typical Florida fashion, the developers donated the tower itself to Miami-Dade College and promised to leave the entire structure intact. Shortly thereafter, plans for the condominium development were approved.

Horatio had driven his Hummer to the tower and gotten the security guard posted there to let him into the building itself. He paced slowly across the concrete floor, between the large white pillars that supported the Mediterranean-style roof overhead, and glanced down at the GPS unit in his hand. Global-positioning technology used thirty Navigation Satellite Timing and Ranging units in orbit to provide precise location coordinates. The satellites each orbited the planet once every twelve hours, covering the same ground once every twenty-four. An atomic onboard clock transmitted a satellite's position and a time signal to earth; by comparing data from more than one satellite at once, a GPS unit could calculate its own position. Most GPS units were accurate to within fifty feet, but Horatio's was equipped with a Wide Area Augmentation System, which further refined the signals through the use of twenty-five ground reference stations. A NAVSTAR signal sent through a WAAS could pinpoint a location to within ten feet.

Right now, it told him that he was practically standing on the item he was looking for. He looked around, but there was nothing in plain view.

And then he looked up.

Suspended in midair, slowly turning in the breeze, was what looked like a small, bright red plastic dinosaur. "Cute," Horatio murmured.

"You see something, Caine?" Sackheim's voice said in his ear.

"I do, Agent Sackheim. A small item suspended approximately twelve feet off the ground by fishing wire. I'm going to see what I can do to get it down."

"What sort of item?"

"A plastic dinosaur, with something around its neck. And there seems to be something metal projecting from it, as well. Hang on."

No stepladder was in sight, but Horatio found an eight-foot length of wood against one wall. He took a multitool out of his pocket and used it to bend a rusty nail embedded near one end of the lumber into a hook. It took only a second after that to reach up and snag the dinosaur.

He paused for a moment before pulling it down. Horatio used to work on the bomb squad, and he was only too aware that he could well be yanking on a trip wire. However, the fishing line seemed to be attached to the ceiling with transparent tape; it didn't feed into any hole he could see, and the ceiling itself didn't appear to have been tampered with. He held his breath and pulled.

The dinosaur fell to the floor with a clatter.

He leaned down and picked it up. "All right. I have the item in question. The metal projecting from it appears to be a USB plug, and the object around its neck is a coin of some sort."

"A USB plug? What—hold on. Your associate is informing me that it's probably a flash drive. Apparently it's some sort of fad to have them embedded in plastic novelties."

Horatio grinned. "Thank Mister Delko for me, will you? I'm going to hook this up and see what's on it."

Horatio's GPS unit was actually an adapted PDA, using Bluetooth technology to connect; it had USB ports as well, and now he used one of them to plug in the dinosaur.

The flash drive contained a digital video file. Horatio opened it.

The face that looked out from the screen was that of Abdus Sattar Pathan. He had a thick, bloodstained bandage taped to the side of his neck, and his shirt was bloodied and torn. His hands were behind his back; he looked exhausted and afraid. Behind him was only a black curtain.

"Lieutenant Caine," Abdus said. "I am relaying this message at the command of my captors. You will follow all instructions to the letter. No one but you must travel to the locations you will be directed to. The hostage will be punished for any deviations."

Horatio studied the man's eyes. He was clearly reading off something in front of him—from the way he bent his body forward and squinted, ever so slightly, it was probably something small. *A computer screen, maybe?*

"You wonder why we have brought you here," Abdus continued. "It is because we want you to see as we do. Look around you, Mister Caine. Is not this place the epitome of Miami? Filled with promise and hope, but so often prey to decay and corruption. A shining example to all who look upon her, but empty inside." Abdus spoke in a hollow monotone, his uninflected delivery giving the words an eerie weight. "One man in Miami might look upon the tower and remember its brilliant lighted eye as his first glimpse of a new home and a new life; another man on the same street might recall living where you stand right now, surrounded by filth and squalor and the incoherent raving of the mad, watching as someone commits slow suicide with a crack pipe or a needle.

"Think about this, Mister Caine. Think about what it means, because it is important.

"The coin around the neck of the dinosaur is a geocaching coin. Printed on the outside is a code. You must enter this code into the geocaching website to obtain further instructions."

The screen went blank.

"I have the results you wanted," the lab tech said.

"Oh, good," Wolfe said. "You're Frankel, right?"

The man with the folder in his hands hesitated. Confusion bloomed in his large, moist-looking eyes, and he glanced nervously down at his right breast where L. FRANKEL was stitched.

"Oh, good," he said nervously. "I thought I'd taken someone else's lab coat again by accident."

"Uh—no, it doesn't look like it," Wolfe said. "The results?"

"Oh, yes." Frankel thrust the folder at him as if it were about to explode. Wolfe raised his eyebrows and took it.

He opened it and scanned the first page. "Hmmm."

"Interesting sample," Frankel said. "Don't see many rare earth elements. Yttrium oxide is commonly used to make europium phosphors—they're what produce the color red in TV screens. Also, its atomic number is thirty-nine, it's named after a small town in Sweden and it's spelled with a *y.*"

"I . . . can see that."

"Oh. Of course. Good-bye." Frankel spun on his heel and left.

"And they say I'm weird . . ." Wolfe muttered.

"So," Tripp said. "You figure out what that white powder is?"

Wolfe looked up from the printout he'd been studying and said, "Hey, Frank. As a matter of fact, the GC/mass-spec just came back. The results were—well, elementary."

"Maybe to you, Sherlock. I'm still in the dark, here."

"Sorry. I just meant that the powder is an element—well, the compound of an element, anyway. Yttrium oxide."

"Don't think I'm familiar with that one," Tripp said, crossing his arms.

"It's commonly found in rare-earth minerals. And some non-earth ones as well."

"Come again?"

"Samples of lunar rock brought back by the Apollo mission were found to have a high yttrium content."

Tripp sighed. "Great. So now we're looking for a female killer Santa from outer space, is that what you're telling me?"

"Not exactly. Commercially, yttrium is extracted from monazite sand and bastanite—you don't have to go all the way to the moon to get it. And it's used for—" Wolfe stopped himself. "Well, a wide variety of manufacturing processes."

"Huh. I don't suppose you've got some brilliant CSI way to link that to fat guys in red suits, do you?"

"Not yet . . . but together with the battery acid, it suggests some sort of industrial procedure."

"Sure. We've stumbled across Santa's secret workshop, now turning out toys and moon rocks."

"Frank, you sound a little stressed."

Tripp ran a hand the size of a catcher's mitt

across the smooth scalp on top of his bullet-shaped head. "Sorry, kid. I hate being laughed at, and this case makes me feel like everyone else in the world is in on the joke except me."

"I know the feeling. But you were definitely right about one thing."

Tripp scowled. "Yeah? What's that?"

"CSIs giving answers that sound like encyclopedia entries."

Tripp paused, and then a grudging smile worked its way onto his face. "So, I guess I've got a firm grip on at least *one* fact."

"You've got to be kidding me," Horatio muttered as he stared at the handheld screen of his PDA.

"Hope you brought your hip waders, H," a familiar voice said in his ear.

"Eric?"

"Yeah. I convinced them to patch me in. Sackheim and his crew are pulling all the data they can get on the next location. They're trying to backtrack where the postings on the geocache site came from—there's at least three more—but they're not having much luck. The messages were bounced all over the net first and heavily encrypted. No way we're going to be able to crack them."

"Then I guess," Horatio said, slipping on his sunglasses as he headed for the exit, "that I'll just have to stick to following orders . . . for now. I'm heading for the next destination."

"Anything you want me to do in the mean-time?"

Horatio emerged into bright sunlight, nodded to the security guard, and headed for his Hummer. "Not just yet. Stick close and keep me apprised of any new developments as they come up." What Horatio meant—and knew Delko understood—was *watch Sackheim and keep him honest.* Horatio had no intention of being blindsided while in the field, and he knew Delko wouldn't let it happen.

"You got it, H," Delko said. "Nothing to worry about."

Horatio pointed the Hummer south, cutting his way through the traffic on Biscayne Boulevard as quickly and efficiently as he could, and got onto Highway 1 heading out of town.

"You have any idea where all this is going?" Delko asked.

"To at least three more locations, if the pattern holds true. But that's not the troublesome part."

"No ransom demand."

"Exactly. Which means either they haven't figured out what they want yet, or this is building to something extremely ugly."

"Yeah. I can't quite figure it out myself—most kidnappers make elaborate plans beforehand, and the geocaching messages definitely indicate fore-thought. But the initial crime scene and lack of a ransom demand suggest hostage takers stalling for time."

"The truth probably lies somewhere in between, Eric. But at least we know Pathan is still alive."

"Or was when the recording was made."

"I don't think they'll kill him just yet. As long as he's alive, he's a bargaining chip—and sooner or later, they're going to tell us what they want."

Wolfe stared at the sheet of paper in his hand. "I don't believe it."

Valera shrugged. "What do you want me to say? I checked three times. The samples you gave me didn't match."

"So Monica Steinwitz didn't have sex with Kingsley Patrick."

"That I don't know. But if they did, I can't prove it."

"Thanks, Valera. I'll break the news to Frank."

Wolfe left the DNA lab, thinking about what the new information meant. If Steinwitz hadn't slept with Patrick, then the mysterious Amelia Claus must have. Therefore, she'd also sent the emails from the abandoned storefront, where she'd been using yttrium oxide to do—what? Yttrium was sometimes used in the manufacturing of laser components; maybe she was building a death ray . . .

"I'm starting to think like Frank," he muttered to himself.

"Hi, Ryan," the gray-haired receptionist said with a grin, standing in his way. He stopped, then noticed she was pointing upward.

At the mistletoe, directly over his head.

*   *   *

Horatio had suspected, from the description on the geocaching site, what the next leg of his journey would entail. Still, it was one thing to suspect; the reality was quite another.

Alligators. Not one, not a dozen, not twenty or thirty or even fifty. Hundreds, sprawled along a narrow length of white sand, lying alongside and on top of one another, as if they had all lined up to buy tickets for some sort of lizard concert and fallen asleep in the sun. Other than the occasional twitch of an immense tail or wrinkled eyelid, they lay torpid and unmoving in the Florida heat. The large, green-scummed pond beside them held more, some floating motionlessly, others moving slowly through the algae-thick water. They were all close to the same size, around seven or eight feet in length.

"Impressive sight, isn't it?" The woman who spoke was dressed in khaki shorts and a short-sleeved shirt, with frizzy brown hair curling out from beneath a white pith helmet that bore the logo GATOR PARADISE. The name stitched over her right breast read BETH.

Horatio stared through the chain-link fence at the crocodilians basking a few feet away. "It is," he said, and pulled his PDA out of his pocket.

"There's more than thirty alligator farms in Florida now," Beth continued. "They produce three hundred thousand pounds of meat and over fifteen thousand skins a year. Plus, farms like this that are open to the public generate tourism revenue, too."

A large sign attached to the fence proclaimed PLEASE DO NOT FEED THE ALLIGATORS. Horatio's attention was caught by a second, smaller sign, a plastic-laminated sheet of paper tacked to the bottom of the first. It featured a photo of a small pile of what looked like corroded bits of round metal. Beneath the photo were these words:

ALLIGATORS WILL EAT ALMOST ANYTHING. MANY PEOPLE LIKE TO TEST THIS BY TOSSING SMALL OBJECTS (LIKE COINS) INTO THE PEN. UNFORTUNATELY, THESE COINS ACCUMULATE IN THE ALLIGATORS' STOMACHS AND THEIR GASTRIC JUICES PARTIALLY DISSOLVE THEM, RELEASING ZINC INTO THE ANIMALS' SYSTEMS AND PRODUCING FATAL ZINC POISONING.

PLEASE DO NOT THROW COINS INTO THE PEN!

"I don't suppose zinc improves the taste any, either," Horatio said.

Beth smiled. "You'd be amazed what people will try to get them to eat. An alligator's digestive system is similar to that of certain kinds of birds; they swallow rocks—they're called gastroliths once they're internal—which stay inside and help grind up things like bones and shells. Since crocodilians tend to swallow things whole if they can, more than one live turtle has found himself at the bottom of a gator's gullet before he could blink."

"And some of the things they eat stay inside?"

"Sure. One gator was found with an eight-inch ball of tightly wrapped roots in its stomach—the cellulose in the roots resisted digestion, and the natural contractions of the gut kept it rotating. It didn't eat the roots on purpose, though; they were ingested accidentally, probably while it was snapping up small fish or turtles on the bottom."

Horatio glanced from his PDA to the gator pen. "How many gators do you have here?"

"Around a thousand. This pen probably holds a third of that."

"So, over three hundred possible repositories . . . if they're telling the truth."

"Uh—what?"

"Beth, I have a bit of a problem here." Horatio pulled out his badge. "I have reason to believe that a vital piece of evidence in a crime has been ingested by one of your alligators. According to my information, it's one of the alligators in this pen."

She looked disturbed. "Is it . . . a body? We have security, but one of our nightmares is someone using the gators to get rid of a corpse . . ."

"Nothing like that. What I'm looking for is much smaller. A coin, in fact."

The look on Beth's face shifted toward skepticism. "Are you sure someone isn't pulling your leg?"

"The only thing I'm sure of at this point," Horatio said, "is that someone doesn't want this to be easy."

      *   *   *

Alexx strode into the lab like she was looking for a cheating husband. Her glare settled on Calleigh, who was studying blown-up photos pinned to a light panel on the wall.

"Ms. Duquesne? May I have a word?"

The edge in Alexx's voice got Calleigh's attention. "Something wrong, Alexx?"

"You could say that. I just got a visit from an extremely distraught Solana Villanova—she wants to go home for Christmas, but she won't leave until we release the body of her ex-husband. The problem is, nobody seems to know whose case this is—I just talked to Frank Tripp, and he mentioned Ryan Wolfe was working on it now. What gives, Calleigh? Hector's being kicked around like a *football.*"

Calleigh ducked her head. "I'm sorry, Alexx. It's still my case. Ryan was just doing me a favor—I promise, I haven't forgotten about Hector Villanova."

"Well, I should hope not. Can I release the body?"

"Yes, that should be fine. Go ahead."

"Thank you." Alexx turned and strode out of the room without saying good-bye.

Calleigh felt bad, but she didn't know what else she could say. The deeper she dug into the Villanova case, the more mysteries she found—now she had to explain how a body could have its hands removed with a corrosive in the middle of a swamp without leaving any trace behind.

A second boat, maybe? One that the body was mutilated in, then was used to ferry the killer out of the swamp?

It was possible—but why use two boats in the first place?

To isolate Villanova, perhaps. Prevent any trace of his body being left in the other craft. But that didn't work, either—why would the killer haul the corpse into the other boat to remove the hands?

She sighed. The problem was, she didn't have enough information. When that happened in a case, the fallback position was almost always the same: go back to the crime scene.

It looked as if she was heading out to alligator country.

14

"BETH," HORATIO SAID, "does the farm have a metal detector on the premises?"

The young woman nodded. "We've got two, actually—it's one of the ways we check the gators if we think they've swallowed something they shouldn't. We only do it if they're acting sick, though."

Horatio rubbed the back of his neck. "And how many staff do you have working right now?"

"Uh—six or seven, I think."

"Okay. What I need is for your staff to check each and every one of the gators in this pen, and I need it done right away. Is that possible?"

"To check all of them? That'll take a while."

"A man's life is at stake, Beth." He motioned to the walkie-talkie clipped to her belt. "Get in touch with whoever you need to, and let's get started. All right?"

"Sure, yeah." She unclipped the walkie-talkie and spoke into it. "Fred? Got a situation here . . ."

Horatio turned back to study the pen full of lazing gators as Beth explained things to her supervisor. One of the lizards seemed to be studying him back, its gold-rimmed eye gleaming in the sunlight. The natural curve of its mouth seemed to Horatio like a mocking grin: *Wouldn't you like to know what I had for dinner? Why don't you climb over the fence and take a closer look?*

"Alligator pie, alligator pie," Horatio muttered. "If I don't get some . . . I think I'm going to *die* . . ."

"So," Caldwell, the clean-cut young FBI agent, said, "Miami-Dade Crime Lab, huh? Nice new digs you've got."

Delko leaned back and cracked his neck. "It's okay, I guess. Lot of glass, lot of grillwork. Can't decide if it makes me feel more like I'm in an aquarium or a jail cell."

Caldwell laughed. "Yeah. Well, I'm sure it beats Quantico. The amount of light that place gets, it's like working in a coal mine."

"Yeah? You there a lot?"

Caldwell got up from his seat, walked over to where the butler had set up a coffee service. "Not really. I just transferred over to the Miami office, was in Nebraska before that. Let me tell you, competition for the Miami office is *fierce*."

Delko grinned. "Well, living in this city does have its benefits."

"I'll bet. Don't get to experience a lot of them on my salary, though. And my free time? You'd have to use a microscope to find it. A scanning electron microscope."

"They work you pretty hard, huh?"

Caldwell poured himself some coffee, then held the china cup under his nose and inhaled deeply. "Ahhh . . . you know what it's like. A tough case, you work it till it breaks. When there's no case, you do paperwork."

"But there's always a case."

"Oh, yeah. There's always a case." Caldwell took a long, slow sip of coffee. "Damn, that's good. I drank so much bad coffee in Nebraska I think I'm still getting the taste out of my mouth."

"Lot of stakeout work?"

"I've done my share. You?"

Delko shook his head. "Nah. I went from the police academy to the underwater body recovery team. Not a lot of submarine stakeouts."

"I've seen a few floaters. Don't envy the guy whose job it is to collect them."

Delko got up, walked over, and helped himself to some coffee as well. "Well, I still do underwater recoveries, but as a CSI I get to cover a lot more territory. It's never boring, I'll tell you that much."

"That why you switched?"

"Partly. Mainly, it was Horatio."

Caldwell took another sip of coffee. "How so?"

Delko shrugged. "He's the best cop I know.

Some guys get into police work for all the wrong reasons—they want the power, the respect. You know the type. Other guys come in with stars in their eyes, think they're going to change the world; a few years on the job and they're as bitter as—well, as the coffee they're always bitching about. No offense."

Caldwell grinned. "None taken."

"Anyway, Horatio doesn't fall into either of those camps. He cares about people, but he manages to be an idealist and a realist at the same time. He cares less about punishing bad guys than protecting people from them."

"Well, that's what it's all about, right?" Caldwell said. "Making the world a little safer. That's why I signed up, anyway."

"How's Sackheim to work for?" Delko said, blowing on his coffee.

"About what you'd expect. By the book, all the way. Stubborn as all hell."

"No wonder he and Horatio butt heads. He's the most stubborn guy I know," Delko said. "Once he gets his teeth into something, forget it. He's like a pit bull."

"Great. A pit bull and a bureaucrat, with us in the middle," Caldwell sighed. "Do me a favor, will you? If they start actually growling at each other, just shoot me. Between the eyes."

"Sure." Delko laughed.

*   *   *

They wrangled 152 gators before they got lucky.

Each gator had to be isolated, held down, and checked with a wand-style metal detector, the kind favored by airport security. Even with two teams working at once, it was a long and exhausting ordeal. Horatio knew he could make it go much quicker by calling in more manpower—but the kidnappers' instructions had expressly forbidden that.

It was full dark now, and they'd dragged out halogen lights on poles to provide illumination. A cold, patchy fog was drifting off the water, chilling Horatio to the bone, and the last thing he'd had to eat was a greasy hot dog from the concession stand hours ago.

"Lieutenant Caine?" a voice called out. "I think we've got something."

"Hang on, Eric," Horatio said into his transceiver. He walked over to the smaller, chain-link-enclosed stall abutting the main pen, where the alligators were being corralled and scanned. "What is it?"

Beth mopped sweat from her forehead with the back of a mud-spattered glove. "Wand's definitely getting a squeal. Could be what you're looking for."

"All right," Horatio said, putting his hands on his hips. "What's next?"

"We flush." Beth pointed to a long board with holes running down its sides leaning against the wall of the stall. "Strap him to that, make sure his head is lower than his tail, stick a PVC pipe in his mouth and a bucket below it. Soon as he bites down, we tape his jaws shut around the pipe and slide a smaller, flexible hose through the pipe and down its throat. We pump a little water in, enough so we can see the stomach swell, then push on either side of his belly. Whatever's inside comes out."

"And if it doesn't?"

"We flush him again. If it doesn't come out after a third flush, we'll have to open him up. Trank him with an intramuscular shot of medetomidine-ketamine—and then wait for him to conk out."

"How long does it take?"

"At least an hour, but it varies with the animal's physiology and size—it can take as long as four."

"Then let's hope we don't have to go that far." *Sifting through lizard vomit,* Horatio thought, *is far enough* . . .

The process worked exactly as Beth said it would. On the second flush, Horatio spotted a copper flash among the half-digested fish and water gushing into the plastic bucket.

He reached into the bucket with a latex-gloved hand and plucked it out. It was a metal geocoin, stamped with a distinctive logo: a hammer and sickle. On the other side was a string of numbers and letters.

"Isn't that a Russian symbol?" Beth said, peering over Horatio's shoulder.

"Yes, it is," Horatio said. "Beth, thank you for your help. I know how disruptive this has been."

"Kind of exciting, actually. Nice break from the routine, anyway. Though I'm glad we didn't have to process all three hundred and fifty."

"I imagine they appreciate it as well," Horatio said with a smile. "Now if you'll excuse me, I have a message waiting . . ."

Hello, Mister Caine. Congratulations on finding the coin—we really weren't sure you would. How many animals did you have to kill?

Not that it matters, of course—not to you. Life is just a resource to be used up, isn't it? For meat or clothing or slave labor, it makes no difference. We're sure that standing knee-deep in the blood and guts of slaughtered animals will cause you no more guilt than ordering a steak in your favorite restaurant.

And for what? To save the life of one man, simply because his father is wealthy? Would you go to such extremes for someone without money, without connections?

We know what you would say if we were to ask you face-to-face. And it would be a lie.

Did you see any children at the alligator farm today? Were they excited to see the big, scaly beasts, did they hold a young hatchling in their hands like a pet? Did you tell them that every creature within their sight would be murdered for profit?

No. You fed them lies, tousled their cute hair, let them pretend that this was a zoo. This is a country, a culture, of falsehoods. We reward the best liars by making them our leaders. And those that don't lie? What happens to them, Mister Caine?

This is the question you should be asking. This is the truth you should be seeking.

But that's not what you want at the moment. You want the next piece of the jigsaw puzzle, the next line of the sonnet. What a sad being you are, Mister Caine; you see only little bits of truth at a time, scraps and fragments of reality, and think this grants you some sort of understanding. It does not.

We understand the truth. And before we are done, you will as well.

We have shown you a promise corrupted, and we have shown you the truth behind a lie. Now you must seek innocence beneath sin, to find a coin of another realm. When you have done this, you will understand what we want.

A list of GPS coordinates followed.

"You got that, Eric?" Horatio said. He'd unlocked the message with the code on the coin and had just read it on his PDA; he knew the FBI was doing the same back at Khasib Pathan's mansion.

"Yeah," Delko said. "Those coordinates are in South Beach, right on Collins—as a matter of fact, they're in the middle of a club called Afterpartylife. Very popular with the elite—the guest list is more exclusive than the president's phone number."

"They'll let me in," Horatio said. "Just what I need after a long day wrangling alligators—a little time with the beautiful people."

"You okay, H? You sound exhausted."

"I'm fine, Eric. Look, I need you to look something up for me while I'm in transit."

"Sure. What do you need?"

"See if Abdus Sattar Pathan has ever performed at the Freedom Tower, the alligator farm, or the place I'm heading."

"I'm on it."

"And I," Horatio said, "am off to do some clubbing."

Afterpartylife was, even by Miami standards, excessive.

It was layered like a cake, three stories deep. The middle layer was a pool ringed by white sand and illuminated with UV light; the water itself glowed an electric blue. The pool's walls were transparent, and the pool itself provided much of the light for the layer underneath it, which was done up to resemble a cave. Crystalline stalactites grew from the ceiling, hanging over plush red leather couches and glowing softly with their own crimson light.

The topmost layer had a dance floor made of glass—or some ultrastrong transparent resin—letting those in the pool look up at the people dancing overhead. Smoke generators puffed out bursts of white mist, generating artificial clouds for the patrons to dance on. The decor leaned toward the heavenly, with waitstaff dressed like angels and brightly colored stuffed parrots on wires streaking by overhead.

Our guy certainly has a thing for metaphor, Horatio thought. He was on the topmost level, staring through the transparent floor at people playing in the pool. A wet bar was set up in the middle, a little tropical island populated by bartenders in swimsuits.

Horatio studied the bar and its patrons, thinking, *Innocence beneath sin. But the upper level represents heaven and the bottom is clearly hell—putting innocence* above *sin, not below.*

Of course, this whole place could be seen as sinful—especially by one as judgmental as our kidnapper. So what lies beneath Hades?

Horatio knew there was such a place—in Greek mythology, at least. Tartarus, the place where Zeus imprisoned the Titans after overthrowing them, taking the crown of Olympus for himself. It was a place supposedly worse than Hades itself—an underworld for monsters and deposed gods.

Tartarus was also where the punishment was supposed to fit the crime—as in the case of Tantalus, who was imprisoned in a pool of clear water, with grapes over his head. When he bent to take a drink, the water receded; when he reached for the grapes, they ascended out of reach. The very word *tantalize* came from his name. His crime? Having dined with the gods, he made the mistake of sharing his dinner conversation with other mortals.

Horatio studied the pool beneath him, glanced at a bowl of fresh fruit on a small marble pedestal a few feet away, then moved his gaze to the young, enthusiastic dancers on the floor. *A veritable cornucopia, in more ways than one . . . All right. So who in Tartarus is an innocent, and how are they being punished?*

His eyes fell on the bartenders below.

The young man dripping water on the floor in front of Horatio was tanned, muscular, and wore only a pair of baggy, floral-decorated shorts. He had introduced himself as Connor Kincaid and taken Horatio down to the lowest level, where young women in skintight scarlet suits and devil horns served drinks to customers lounging around on the many couches and overstuffed chairs. Soft electronica warbled from hidden speakers. "It's where people go to chill," Connor had told him. "Despite the whole infernal-pit-of-hell thing."

Connor had grabbed a white towel along the way, and now he was briskly drying himself off. "They heat the pool and crank the air-conditioning," he said. "You get wet, you lose heat fast. And working on the island, you get wet all the time. They give the customers those giant pump-action water cannons to play with, which is lots of fun—for them."

"But not so much for an employee caught in the cross fire?"

"Cross-drenching is more like it. And since nobody carries money in their swimsuit, the club hands out plastic cards on lanyards, which get used to pay for drinks at the island. Pay, yes—tip, no. People who wouldn't think anything of dropping a twenty on a table won't give you a dime if they have to key it in."

"So there's no traditional tip jar on the island? Nothing to put coins in?"

Connor draped the towel around his neck. "Nah. The only coins I see are at the end of my shift, when the other floors give me a cut of their take. They know how tough it is working the pool."

"One more question, if you don't mind, Connor; what's management's policy on fraternization with the customers?"

Connor rolled his eyes. "Completely off-limits. One of the places down the street got hit with a lawsuit when a bartender groped some student on vacation, and since then there's a strict hands-off policy. They fired a waitress who was a little too friendly just to show us they meant business."

No consorting with the gods, Horatio mused. *Tantalizingly close—but no closer. Trapped between heaven and hell, but not for any crime. An innocent . . .*

Horatio thanked him and let him go back to work. He sat, chin in hand, and thought, *I'm missing something here.*

"No luck, H?" Delko asked in his ear. *Like having an invisible sidekick*, Horatio thought. *Or maybe a Greek chorus.*

"Not yet," Horatio said. "How about you?"

"Nothing on the Freedom Tower, but the Brilliant Batin did perform a show at Gator Paradise six months ago. Found something strange about Afterpartylife, too—the place is owned by some sort of offshore consortium, but I'm having trouble tracing it back."

"What kind of trouble, Eric?"

Delko hesitated. "It's hard to say, H. Might just be a coincidence, but databases I should have no trouble getting into seem to be having problems. I keep getting rerouted to dead ends. You know?"

"Yes, I do." Delko hadn't come out and said it— not over an FBI channel—but Horatio understood what he'd meant. He meant the kind of interference you got when someone didn't want you snooping around; someone inside the power structure itself.

Someone bureaucratic.

He took out his PDA and called up a website with a mythology database. Tartarus, it seemed, had played host to a number of famous miscreants, including someone named Ixion. When Horatio read the description of the man's crime—and punishment—he smiled, shook his head, and stood up.

He made his way back to the middle floor. The white-sand beach around the pool was around ten feet wide, bounded by a raised tile rim next to the water and a gentle incline at the opposite edge. Horatio stepped onto the sand, walked over to poolside, and dropped to one knee. He dug his hand into the sand, forced it as deep as it could go; he got as far as his wrist before he hit bottom. Call it nine inches, give or take. He nodded.

"Eric? I think I know where our next coin is."

"Where?" Sackheim's curt voice said.

"Buried in an artificial beach." Horatio described where he was.

"We'll get you another metal detector, have you sweep the site," Sackheim said. "Shouldn't take you more than an hour—"

"Our perp isn't going to make it that easy," Horatio said. "The previous message referred to a 'coin of another realm.' If it's made of wood or plastic, we'll have to sift through every square inch."

"Then that's what you'll do," Sackheim said. "Even if it takes all night."

"Which is exactly what our guy wants. He's wasting our time on purpose."

"To what end?"

"I don't know yet. But I'll tell you what I do know—our kidnapper is far too impressed with his own cleverness. He picked the last two places for their metaphorical relevance to Miami itself, and this one because it represents the afterlife—specifically, the mythological version called Tartarus."

"So what's he trying to tell us? That Pathan is already dead?"

"I don't think so. One of the souls imprisoned

in Tartarus is a killer named Ixion—he was the first Greek to murder one of his own relatives."

"So?"

"So Ixion is the Greek version of Cain. Would you like to know what his punishment was?"

"I can't wait."

"He was strapped to a spinning wheel. Doomed to go in circles forever—around and around and around . . ."

"Sounds like you're reading a lot into this, Lieutenant," Sackheim said. "I've got teams going over data on Cuban refugees, arrests made connected to the Freedom Tower, and crimes relating to alligators. Plus the last coin had a Communist symbol stamped on it, which opens up a whole different can of worms. Our kidnappers could have some sort of grievance involving any one of those factors—"

"I don't think so," Horatio said. "Criminals with a political point to make aren't known for their subtlety or their patience. So far, we don't know who they are or what they want—and while the first fact makes sense, the second doesn't. They want us guessing, and that's exactly what we're doing."

"The FBI doesn't *guess*, Lieutenant. The FBI *extrapolates*."

"Extrapolating from faulty data is a waste of time," Horatio said patiently. "The only data we're collecting at the moment is what's being fed to us—"

"And you don't like the taste? Too bad. You

wanted to be involved in this case, you're involved—but *I'm* in charge. Whatever information
this investigation generates will be evaluated *thor-
oughly*, and I will make my decisions *based* on those
evaluations. Am I clear?"

"As crystal."

Horatio pulled the earpiece out and dropped it
in the pool.

Afterward, Horatio blamed himself for what happened.

He'd left the club. He wasn't sure where he was
going to find answers, but it wasn't sifting through
a few thousand tons of sand.

Sackheim knew as soon as Horatio walked out
the door, of course; he'd been shadowed by FBI
agents the entire time, just out of sight. When Horatio walked, Sackheim sent in a ringer, an agent
named Hargood in a red wig that wouldn't have
fooled a blind man three blocks away. The agent
also carried a metal detector, to do the job Horatio had figured out was pointless.

A metal detector worked by generating a strong
electromagnetic field, causing a current to flow
through nearby metal objects and then measuring
it. Such a field, unfortunately, was also easily de-
tectable by other devices—such as the electronic
fuse attached to the bomb buried in the sand, mid-
way between the pool and the edge of the beach.

Hargood died immediately. Seven other patrons

of the club were injured by shrapnel, two of them badly. Three more died in the rush to leave the club, trampled to death in the crowd's panic.

Less than an hour later, Horatio stood in front of Afterpartylife once more, awash in the cycling red flash of emergency lights. The wail of approaching sirens sounded like a damning chorus to his ears.

This time, Delko's voice came from behind him. "It's not your fault, H."

Horatio didn't turn around. "Isn't it? That bomb was meant for me. The only reason I'm not being carried out on a stretcher right now is because I walked away."

"It was the right call, Horatio. You know that."

"The only thing I know right now, Eric," Horatio said, "is that four people are dead, and seven others in the hospital. That," he said, turning around and meeting Delko's eyes, "and the fact that I'm going to nail this son of a bitch . . ."

15

WOLFE HAD DECIDED that he was quitting Christmas.
No more presents, no more carols, and especially
no more Santa. From here on in, he'd just find a
nice damp cave somewhere around the end of No-
vember and stay there until the first week in January. He announced this in the lab to Calleigh—in a
committed, but ever-so-slightly-sad way that he
thought was rather poignant—and got a muttered
"Uh-huh" in return.

"If your brow gets any more furrowed, you'll be
able to screw on your hat," Wolfe said. "What's up?"

"It's this damn Villanova case," Calleigh said.
"You know, I went all the way back to the original crime scene, took a ton of photos, went over
the place with a fine-tooth comb, did everything
but actually get in the water—and now I'm wondering why I bothered. There's nothing new here,
or at least nothing I can see."

"Well, you might not have to suffer much longer."

"Why? You going to put me out of my misery?"

Wolfe shook his head. "No, but H might. He's got Delko processing the nightclub bombing, but that leaves him shorthanded on the kidnapping case. Can't see him leaving one of his top CSIs on the bench."

Calleigh frowned. "Then you don't know Horatio very well."

"What do you mean?"

"I mean, I'm not on the bench, Ryan. I'm working a case. And this case is just as important as any other—a man lost his life, and it's our job to find out how and why. Horatio isn't going to suddenly forget that. The bombing is just another facet of the kidnapping case, and unless things drastically change, Eric will work both."

"Right. I guess I should concentrate on my own case, then."

"Good idea."

"Except that I *hate* this case. Have I mentioned that?"

"Several times."

"I mean, it's got everything except exploding Christmas trees. Drunken, sex-crazed Santas, suspects named after reindeer, poisoned pickled herring, homicidal snowmen—"

"Homicidal snowmen?'

Wolfe gave a large, theatrical sigh. "Okay, I

made that part up. But they're waiting in the wings, armed with yttrium-powered lasers and razor-sharp icicles. You'll see."

Calleigh smiled. "What I see is someone almost as stumped as I am. The lead I got you didn't pan out?"

"No. We found what we were looking for, but we can't tie her to the vic—"

His cell phone rang. "CSI Wolfe."

"Mister Wolfe? This is Valerie Blitzen. I just remembered something Santa Shaky said to me, and thought you should know."

"What is it?"

"The name of the hotel he said he was going to for that big Christmas Eve party. It was the Byzantia."

He thanked her and hung up. "Well, well, well," he said. "The reindeer just gave me a tip."

"Better tell her to be careful, then."

"Why?"

"Because killer snowmen," Calleigh said sweetly, "*hate* informers."

"It was a land mine," Delko told Horatio. He had the recovered fragments of the device laid out on the light table in front of him. "The type that used to be called a bouncing betty."

Horatio nodded. "Uses a small charge to propel itself out of the ground and into the air before detonating, thereby doing maximum damage to the enemy."

"Yeah. This one went off about waist height—cut Hargood in half."

"Can you identify the make?"

"At first I thought it was an Italian model, something called a Valsella Valmara 69. But after closer examination, I can safely say it wasn't—it was a copy. A lot of countries will simply imitate a successful design rather than come up with one of their own, and that's what this was. I can tell you where it's from, too."

"Let me guess. Somewhere in the Middle East?"

"Iraq."

"Which suggests that our kidnapping is political in nature," Horatio said. "The problem is, too many suggestions have already been made. . . . Eric, we need to stop playing this guy's game and start playing our own. I'm tired of the scavenger hunt."

"What'd you have in mind, H?"

"Something we're very good at, Eric. A little old-fashioned kick the can . . . and it's *his* can we're going to kick."

"That's commendable," Agent Sackheim said, striding through the doorway with four agents in tow. "One of my men is dead and you're comparing this to a child's pastime."

"Agent Sackheim, I deeply regret—" Horatio began, but Sackheim cut him off.

"Save it, Caine. I made a mistake letting you and your people get involved in this investigation in the first place, and now it's cost me one of mine. That's over." He nodded to his agents, and they began to pack the fragments on the table into evidence boxes.

"Hold it!" Delko said. "You can't just confiscate—"

"I can and I am," Sackheim said. "Everything you have is being shipped to Quantico, where *competent* technicians will examine it. Since Lieutenant Caine seems to have lost interest in acting as a go-between, your services are no longer required. Send everything you have on file to me in the next hour, or I swear I'll see you up on federal obstruction charges."

Delko caught the eye of Caldwell, the agent he'd talked to at the Pathan house. Caldwell gave him an almost imperceptible shrug and widening of his eyes, as if to say, *What do you expect?*

"Yeah," Delko said coldly. "Sure. We'll do that."

"And when you've got what you came for," Horatio said, putting his hands on his hips, "I want you and your people out of my lab . . ."

Wolfe wasn't that familiar with the Byzantia Hotel. He knew it had been around for a while, was one of Miami's art deco buildings, and was considered pricey but not in the same league as one of the überhotels on Ocean Drive. It was decorated for Christmas with strings of lights around the trunks of the palm trees outside, but nothing too overblown.

The lobby was cavernous, with vaulted, white ceilings and an old-style crystal chandelier. Wolfe glanced around, noted the smallish Christmas tree beside the front desk, and felt unaccountably relieved.

He studied the glass-encased black signboard on the wall, where they posted events taking place at the hotel. On Christmas Eve, the Alexander Ballroom was hosting something called the Christmas Carnival.

He followed engraved brass signs down hallways and through foyers until he reached a set of double doors, twelve feet high and carved of oak, with ALEXANDER BALLROOM on a large gold plaque to one side.

They weren't locked. He pulled one open and stepped inside.

"Ohhhhh . . . *boy*," he said faintly.

Whoever coined the term winter wonderland *was clearly thinking about this place. And whoever thought of* this *place had more than sugarplums dancing in their head.*

Dazzlingly white fake snow—made of something the consistency of Styrofoam—covered the floor and rose in sloping drifts a good six feet up the walls, creating the illusion he was in a sunken, arctic valley. Little paths were carved through the snow, leading to islands of seasonal cheer: dozens of themed kiosks, made of toys or Christmas trees or gingerbread. Full-size animatronic reindeer swiveled their heads to look at him from behind a candy-cane corral, while dozens of inflatable snowmen drifted slowly through the air like grinning zeppelins, propelled by tiny electric motors; every now and then one would bump into a wall or another of its kind and reverse direction until it hit something else.

And in the center, Santa's workshop.

More like Santa's coliseum, Wolfe thought. It was built of something that resembled white marble but was probably Styrofoam, with more silver trim than an old Chevy. Four thick columns supported an elaborate, multigabled roof that reached to the ceiling of the ballroom; beneath was a sort of red-velvet ziggurat with an elaborate, plush throne at its apex. From the huge, neon *S* worked into the fabric, Wolfe surmised it belonged to Santa—either that, or Superman.

None of the ballroom lights were on, but there was plenty of illumination—strings of colored lights were wound around the columns, the throne, the kiosks, practically every available surface.

Abruptly, one of the snowmen ran into the spire at the very top of Santa's edifice. It deflated with a discouraged whooshing noise, and a voice called out, "Hold it! Hold it, everyone! Lights!"

The overhead fluorescents came on, changing the rich, multihued light into the flat, white glare of a supermarket. Wolfe noticed for the first time a large white screen at the far end of the ballroom, taking up most of the wall, with a raised stage in front of it. Floor-to-ceiling black curtains flanked the screen, and a man and a woman now emerged from behind each, walking across the stage to meet in the middle. The man's words carried clearly to Wolfe's ears as he approached them.

"My God, my God, my *God*!" the man said. He had a narrow face, accented by a thin black mustache and slicked-back, dark hair. He plucked nervously at the sleeve of his lime-green silk shirt as he paced. "Chandra, *why* didn't we see this coming? I mean, it should have been *obvious*, right? I mean, *hello*, the *Hindenburg*?"

Chandra was an attractive, brown-skinned woman in jeans and a yellow belly shirt, with something green glinting in her navel and just above her upper lip. She had a remote control in her hands, big enough for two joysticks side by side.

"Calm down, Wiggy," she said. "The snowmen are filled with helium, not hydrogen—they're not going to explode. And we'll just stick an ornament or something on top of the spire, it'll be fine."

"Excuse me," Wolfe said. "I was wondering if I could talk to someone in charge."

The man turned and gave him an evaluating glance. Apparently he didn't like what he saw, because he let out an immediate moan. "*Ohhh*, no. It's the flowers, isn't it? I *knew* trying to bring in that many snowdrops at this time of year was a mistake. We should have just gone with the poinsettias—"

"It's not about flowers. My name is Ryan Wolfe. I'm from the Miami-Dade Crime Lab."

"Crime Lab?" the man said. "I have no response to that."

"What can we do for you, Mister Wolfe?" Chandra said. "Is there some sort of problem?"

"That's kind of hard to answer. I mean, there *is* a problem, but it's mine, not yours. I was hoping you could help me with it."

The man rolled his eyes so far up into his head for a second Wolfe thought he was fainting. "Look, I'm all for doing my civic duty, but you have no *idea* how busy we are right now. Do you?"

"This'll only take a minute—"

"A minute. A minute. This has *already* taken a minute, sixty precious seconds that I will never, *ever* get back, sixty seconds that I should have been using to fix the ump*tillion* problems that need fixing before this entire ghastly mess collapses around my ears . . ." He paused, then deflated as abruptly as the snowman had. "Oh, what the hell," he sighed. "Go ahead. But you have to promise to shoot me afterward."

"Ludwig—take five, will you?" Chandra said gently but firmly. "Go have a cup of chamomile. I'll talk to Mister Wolfe, and then we'll get back to work. All right?"

He gave her a long-suffering look. "You're humoring me. I *hate* it when you humor me."

"I know. That's why I do it."

"I'll make you a cup, too. Don't take too long." He disappeared behind the black curtain.

Chandra hopped off the stage, the control tucked under one arm, and landed in front of Wolfe. "So—what's your problem?"

"My problem is murder," he said. "Literally. I have a corpse and a case that's getting colder by the minute, and the best lead I have is this place."

She looked intrigued. "How so?"

"The Christmas Carnival. It's the only big event happening at the hotel Christmas Eve, right?"

"Yes. We're taking over all their function space and most of their rooms. It's kind of a big Christmas-themed convention—most of the people coming are connected to the Christmas industry in one way or another."

"The Christmas industry? I know it's gotten awfully commercial, but I don't think I've ever heard it called *that*."

She started walking, and he fell in step beside her. "This is a little more specialized—ornament manufacturers, specialty retail stores, places like that. And this year there's the television show, too."

"What televison show?"

She stopped in front of a booth decorated entirely with different types of tinsel and tucked a dangling length of glittery red behind a pole. "It's called *Sudden Success*. It's a reality show where they take some random, ordinary person and let them live like they were a billionaire. Private jets, hanging out with celebrities, living in a mansion in Beverly Hills. They're shooting a segment here—the Carnival is going to be the backdrop for a really lavish party Christmas Eve. I've even heard rumors U2 is supposed to drop by, but what do I know? I'm just the party planner."

"Does the name Kingsley Patrick mean anything to you?"

She thought about it for a second, then shook her head. "No. Should it?"

"He claimed he was attending this party."

She walked over to the reindeer corral and looked them over critically. "I guess it's possible. The name doesn't sound familiar, but he could be on the guest list."

"Can I get a copy of that? I'd also like to see a list of people who are going to be working the event."

"I guess I can do that—for our people, anyway. You'll have to talk to the hotel about their employees. Exactly what are you looking for?"

"I'm . . . not really sure," he admitted. "But when in doubt, follow the money. This seems to be the only big thing my victim was connected to, though I'm still not sure how. It might have just been a party he was going to."

"Then he must have had some impressive connections." She vaulted easily over the candy-cane fence and took a closer look at one of the reindeer that wasn't moving. She popped open a panel in its side—a sight Wolfe found oddly disturbing—and fiddled with something inside. "This party is gonna be *extremely* exclusive, even for Miami." After a second, the reindeer's nose lit up with a red glow, and its head started to nod up and down. She shut the panel with a satisfied smile on her face.

"Well, he was an actor, so I suppose he might have those types of connections," Wolfe mused. "But that still doesn't tell me why someone would want to kill him . . ."

"If Wiggy were here, he'd say, 'To put him out of his misery.' And then he'd pretend he was going to commit suicide with a plastic icicle."

"Yeah, he seems a little—high-strung," Wolfe said. "Opening-night jitters?"

"More or less. He's always pretty wound up before a show, but he's the best man in Miami when it comes to set dec. In the five years we've been working together, I've never actually seen him reach critical mass; he just gets up to a roiling boil and stays there until he runs out of steam. Then he starts drinking wine and everybody's his best friend."

"Sounds like an interesting relationship."

"Well, when you work with genius, you have to make allowances for personality quirks."

"I know what you mean," Wolfe said.

*   *   *

"I can't believe they just hijacked our investigation," Delko said. He leaned against the break-room table with both arms, gripping the edge with his hands as if he wanted to flip the thing end for end.

Horatio leaned forward in his chair and said quietly, "It doesn't matter, Eric. We have copies of all the documents, all the photos. The only thing we don't have anymore is the physical evidence, but I think we've already learned all we could from that. If not—well, the boys at Quantico are welcome to take a swing. They know what they're doing."

"And we don't?"

"What we know, Eric, is only as much as we're being *allowed* to know. But that," Horatio said, getting to his feet, "is about to change . . ."

Tripp ran his eye down the guest list and whistled. "Lot of heavy hitters in this crowd. Models, rock stars, actors, lot of local players in the hotel biz . . . doesn't really sound like the kind of people Kingsley ran with, though. Out of his league, wouldn't you say?" He passed the list back through the car window.

Wolfe took it and leaned against the side of Tripp's car. "I would—which would explain why he's not on the list. But it's definitely a league he would have given almost anything to play in."

"You figure he was planning to crash it?"

"I don't think so—according to the party planner, security's going to be tight. Nobody gets in without a bar-coded invitation, and we didn't find one at Kingsley's apartment."

"Maybe that's what was stolen," Tripp said. "The place was broken into, but nothing seemed to be missing."

"Could be—but that doesn't help us much. If the killer has one of the invites, it's not in Patrick's name; we don't know whose name *is* on it, or where Patrick got it in the first place. There's also no way we can run down everyone on this list before the party tomorrow night, even assuming that whoever gave up the ticket will admit to it."

"You're right about that. Just getting access to some of the people on that list would take most of a day, and if some midlevel gofer scammed one and sold it, we'd never track it down."

Wolfe folded the list and slipped it into his jacket pocket. "Well, there's another possibility. Could be that Patrick found himself another way in; a little less dignified, but still guaranteed to get him in the door—and maybe even help him pay the rent."

"Hotel staff, you mean? Well, he wouldn't be the first actor to put *waiter* on his résumé."

"Which is why I asked you to meet me here, Frank. I'm getting the runaround from hotel management and I was wondering if you'd lend a hand."

Tripp grinned. "I see. Need the big dog to do a little barking, huh?"

"Actually, I was just hoping you'd help me cover

a little more ground. Every time I try to pin the manager of the hotel down, he vanishes—I get the feeling he really doesn't want to talk to me."

"We'll see about that," Tripp growled, opening his car door.

The clerk at the front desk, a tiny blond woman with a ponytail, gave Wolfe an open, sunny smile as they approached, a smile Wolfe had analyzed as meaning *I can't help you but I'm going to be really cheerful about it.*

"Did you find him?" she asked. Cheerfully.

"No, I'm afraid not," Wolfe said.

"I can page him again for you—"

"I'm afraid that's not gonna do it, sweetheart," Tripp said. His badge was already out. "We need to talk to your boss, and we need to do it *now.*"

Her cheerfulness faltered like a seagull in a high wind, then self-corrected and came back up. "I'm sorry, but there's really nothing I can do—"

"Look," Tripp said in a low voice, "I understand it's your job to run interference, but he can't blame you if he doesn't know it's your fault. So here's how it's going to go: you can tell me where he is and exactly how to get there, and I won't mention how I found out—or I can make things so unpleasant down here that he'll be forced to put in an appearance. I don't think he'd appreciate that much, do you?"

She blinked at Tripp rapidly, the visual equivalent of a stutter. "Is that a . . . a threat?"

"I can have six squad cars here, lights going and sirens screaming, in under a minute. And I can make sure they park right in that turnaround out front and stay there, too. How many guests do you want to rethink their travel plans because this part of Miami isn't quite as safe as they thought it was?"

She only hesitated for a second, and when she answered her voice was considerably less cheerful. "He's in the Caesar Room. Third floor, first door on the left when you leave the elevator."

"And he's not going to vanish between now and the time I get there, is he?"

"No. He's in a meeting."

"Good. Thank you. You have a real nice day."

As they walked toward the elevator, Wolfe said, "I'm impressed, Frank. It never occurred to me to just *bully* it out of her."

"Kid, sometimes it's better to go straight through the fence instead of looking for the gate. Not to mention a lot more satisfying . . ."

Wolfe rapped on the dark, polished wood of the door to the Caesar Room. A Hispanic woman in her fifties opened it. "Yes?"

"We'd like to talk to Mister Fergusson, please," Wolfe said.

"He's busy at the moment. Can you come back in half an hour?"

"No, ma'am, we can't," Wolfe said firmly. "Tell him the Miami Police Department would like to have a few words with him—and we'd like to have them *now*."

The woman didn't seem fazed. She said, "Just a second, please," and closed the door.

"Nice try," Tripp said. "Course, she looked a little harder to intimidate."

Before Wolfe could answer, the door opened again. The man who stood there was short and pudgy, with a wide, freckled face and wispy ash-blond hair. He gave them the professional smile of someone in the service industry, without any of the underlying resentment usually simmering just below the surface.

"Gentlemen," he said. "I'd be happy to talk to you—would my office be all right?"

"That'd be fine," Wolfe said. Fergusson stepped out into the hallway, closing the door behind him, and headed down the hall. Wolfe and Tripp followed him through an unmarked door, which led to a service corridor of considerably less glamour.

Wolfe was always intrigued by the secret spaces behind what was presented to the public. He could remember as a child being taken to use the restroom in a mall, and somehow getting away from his parents and wandering down a seemingly endless hallway, punctuated by doors with names of stores on them. It was like an entire other world hidden away, the bones and guts and arteries of the mall. It had changed the way he thought; after that, he was always looking for what lay underneath.

He supposed he still was.

More than anything, what lay behind the Byzantia's polished and gleaming exterior reminded him of being backstage at a theater. There was the same complete disregard for appearance, the bare plaster and exposed ductwork and scuffed floors, the harsh fluorescent light and stacks of chairs. Maids pushing carts of laundry, waiters carrying trays, kitchen staff manhandling tall wheeled shelves loaded with produce; everything had the same sort of steady, purposeful pace of people with work to do.

It was only a shortcut, though—they took a service elevator back down to the main floor, where Fergusson's office turned out to be just off the lobby itself. Wolfe got the message: *This is a place of business, and we're* busy. *Don't take up too much of my time.*

The office was clearly part of the external sheen, as befitted the person who ran the place. A floor-to-ceiling window looked out on South Beach; his desk was large and sculpted out of brushed aluminum, glass, and chunks of raw mahogany. He took a seat behind it and motioned for Wolfe and Tripp to sit as well.

"Now—what can the Byzantia do for you?" he said pleasantly.

"Supply us with a list of your employees," Wolfe said. "And I need to know which ones are going to be working tomorrow night."

"May I ask why?"

Wolfe paused. When he hadn't spoken for several seconds, Tripp said, "It's part of an ongoing investigation."

"Into what?"

"We're—not exactly sure," Wolfe said. Tripp's sigh let him know he'd said the wrong thing, but he plunged on anyway. "Our evidence suggests a murder was committed in order to gain access to your Christmas Carnival. We're concerned that it was in preparation for a crime."

"What sort of crime?"

"We don't know. Yet."

Fergusson spread his hands in apparent puzzlement. "So, you have the *suggestion* of an undefined *potential* crime. Is that right?"

"Look, we're not asking you for much," Tripp said. "Just a little information. We'll check it out—quietly—and alert you to any possible problems. Everybody wins."

Fergusson considered this for a few seconds. "Let's say I do. And you discover that one or more of my employees has, I don't know, a criminal record or something. Can you guarantee this isn't going to show up on the news?" He stared pointedly at Wolfe.

Erica Sikes, Wolfe realized. *The reporter who shafted me. He's seen me on television, talking to that—* "I can assure you," Wolfe said, "my days of talking to reporters are *over.* We'll be discreet."

Fergusson shook his head. "If there was some sort of definite threat to the hotel or my guests, I'd be more than happy to cooperate. But this—it seems to me you're chasing ghosts."

"Maybe," Wolfe said, "but this particular ghost has already killed one person."

"I'm sorry, but I have to think of my employees' rights as well as the well-being of the people staying at the hotel."

"Course you do," Tripp said. "Lot of your staff is Latino, isn't it? Hard to tell nationality just by looking—might be Cuban, Cuban-American, Guatemalan, Colombian, Argentinean . . . some of 'em probably immigrated from countries where the police aren't so polite. Having cops around could make them nervous, right?"

"Regardless of where they're from," Fergusson said, "they still have a right to their privacy."

"Depends on who you talk to," Tripp said. "Wolfe and I, we're kinda focused on just catching one particular bad guy. We may be fishing, but we're not interested in small fry. Now, a federal agency—like the INS, for instance—would take a very different approach. They'd just throw out a net and see what they could haul in."

Fergusson's eyes narrowed, but he didn't reply.

"So," Tripp continued, "in the interests of everybody involved, I'd advise you give us that list of employees. We can always go to a judge and get a warrant—but all that's going to do is make us unhappy, and pretty soon *everyone's* unhappy. You don't want that, do you, Mr. Fergusson?"

Fergusson stared at Tripp for a moment, then smiled. "No," he said. "I don't think anybody wants that . . ."

16

HORATIO AND DELKO MET in the conference room.

"Okay," Horatio said. He was already seated and waited for Delko to sit down as well. "Let's see what we have."

Delko flipped open the file folder he was carrying. "Khasib Pathan, our kidnapping vic's father. Citizen of Saudi Arabia and member of the royal family; seventy-third in line for the throne. Started out rich and got a lot richer by making some smart moves in the stock market; he's a billionaire, in the top hundred of the world's wealthiest men. He's got four wives and nine children—seven male, two female. Abdus is the first child of the fourth wife."

"Where are the other children?"

"They're all back home, working for the family business. The boys went to school here, while the girls never left Saudi Arabia. Abdus was the only one who came to America and decided to stay."

"To his parents' everlasting regret," Horatio mused. "Or his father's, anyway. . . . What about his mother?"

Delko pulled out a laser copy of a photo and handed it over. "Bridgette Pathan."

The picture showed an attractive, smiling blonde in her forties. "Maiden name is Annik," Delko added. "Originally from Stockholm. His other wives are all Saudi."

"I see . . . this could explain why Abdus chose a different path from his brothers. Did she have any other children?"

"None I can find a record for."

Horatio nodded. "What about his politics?"

"This is where it gets interesting, H. Khasib Pathan has been linked to a number of Islamic fundamentalist factions—including those known to have committed acts of terrorism."

"Now that *is* interesting. It may also explain why an Iraqi mine was used in a Miami nightclub."

Delko shook his head. "I don't get it. If this guy is funding terrorists, why is the FBI falling all over themselves trying to help him?"

"Politics makes for strange bedfellows, Eric. And sometimes, for blackmail."

"You think this might be part of an internal power struggle? Like one Mafia family kidnapping the member of another?"

"Possibly. If so, the State Department almost certainly has a vested interest in who comes out on top."

Delko tossed the file folder onto the table. "You know, I'm starting to feel a little out of my depth here. Billionaire royal families, international terrorism . . . didn't this case start out in a convenience store?"

"It doesn't matter, Eric," Horatio said, getting up from his seat. "We go where the evidence leads us. We've dealt with foreign nationals and billionaires before—drug money or oil money, it makes no difference. The person to keep in mind isn't Khasib Pathan—it's Talwinder Jhohal."

"The owner of the convenience store," Delko said. "The guy who got attacked."

"Yes. A hardworking citizen of Miami that deserves justice just as much as someone living in a mansion on Fisher Island. Let's not forget about him—or any of the victims of that bomb."

"I'm not ready to quit, H—I'm just not sure where we go from here."

"We go back to the beginning, Eric. To the initial assault that started this chain of events. Technically, it's a separate case . . ."

"Which means we still have jurisdiction," Delko finished, a smile appearing on his face.

"And all the evidence we collected. Which we will go over again, side by side with what we have from the kidnapping, and look for connections."

Delko grabbed the folder from the table and stood. "Well," he said. "What are we waiting for?"

*   *   *

The reality show *Sudden Success* had taken over the entire top floor of the Byzantia. Wolfe and Tripp had to dodge a burly man in a baseball cap hauling a cart full of lighting equipment and a woman pushing a wheeled rack full of clothing before they got to the door of the penthouse suite, an elaborately carved slab of blond wood with inlaid mother-of-pearl trim.

The door was opened by a harried-looking woman in a red baseball cap, baggy black shorts, and a loose-fitting T-shirt with a picture of Marilyn Monroe on it. She had a hands-free headset on and was already in the middle of a conversation.

"No, no, they say they'll edit that later—Hi, come on in—yes, that's exactly what I want—just have a seat, someone'll be right with you—I don't care if the guy in wardrobe hates you, we need it for segment seven—have some fruit or coffee, there's plenty—no, not you, I'm talking to someone else—what, you think I'd call you that? Honey, if I wanted to insult you I'd be a lot more original . . ."

The suite was large, the view amazing, the furnishings extremely expensive. It was also half-filled with lights on stands, camera equipment, empty foam-lined AV crates, and loops of cable. Production assistants came and went, ferrying coffee or duct tape or clipboards, and in the middle of it all stood a young woman in a cocktail dress. She was tall and beautiful, with long, dark hair that fell in waves halfway down her back. The dress was made of some sheer, slightly iridescent fabric, its color a deep, rich blue. It was cut low in the front and even lower in the back and slit from ankle to hip. The woman was holding perfectly still while another woman, dressed in jeans and a plaid shirt, dusted her cheekbones with a makeup brush.

The woman who had let them in had wandered away, still talking to her cell phone. Wolfe wondered whom he should talk to; there was no one obviously in charge.

"Where should we start?" Tripp asked.

"Pick the biggest visible target and go from there." Wolfe headed straight for the woman in the cocktail dress.

Up close, she was even more lovely. Her eyes were dark, her lips red and full, her teeth a sparkling white.

Wolfe made eye contact and smiled. "Hi. You must be the star of the show."

She gave his smile back, with interest. "I guess. Are you from the network? Madeline said they were sending somebody over today."

"No. I'm—"

"—not anyone you need to concern yourself with," a voice said briskly from behind Wolfe.

He turned. The man who'd spoken was broad-shouldered, with long, unkempt salt-and-pepper hair. He wore a khaki vest with too many pockets and a stern expression on his face.

"Anitra has too much on her mind already. I'm Jeff Walderson, the director. Let's go in the other room where we can talk, and let Anitra concentrate on her glamour shots, all right?"

"All right." Wolfe nodded to Anitra. "Break a leg, I guess."

"Thanks," she said.

Wolfe and Tripp followed the director into the next room, a massive bedroom suite with a hot tub in one corner and a bed that looked as if it belonged to a French emperor. Walderson closed the door behind them, then said, "Now. The manager said the Miami PD had some concerns about tomorrow night's party?"

"That's correct," Tripp said. "We're running background checks on anybody working the event, and we've got employee lists from the party planner and the hotel. We'd like one from you as well."

"I don't understand. What is it you're looking for?" Walderson sounded genuinely puzzled.

"We're not at liberty to discuss details of the case," Wolfe said. "But we're trying to prevent problems, not cause them. Providing us with a list shouldn't be hard, right?"

"Well . . . no. I guess that would be all right. As long as this isn't going to interfere with the shoot."

"Don't see any reason it should," Tripp said.

Walderson sighed. "Okay, then I guess you should talk to Chuck. He's the on-site head of security.

He'll give you a list, and you can discuss whatever problems might come up with him. Okay?"

"That sounds fine," Wolfe said.

Walderson pulled out his cell phone and made a call. A minute later, a squat, powerfully built man with a bushy orange mustache opened the door. He wore a dark blue jacket with CELEBRUS SE-CURITY emblazoned on the breast.

"How do," the man said, nodding. "I'm Chuck Keppler."

Walderson introduced Wolfe and Tripp. "Give these guys full access, okay?" Walderson said. "You run into any serious problems, let me know. Now, if you'll excuse me, I have to get back to work."

Keppler was an ex-cop himself—not unusual in the security business. He'd worked for both the Atlanta and Miami police departments before deciding to go the private route and now made his living arranging security for everyone from supermodels to CEOs. He had no problem with discussing his current job with Wolfe and Tripp, and supplied them with a complete list of personnel associated with the show.

Keppler took them to another, much smaller hotel room down the hall, and they sat down on the balcony, at a patio table beneath an umbrella.

"So, your trail leads here, huh?" Keppler popped open a can of soda with one thumb and poured it into a glass full of ice. "Yeah, that's what it's like, sometimes. What's your gut say?"

"At the moment," Tripp said, "my gut's telling me I'm in the wrong business."

Keppler grinned. "Oh, it ain't all skittles and beer. The money's good, but I'm really just a glorified babysitter. Aside from the occasional nut job with a grudge, it's about as exciting as watching paint dry."

"Yeah?" Wolfe said. "You get many of those?"

"Not on this gig. See, the whole idea behind *Sudden Success* is to take a regular citizen and let them experience what it's like to be rich. Not exactly original, but it seems to be a formula that works. Thing is, the focus of the show is—by definition—a nobody. So the whole celebrity-stalker thing doesn't usually come into play."

"Usually," Tripp said. "But this party is gonna feature a whole mess of 'em, isn't it?"

"Yeah. So security there is going to be tight. I've got twenty guys working the room, I've done background checks on every person working the event, and there's cameras everywhere. Sorry, but it sounds to me like your guy was just a would-be actor trying to crash a party and make some connections."

"Maybe so," Tripp said, "but somebody went to a lot of trouble to kill him, just the same."

"I'd like to talk to the woman—Anitra?—that's the subject of the show," Wolfe said. "I met her briefly, but the director cut in before I had the chance to ask her any questions."

"Well, they keep her pretty busy," Keppler said. "Gourmet meals, dates with celebrities, Hollywood premieres . . . basically, they try to keep her in a permanent state of overload. I heard the director say once, 'Stars in her eyes mean eyes on our star.' It's the American dream, right? Get everything you ever wanted handed to you on a silver platter."

"For a while," Tripp said. "Wouldn't want to be in her shoes when the show ends. Seems awful cruel to give someone that much and then take it away again."

Keppler shrugged his massive shoulders. "Is it? Personally, I'd rather have a taste of the good life than go hungry—after all, who knows what might happen? Maybe one of those movie stars will fall in love with her, or one of the millionaires she meets at a cocktail party will offer her a job. That's part of the American dream, too, right—endless possibility?"

"Right now, I could do with a few less possibilities," Wolfe said. "Can you get me some time to talk with her?'

"I think I can swing something. They give her a little downtime every day to spend with her daughter—she's a single mom. You might be able to get a few questions in then."

Wolfe looked out over the steady crawl of traffic down on Ocean Drive, the strip of white beach just beyond it scrawled with the dots of shade umbrellas and dashes of towels, the steely blue glint of the Atlantic reaching to the horizon. *It's a long way down,* he thought. *A very long way . . .*

On the theory that fresh eyes might see something new, Horatio had Delko examine the convenience-store assault evidence, while he scrutinized the kidnapping case data.

Horatio spent a lot of time going over the photos from the kidnap site. Something about the blood-spatter pattern bothered him . . . and abruptly he realized what it was.

"Eric, take a look at this," Horatio said, proferring a photo.

Delko took it, studied it. "The blood spatter on the wall. You see something I don't?"

"It's what I don't see that's bothering me. We hypothesized that the attacker slashed at Pathan's throat while he was standing here. Pathan spun, splashing blood along this arc—but his attacker had to have been standing in this spot here. And what do we see on the wall behind that spot?"

"More spatter," Delko said. "Where we should see ghosting from the attacker's body blocking the spray of blood."

"Correct. Which means our attacker was a ghost himself."

"You're saying he never existed? That Pathan slashed his own throat?"

"Pathan's a professional illusionist, Eric. If he

could fake fingerprints so perfectly we can't tell the difference, he could fake this."

"I'm with you, H—but how do we prove it?"

"We follow in his footsteps, Eric. We may no longer have access to Pathan's workshop, but we have plenty of photos. We can duplicate his tools and supplies . . . and then make our own magic."

"A reconstruction?" Delko asked. "If we can show how Pathan fooled us, maybe we can push the Bureau into taking a closer look at the actual evidence?"

"And a closer look at Pathan himself . . ."

Looking at Anitra Farnsworth, Wolfe thought, you'd never guess she was a waitress at a Denny's in Sparrow Falls, Michigan. She had exchanged the blue cocktail dress for something even more elegant in black, which was apparently a Vera Wang original worth what Wolfe made in a year. Her hair was up now, exposing a long and elegant neck that a matronly assistant was draping a necklace of pearls around. The director, Walderson, was studying her critically.

"What do you think?" the assistant said, a proud smile on her face.

"I don't know," Walderson said. "I think we should stick with the other one—that green set off her eyes beautifully."

Anitra rotated slowly, her hands out at her sides. "Oh my gosh. This makes me feel like—a princess. Or a movie star. Or maybe a movie star playing a princess."

Walderson chuckled. "Well, that's exactly what you look like, sweetheart."

At that moment the door opened and a blond girl of six or seven, dressed in denim overalls, walked in. She looked around self-consciously, clearly a little spooked at all the activity, and then she saw Anitra.

"Mommy! You look *beautiful*." She pronounced the word carefully.

Anitra beamed at her daughter. "Don't I, sweetie? Mommy's all dressed up for the party tomorrow night."

"Can I go, Mommy?"

"Maybe for a little while. But I think it's going to be a little past your bedtime. Are we done for now, Jeff?"

"Sure." Walderson motioned to the assistant, and she stepped forward and unclasped the necklace from around Anitra's neck. She took it over to a black velvet case on a table and placed it inside, then handed the case to Chuck Keppler. Keppler immediately spoke a few words into the throat mike of his headset, and two men in identical security blazers stepped into the room. Keppler left, flanked by both men.

"Okay, Coral," Anitra said. "Mommy's all done for now. Did you eat lunch?"

"Yessss . . ."

Wolfe picked that moment to take a step forward. "Uh, excuse me, Ms. Farnsworth. I was wondering if I could talk to you for just a moment."

"Are you a reporter? Because I'm only supposed to talk to reporters that have been okayed by Jeff, it's some kind of confidentiality thing—"

"No, I'm a crime-scene investigator with the Miami Police Department. We're following up a few leads that may have a connection with tomorrow night's party."

She sighed. "Well, I knew it couldn't last forever. . . . Last week I went heli-skiing with a boy band and then had lunch with the eleventh-richest man in the country, but I guess my luck has run out. Take me away." She held out her hands as if proferring them for handcuffs.

"No!" Coral proclaimed loudly. She ran in front of her mother and glared up at Wolfe defiantly. "You're not taking my mommy away!"

Wolfe took a startled step back, then laughed. He knelt down in front of the child. "It's okay. I'm not here to take your mom away—she's just making a joke. We're just going to talk, all right?"

Coral looked up at her mother for confirmation.

"It's okay, Coral," Anitra said, grinning. "I was only kidding. Go play in the bedroom for a little bit, okay?"

"Welllll . . . okay." The girl marched off to the next room, throwing a suspicious look over her shoulder that made it hard for Wolfe to keep a straight face.

"So—what's this all about?" Anitra asked.

"It's kind of hard to explain," Wolfe admitted. "My first question is, did the producers give you any comped passes to tomorrow's party? For family or anything?"

"No. They're very strict about who I interact with on camera. They don't want me to get too comfortable, I guess. Me hanging out with old friends or relatives doesn't make for great TV."

"How are you finding the whole experience?" The question wasn't really relevant to the investigation, but Wolfe was curious.

"Honestly? Exhausting. It's like—well, like Christmas every day, and New Year's every night. After a while, you feel like there's this big, frozen grin on your face all the time. It's getting so all I want to do is sit down with some fast-food takeout and read a newspaper—something with a big, nasty headline about a disaster somewhere. Isn't that *awful*?"

"Well, too much of anything isn't good. How's your daughter holding up?"

"She's a trouper, but it's hard on her, too—not to mention the bedding. I can only guess what she'll think about all this when she gets older."

"One final question, then I'll stop cutting into your mom time. Does the name Kingsley Patrick mean anything to you?"

"Who?"

Wolfe repeated it. She frowned, then shook her head. "No. Sorry, I thought it rang a bell for a second, but I'm drawing a blank."

Wolfe pulled out his card and gave it to her. "Well, if anything comes to mind, please give me a call, okay?"

"Sure."

"Okay," Delko said. "Most of the stuff in Pathan's—sorry, the Brilliant Batin's—workshop was pretty easy to duplicate. He had a bunch of standard magic props, plus supplies like tubing, balsawood, monofilament line, and a range of glues and paints. The tools weren't that esoteric, either—power drill, jigsaw, a few vises, and assorted other woodworking equipment. He also had some jeweler's tools—for really fine precision work, I guess."

Horatio nodded, hands on his hips. "I see you've assembled something, as well."

"Yeah, I call this the Frankenstein pump." Delko held up a small device with a nozzle projecting from one end and a short length of surgical tubing hanging down. "The average human heart beats seventy-five times a minute, which is enough to circulate the five or six liters of blood in most people's bodies. Mechanically speaking, it generates around one and a third watts of power, but it needs thirteen watts of energy to keep it going; its efficiency is only around ten percent.

"That's under normal conditions. Under stress, the heart can deliver up to five times as much blood—peak blood pressure is around a sixth of an atmosphere. I figure Pathan's trying to duplicate a highly stressful situation, so I took that into account.

"The electrical stimulus that makes the heart contract is produced by a group of cells in the right atrium called the sinus node. I used a standard nine-volt battery."

Delko inserted the dangling tube into a beaker filled with red fluid. "The pump I'm using is from a kit called the Mystical Fountain. It's supposed to let liquid flow from unlikely sources—midair, a volunteer's ear, that sort of thing—but it didn't take much work to adapt it. Pathan didn't actually have one in his workshop, but they do carry them at the magic shop we know Pathan frequents."

"And if he did use one, he would have disposed of it afterward," Horatio said. "So how does it work?"

"Pretty simple." Delko had movable wall dividers covered in white paper placed to simulate the dimensions of Pathan's living room; he picked up the pump and flask and walked over to an *X* taped on the floor.

"This is where Pathan was supposedly standing." Delko brought the device up to chin level, closed a switch on the pump, then turned in a steady circle as crimson liquid jetted out of the nozzle, arcing through the air to land with a splash on the white surface of the paper walls.

Horatio held up a photo of the crime scene at Pathan's apartment and compared it to what Delko had just done. "Eric, I believe we have a match. But one thing still troubles me . . ."

"The amount of blood? Yeah, there was a lot. Using the Frankenstein pump, I've figured out there has to be about a liter of Pathan's blood on the walls."

"One liter of his own blood." Horatio rubbed his chin thoughtfully. "Hypovolemic shock occurs when the victim loses between ten and twenty percent of blood volume—which is roughly from half a pint to just over one."

"But there are ways around that," Delko said. "EMTs give oxygen to people suffering from blood loss, to hyperoxygenate their blood and temporarily make up for the loss of volume."

"True. And while we didn't find any anticoagulents in the blood on the walls, he could still have stored his own blood beforehand, to replace whatever he withdrew for the staging. A quick transfusion plus a few hits of pure oxygen would put him right back on his feet."

"So we know how he did it," Delko said. "But we still can't prove it. We didn't find oxygen, blood-transfusion supplies, or a pump at the crime scene."

"That's because the Brilliant Batin is too clever

to leave any of those things behind. But knowing they exist is the first step toward finding them."

"So, the black sheep of the family decides to pull the wool over his father's eyes—that part I get," Delko said. "But why ask for you as the go-between, then give you the runaround? If he wants money, why not just ask for it?"

"That part I'm not sure about. It can't be just ego; Pathan's already convinced he's beaten me once. This almost has the feeling of a personal vendetta—but I'm not sure why he's singled me out. It makes more sense for this kind of anger to be directed at his father."

"Sure," Delko said, nodding. "It's not enough that he's rejected his father's beliefs—he has to prove he's right and his father's wrong. Which, when it comes to religion, is pretty well impossible."

"Yes, it is," Horatio said. "So he'll settle for emotional punishment and monetary compensation. The longer this drags on, the worse it is for Khasib . . . and Abdus can make it last as long as he wants to. He's the one in control."

"But if Abdus is behind all this, then he's the one who tried to kill you. Why? Killing a police officer in the middle of a federal investigation is insane."

"I disagree. Whatever Abdus Sattar Pathan is, Eric, I don't think he's irrational. A lot of careful thought and planning has gone into this . . . and it all started in that convenience store."

"Yeah. That doesn't make sense, either. Why would Abdus suddenly go off on revealing pictures of a woman he doesn't know? Unless . . ."

"Unless it was a setup from the beginning," Horatio said. "Specifically designed to draw me in."

"You think Pathan has some connection to one of your old cases?"

"If so, I don't know which one. But maybe it's time I did a little reviewing . . ."

Every cop made enemies. The better you were at the job, the more enemies you made . . . and Horatio was extremely good at what he did.

This wasn't the first time someone had come after him. He'd been targeted by a bloodthirsty gang called the Mala Noche, by a corrupt judge, by serial killers—even by his own mentor on the bomb squad.

But few of those people were still around. Some were dead, some in prison, and he couldn't find a connection to Abdus Sattar Pathan for any of them. Besides, none of them felt right; Horatio's gut instincts were telling him there was more going on here than what he was seeing.

Which is the one element that does *make sense. Pathan makes his living creating illusions, and that's just what he's done here: created the illusion that he's been kidnapped. The why should* be obvious: *he wants something. But whatever that is, so far he hasn't asked for it.*

Horatio believed that forensic concepts could be applied to all aspects of life. There was a thing he thought of as mental DNA, the distinctive pattern of thought that underlay each individual's behavior; the stronger a person felt about something, the more evident the behavior became. It was there in the photos of a serial killer's victims; it was there in a bomber's choice of detonator. Profilers referred to it as a signature, but Horatio knew it was more than just an identifying attribute—it was a clue to the criminal's approach, their worldview, an entire pattern of thinking.

And what was the defining characteristic of the Brilliant Batin, the underlying metaphor by which he lived his life, that informed, no matter how subtly, his every word and deed?

The obvious answer was *magic*. But Horatio had been in the man's house, and it was no shrine to legerdemain; his workshop had been the only indication of his craft.

Besides, Horatio thought, *nothing about Abdus Sattar Pathan is obvious.*

So. Go deeper. My place isn't filled with old microscopes and posters of Quincy, but that doesn't mean my job hasn't influenced my thinking—in many ways, it directs how I think. So what gives direction to the thoughts of a magician?

No. Not direction.

Misdirection.

One of the fundamental principles of stage magic.

Focus the audience's attention on the left hand, so it doesn't notice what the right hand is doing.

He'd been wrong about Abdus not asking for anything. He'd not only made his demands, they'd already been met. What he'd wanted was Horatio's attention, his *full* attention—not because what Pathan was doing was important, but because he wanted to ensure Horatio *didn't* notice something else.

It kept coming back to the original case, the convenience-store assault. Pathan had walked into a store, noticed a nude pictorial of a Middle Eastern woman, and flown into a rage. He'd contacted someone while in the hospital, someone who'd posed as his lawyer and smuggled in whatever was necessary to fake his fingerprints and then disappeared. Someone, presumably, who'd later threatened Talwinder Jhohal into silence.

Someone Pathan didn't want Horatio to find.

Someone who had just become his number one priority . . .

17

CHRISTMAS EVE.

All over Miami, some stores were shutting down early and others were staying open late for last-minute shoppers. Some people hurried home to be with their families, while others, fleeing colder climates in favor of a snow-free holiday, celebrated in restaurants and bars, on cruise ships and beaches. Radio stations pulled out every artist who'd ever recorded a Christmas album or song and filled the airwaves with roasting chestnuts, reggae carols, and novelty tunes featuring homicidal reindeer.

And Horatio gathered his staff for an important meeting.

Alexx, Wolfe, Delko, and Calleigh were already seated at the conference table when Natalia entered the room. Horatio was at the head of the table, waiting patiently as she took her seat.

"Everyone's here," Horatio said. "Good. Time to get down to business. Calleigh, would you mind starting?"

"Not at all, H." Calleigh picked up the large evidence envelope on the table in front of her and dumped it out on the table.

A small, neatly wrapped Christmas present.

"I drew Delko," Calleigh said with a smile. "And while I couldn't find a South Beach supermodel that would fit into an evidence envelope, he was still pretty easy—to buy for, I mean."

Delko leaned forward and grabbed his gift. He opened it to reveal a baseball card mounted on a Lucite stand.

"Orestes Destrade," he said. "How'd you know I don't have this one?"

"That would be the *I* in CSI?" Calleigh said.

"Thanks," Delko said, grinning. "Guess that means I go next."

He picked up his own evidence envelope, pulled out a small box and handed it to Wolfe. "Merry Christmas."

"This should be good." Wolfe tore off the wrapping to reveal a plastic device around the size and shape of a garden-hose sprayer.

"Contact-free thermometer," Delko said. "Uses infrared to record temperature from a few inches away. Good tool when you don't want to disturb a crime scene."

"Yeah?" Wolfe said, examining it critically. "If

it's such a good tool, why don't you have one?"

"Hey, someone's got to be the test case," Delko said.

"Just wait," Calleigh said. "Two weeks from now he'll be borrowing it from you."

"And in three," Alexx added, "he'll have ordered the *advanced* model for himself."

"All right, all right," Delko said, laughing. "Who's up?"

"That would be me," Wolfe said, putting down his new toy. He opened his own evidence envelope, pulled out a small, gift-wrapped box and handed it to Calleigh. "Merry Christmas."

"Thank you, Ryan," Calleigh said. "I can't wait to see what it is . . . oh."

"I hope you like it," Wolfe said. "I'm not really good with gifts, so I guess I went with something obvious . . ."

Calleigh held up her gift, a small golden bullet on a chain. "It's lovely. But—"

"You do know what those things are used for, right?" Delko asked, his grin getting bigger and bigger.

"Bullets?" Wolfe asked, confused.

Calleigh sighed. She unscrewed the tip of the bullet, revealing a small compartment within. "Some of Miami's more flamboyant criminals like to use them to stash cocaine," she told Wolfe. "This wouldn't be in reference to that little accident I had with the cocaine dust in the air, would it?"

Wolfe swallowed. "No. Definitely not. I'm sorry, I just—I mean, Bullet Girl, right? I would *never*—" He shook his head. "I *hate* Christmas."

Calleigh smiled. "Don't worry about it, Ryan; it's actually very sweet. Despite the nickname, nobody's ever actually given me a bullet before. I suppose most people think it's too . . . on the *nose*."

Wolfe winced.

"Since Ms. Duquesne has already given out her present," Horatio said, "I think we'll ask our resident DNA expert to go next. Natalia?"

Natalia smiled. "Uh, first, I'd just like to thank you guys for including me. Never easy being the new kid, right? Anyway, I drew Alexx—hope you like it." She handed her envelope over to the doctor.

Alexx opened it and pulled out a small, leather instrument case.

"I didn't wrap it," Natalia said. "Sorry if I got the protocol wrong—"

"Oh, honey, this is *beautiful*," Alexx said. "One of my colleagues in New York has one just like it. Hand-stitching, calfskin leather, brass zippers—you have to have them custom-made, don't you?"

"Well, yeah. I asked around and other doctors seem to like them, so I had one made for you. I hope it's okay."

Alexx raised her eyebrows. "I'm not gonna ask how much it cost, but—girl, this is a pretty pricey gift."

"I can afford it. And the only parameters you gave me were that the present had to fit in the evidence envelope."

"Those *are* the rules," Calleigh said.

"If you get *me* next year?" Wolfe said. "I won't object to bundles of hundreds. Really."

"Or gold," Delko said. "Bet you could fit an entire brick—"

"Gentlemen, that's enough," Horatio said. "Alexx, it's your turn."

"Oh, no, Mister Caine," Alexx said. "It's *your* turn." She picked up her envelope from the table in front of her and tossed it to Horatio.

Horatio caught it with one hand, then held it up to his ear and shook it gently. "I don't know. I think I might have this X-rayed first . . ."

"C'mon, H, don't keep us in suspense," Delko said. "Alexx wouldn't tell any of us what she was getting you, either."

Horatio gave him a mock frown. "Oh? I thought this was supposed to be *Secret* Santa?"

"Please," Wolfe said, "*please*, don't say Santa."

"Very well," Horatio said, opening the envelope. "And it appears to be . . . well, well. *Very* nice."

It was a double CD set. "Robert Johnson, honey," Alexx said. "The complete works of. I thought to myself, if anyone can identify with the blues, it's Horatio."

"Who's Robert Johnson?" Wolfe asked.

Alexx gave him a look that managed to convey

equal amounts of pity and disbelief. "Who's Robert Johnson? Only the godfather of the blues, that's all. Hadn't been for him, rock and roll wouldn't exist."

"Also, he supposedly sold his soul to the devil in return for becoming the greatest bluesman of all time," Delko added. "If so, he got a raw deal—only recorded twenty-nine songs in his whole life and died when he was twenty-seven. Somebody poisoned his whiskey."

"It wasn't the poison that did it, though," Alexx said. "Pneumonia got him a few weeks later, finished the job."

"Well, this is festive," Calleigh said. "Can't we even exchange gifts without the subject of homicide coming up?"

"Apparently not," Horatio said with a smile. "But we'll all have another chance in a week or so. Natalia, I hope you don't mind, but my present to you is something I'd like everyone else to share, as well."

"Uh, no, of course not. What is it?"

"A chance for a little rest and relaxation. I know the manager at Toranado's, and I've booked us a table for New Year's Day. Drinks and dinner . . . on me."

"Toranado's," Delko said. "Wow, that's pretty upscale. Thanks, H."

"What I want to know," Calleigh said, "is how he plans on getting all that food and drink into an evidence envelope."

Horatio put his hands on his hips. "Well, I could point out that the bill for this get-together will fit into the envelope quite nicely—but that wouldn't really be fair. Instead, I think I'll just pull rank . . ."

"Works for me," Delko said.

"Don't argue with the boss," Wolfe said.

"When he's right, he's right," Calleigh added.

"I'll even let him pay for cab fare," Alexx said.

"Hey, I'm still learning the rules," Natalia said.

"All right then," Horatio said. "Now that that's settled, let's all get back to work."

The Christmas Carnival party at the Byzantia had at least two uninvited guests: Ryan Wolfe and Frank Tripp. Wolfe had tried to convince Tripp to go home to spend the evening with his family, but the cop had insisted on coming along. "Where I come from, you dance with the one that brung you," he'd said. "If you're going to this shindig, I am, too."

Even though we don't know what or who we're look-ing for, Wolfe thought. *Even though the place is al-ready crawling with private security. Even though we don't know if a crime is actually going to be committed.*

Still, Wolfe hadn't really tried to argue with the stubborn Texan. He had the definite feeling that something was going to happen—and when it did, he'd appreciate having Frank Tripp covering his back.

So far, though, all that had happened was a steady parade of wealthy people in expensive outfits, wandering from booth to booth, sipping holiday-themed drinks and munching on canapés.

Wolfe eyed the Santa occupying the raised throne suspiciously. Keppler had insisted his background check had been clean, but at this point Wolfe would have preferred to ban all Santas on sheer principle. Santa seemed especially jolly tonight, probably because the people lining up to have their picture taken on his lap were mostly women in slinky dresses instead of screaming children.

Tripp was making a circuit of the room while Wolfe stood by the door, and now he was back. He had a glass of eggnog in one hand.

"How can you drink that stuff?" Wolfe said.

"It's nonalcoholic."

"Tell that to your arteries. It's like flavored cholesterol."

Tripp took a long swallow. "Maybe so, but it tastes awful damn good to me. C'mon, Wolfe, loosen up. It's Christmas Eve, after all."

"Yeah, and I'm in Christmas Hell," Wolfe muttered. "I think I'm developing an actual physical allergy to the color red."

"Yeah? Then Miss Farnsworth's outfit must be giving you hives."

Anitra had shown up wearing an elegant gown covered in red sequins, with her hair piled up in an elaborate style and a dazzling necklace of emeralds around her throat. She was currently chatting with a well-known rapper, an NFL quarterback, and the lead in a sitcom that had just been canceled.

"Looks like she's adjusting pretty well," Wolfe said. "Wonder where her daughter is, though."

"It's getting pretty late. Probably put her to bed before she came down."

"That's a shame. I mean, this is a little too much holiday cheer for me, but I bet a six-year-old would be in heaven."

"She'll get her heaven tomorrow," Tripp said. "Kids live for Christmas morning, and parents live for their kids. I'm sure the producers of *Sudden Success* will have a whole extravaganza set up, complete with cameras."

"Great. The commercialization of December twenty-fifth is complete. It's not enough to sell us toys—now they can market the happiness generated by children *getting* toys."

"Long as the kids are happy, right?"

"Yeah . . ." Wolfe frowned. "Something Anitra said about her daughter has been bugging me. Can you spare me for a minute? I want to run something down if I can."

"Knock yourself out. I'll stand on guard against an aerial assault by the Frosty squadron."

Anitra had joined the line to see Santa. Wolfe paused to watch her plop herself down on his lap and throw her arms around him, laughing.

"You know," Tripp said, "I'm starting to think this was a big waste—"

Abruptly, all the lights went out—

"—of time," he finished.

"Emergency lights aren't coming on," Wolfe said. The room had gone completely silent for a second, but a murmur of voices was rapidly rising from the crowd of partygoers. "This is it, Frank. Whatever's going to happen is going to happen *now.*"

Wolfe moved to block the front door and shouted, "Everybody please stay calm! We'll have the lights on in a moment, but I have to ask that everybody just stay put!"

He pulled out a small flashlight and turned it on. Tripp was already speaking into a radio, calling for backup.

"Don't let anybody leave," Wolfe said. "I'm going to see if I can find out what's going on." He slipped out the ballroom doors.

The hall outside was almost as dark, but emergency exit lights cast a dim glow over doorways. Two Celebrus security men flanked the door; Wolfe pulled his badge and told them the same thing he'd told Tripp.

It didn't take him long to get to the lobby—the emergency lights were on there and in the stairwells. The Alexander Ballroom seemed to be the only place they *hadn't* come on.

The hotel manager, Fergusson, was at the front desk, talking in a low voice to the staff. No one was panicking, and the few guests in the lobby seemed more amused than frightened.

"Officer Wolfe," Fergusson said, recognizing him. "Can I have a word?"

He pulled Wolfe aside and said in a quiet voice, "There was this muffled sound just before the power went out. Like an explosion underneath the hotel."

"You have an engineer on duty?"

"No, he's gone home. But I have master keys to every area."

"Take me to the electrical room," Wolfe said.

They used the stairs, going down several dimly lit flights and through a metal door that led to a service corridor. This wasn't just backstage at the theater, Wolfe thought. This was down in the dusty, secret places below the footlights, the kind of catacombs the Phantom of the Opera liked to hang out in. These were the guts of the hotel, the internal workings of gas and water and electricity that kept its heart beating, its senses alert, its body warm.

And now, it had an invader.

The door into the electrical room had been forced open with a crowbar that lay inside. Acrid smoke hung in the air, making both of them cough, and what had once been a bank of equipment was now a charred, twisted ruin.

"No alarms on the door?" Wolfe asked.

Fergusson shook his head. "Not this far down. You need a passkey to get into this part of the basement."

"Well, someone managed to get in and do this. This was no industrial accident—that's blast damage from an explosive device."

The lights flickered, then came back on. "Backup generator," Fergusson said. "It's located in another room. I sent someone to turn it on as soon as the power went out."

"This is a crime scene, now. And if I'm right, it's not the only one in the hotel."

"Is this—is this a terrorist attack?" For the first time, Fergusson's voice sounded nervous.

"I don't think so," Wolfe said. "But as to what it *is*—I'm just as much in the dark as you are . . ."

Horatio spent his Christmas Eve looking through photos. Not family pictures—shots of the crime scene at Abdus Sattar Pathan's house. He was looking for ghosts.

He studied the picture of Pathan's bedroom for some time, looking for what wasn't there. There was a small personal stereo, but no CDs, no tapes, no records. He used a magnifer to zoom in on the face of the stereo and identified which station it was tuned to—an all-talk format.

The bathroom was next. He remembered the toothpicks, but now he noticed the absence of either toothpaste or a toothbrush.

They'd inventoried all the items in the workshop and taken pictures of the props. Horatio went through them until he found what he was looking for: a deck of cards. The pack was closed, though, which was less than helpful. He thought for a moment, then looked up a number and made a call.

"Hello, Mister Fresling? This is Lieutenant Caine. I'm sorry to bother you at home on Christmas Eve, but I have a quick question about the Brilliant Batin's act. Did he use a standard deck of playing cards for any of his tricks?"

Horatio listened to the answer.

"Really. Had them specially made by your shop. And what was the pattern used? I see . . . thank you very much, Mister Fresling. Merry Christmas to you, too."

Horatio hung up. He knew something important now . . . but he still didn't know what it *meant*.

"We got one ticked-off group of people in that room," Tripp said. He stood with his arms folded across his broad chest, standing outside the closed ballroom doors as if he were personally going to tackle anyone trying to leave. "One group of ticked-off, rich, and famous people—and not one of 'em wants to be locked in a ballroom on Christmas Eve."

"Just give me a second, Frank—I want to confirm something."

Wolfe slipped into the ballroom, where the guests had gone back to milling around and enjoying themselves as if nothing had happened. Most of them, anyway; a small group was clustered near the door, talking to Chuck Keppler. He was trying to explain to them why they couldn't leave, and not doing a very good job.

Wolfe hopped over the candy-cane fence surrounding the animatronic reindeer and walked over to the nearest wall. An emergency light was mounted about ten feet above the ground; he looked around for something to climb on and finally clambered onto the back of one of the reindeer. He stood, balancing carefully, and used a multitool to pry free the top of the battery that provided power to the light. When it was off, he pulled a salt shaker out of his pocket, filled now with baking soda he'd gotten from the hotel kitchen. He sprinkled a small amount into the battery.

Nothing happened. He added more, but there was still no reaction.

He sighed, replaced the top of the battery, and climbed back down. Keppler was waiting for him by the door.

"Look, I can't keep these people here all night," Keppler said. "I mean, what does the power being cut off have to do with this event? All that happened was the lights went off for a few minutes. Nobody was killed or kidnapped or robbed. I understand you guys wanting to control a crime scene—but where's the crime?"

"Right in this room," Wolfe said. "I'm sure of it. The battery acid in all the emergency lights here

has been replaced with something else—probably
plain water. I found traces of battery acid at another site linked to the Patrick homicide; this must
be where it came from."

"Okay, I'm with you so far—somebody wanted
this room completely dark for a few minutes. But
unless you can tell me why—"

"I know, I know. These aren't the kind of people who like to be told what to do. Just keep a lid
on them for a little while longer, okay?"

"I'll try," Keppler said.

Wolfe rejoined Tripp outside and explained
what he'd found.

"Yeah, something's definitely up," Tripp said.
"But I'll be damned if I know what."

"I'm going to process the electrical room," Wolfe
said. "Call me on my cell if anything happens."

Delko wasn't crazy about working on Christmas
Eve, but he couldn't go celebrate with his family
while somebody was trying to kill Horatio. Horatio
was family, too.

He didn't bother rechecking the fingerprint data
from the Pathan assault—if Calleigh had done it
and Horatio had reviewed it, the data was solid.
He and Horatio agreed that the key to the case was
Francis Buccinelli.

He studied the picture from the Detention Center's security camera. Beard, glasses, thick hair; it
could easily be a disguise. But whoever Buccinelli

really was, Pathan had managed to contact him while in custody. The arresting officer figured he'd done it in the hospital.

Delko thought it was time to pay a visit to Dade Memorial. *At least it's guaranteed to be open on Christmas Eve,* he thought.

He ran into Calleigh as he was headed for the elevator. "Hey," he said. "On your way home?"

"Afraid not," Calleigh sighed. "I'm still working on the Villanova case. The body's being shipped back to Brazil the day after Christmas—apparently it's hard to get a flight before then. His widow is going to spend the holiday in a hotel room, probably dealing with paperwork, and I still can't give her any answers. I feel too guilty to go home."

"I know how you feel," Delko said. "Knowing that whoever tried to kill Horatio is still out there . . . I just can't imagine putting that on hold while I watch *It's a Wonderful Life* for the umpteenth time."

"Where are you headed, if not home?"

He told her. "If I can figure out how he made the call, maybe I can track it back to its source. And figure out who Francis Buccinelli really is."

"At least you have a name, even if it's fake. My killer might as well be the tooth fairy for all the proof I have."

"Don't give up," he said.

"You either," she answered with a smile.

*   *   *

Wolfe was almost finished processing the electrical room when his cell phone rang. It was Tripp, with bad news.

"We're letting them go. I just got a call from the chief of police himself, who just got a call from someone in the ballroom. Unless you can give me a solid reason to hang on to any of them, this party's over."

"Sorry, Frank. I haven't found anything down here that might tell us what's going on. I'll keep looking, but I'm just about done."

"Sounds like we both are, kid." Tripp hung up.

Wolfe sighed. He was so close to cracking the case he could feel it . . . he had all the pieces, all he had to do was put them together. He slumped against the wall, staring at nothing in particular; his eyes fell on a small, winking green light on a panel of equipment. *Nice to see* something's *working*, he thought gloomily. *Though I'm almost as tired of green as I am of red . . . Red and green. Two elements of the compound known as* christmasium.

Red and green. For some reason, he couldn't get the colors out of his head. Something was nagging at him.

And suddenly, he had it.

He called Tripp on his cell phone. "Frank? Listen carefully . . ."

After he'd told Tripp what to do, he headed for the elevator. He asked a few questions at the front desk, then headed up to the penthouse floor.

He found the maid in the area beside the service elevator, refilling her cart with cleaning supplies; according to Fergusson, she was the same maid who took care of the penthouse suite every day. Wolfe showed her his badge and asked if the laundry on the cart had come from the suite.

"Yeah," she said. "Why?"

"I'm going to have to take a closer look at it," he said. *Public area, in plain sight.*

The maid, a young woman with blond streaks dyed into her hair, shrugged. "Fine by me. Kinda smelly, though."

"Oh? What kind of smell?"

"The bed-wetting kind. Kid's got a nervous bladder, I guess."

"Right. Well, it's a lot of excitement for someone her age." Wolfe bundled up the sheets in a plastic laundry bag, thanked her, and went back down to the lobby.

"Merry Christmas to me," he muttered to himself in the elevator. "I think I *finally* have an idea what's going on . . ."

The hospital ward was quiet this evening, a carol playing softly on a radio somewhere and a small artificial tree glowing with multicolored lights on the nurses' station. Delko was in luck; the room Abdus Sattar Pathan had been put in after the police brought him in had one other occupant, and he was still there.

"We normally don't put criminals and regular patients together," the nurse told him. She was young and Hispanic, with chubby cheeks and an overbite. "But we were short of room, he was unconscious and handcuffed to the bed. We didn't think there'd be a problem."

"How did the other person in the room feel about it?"

She looked a little uncertain. "Mister Johnson? Well, he's comatose, so we couldn't exactly ask his permission."

"Is there a phone in that room?"

"There's a jack, but you have to arrange to have access. There's a fee."

"Are Mister Johnson's personal effects stored in the room?"

"Yes. There's a small cabinet for clothes."

"I'd like to take a look at that, please."

She led him to the room. A black man in his forties or fifties lay in one bed, an IV drip taped to the back of his hand, a softly beeping monitor beside him. The other bed was occupied by a much older man, with a wreath of white hair spread out on the pillow around his head like a halo. He was also hooked up to an IV and biomonitor.

The nurse indicated the black man. "This is Mister Johnson. His things are in that cabinet over there."

Delko went over, knelt down, and opened the cabinet. Inside were a pair of shoes, some clothes, and a hat. He searched through the pockets until he found what he was looking for: a cell phone.

He pulled it out carefully. He might be able to pull a print off it, but he was more interested in the last number called.

He hit redial. After a few rings, a voice-mail message kicked in.

"Hello. This is the Brilliant Batin. I'm currently unavailable, but please leave a message and I will contact you . . ."

Delko hung up and stared at the phone as if it had just bit him. "He called *himself*?"

By the time Wolfe got back to the ballroom, all the guests were gone. The only people left were the film crew, busy packing up the last of their equipment, Chuck Keppler, and Anitra Farnsworth. She was sitting on the steps of the Santa throne, her shoes off, looking tired but happy, talking to the security chief.

Wolfe walked up and said, "No more filming today?"

"God, I hope not," Anitra said. "I just want to go upstairs and go to sleep. Coral will have me up at the crack of dawn, and then—well, I don't know what Jeff has planned, but I'm sure it'll be impressive. I'm guessing Santa himself will show up to shower us with gifts."

"Well, you never can tell where old Saint Nick will show up," Wolfe said. "Or which one, for that matter."

Anitra frowned. "I don't get it."

"Well, there's more than one Santa Claus. Some are nice—and some are naughty. For instance, the Santa that was here tonight—he wasn't so nice."

"Hey, we checked that guy out," Keppler said, suddenly looking worried.

"No, you checked out a guy named Kyle Dickerson," Wolfe said. "And you're right, he was clean. His biggest crime was probably firing his agent . . . see, Dickerson used the name Kingsley Patrick as an actor. But he was down on his luck, so far down he took a gig playing Santa Claus. He was too embarrassed to use his stage name, so he used his real one."

"Patrick was the name of your stiff, right?" Keppler said.

"Yeah. Someone killed him, stole the ID badge he was given when he was hired, and played Santa in his place."

Wolfe looked Anitra in the eye, then let his gaze wander a little lower—to her neck. "That's a beautiful necklace. I'm guessing that as part of the show, the director arranged the same sort of deal movie stars get for high-profile premieres—the loan of a very expensive piece of jewelry in exchange for publicity. How much are those emeralds worth?"

"Two point seven million," Keppler said quietly. He was looking at Anitra in a very different way now; it seemed more sad than angry to Wolfe.

"You were sitting in Santa's lap when the lights went out," Wolfe said. "One of you used a radio-controlled detonator to set off the bomb and douse the lights, letting you swap the real emeralds for fakes. The ones you're wearing right now were manufactured by you and your associate, using a method called the Czochralski process. When I found traces of yttrium oxide at the storefront your partner was using as a base of operations, I couldn't figure out what it was for; it's used to make red phosphor dots for TV screens, but the color I *should* have been thinking about was green. Once you added aluminum oxide and melted the two together in an iridium crucible, you created a compound called yttrium aluminum garnet—one of the simulants used for synthetic emeralds."

Anitra's face hardened. She got to her feet and stared right back at Wolfe defiantly. "Well, there's no point in denying it—I'm wearing the damn thing, aren't I? But don't expect me to pretend I'm sorry."

"Jesus, Anitra," Keppler said. "How could you think you'd get away with something like—"

"Don't you *dare* lecture me," she said coldly. "I don't owe you or Jeff or the damn studio a thing. Am I supposed to be *grateful* for letting them take pity on me? Take the poor little white-trash girl and give her a taste of the good life, parade me around in front of the whole world while I act all big-eyed and awestruck? None of you give a damn about me or Coral—you were just *using* me. Well, I decided to use you right *back*."

"You did more than that," Wolfe said. "You killed an innocent man—and you used Coral's medication to do it. She takes imipramine to control her bed-wetting, doesn't she? And you take phenelzine as an antidepressant.

"What was the plan for your getaway? Slip onto a boat and head for the Bahamas, hoping that the switch wouldn't be noticed until after the holidays?"

"Something like that."

"We've already arrested your partner in the Santa suit as he left the hotel," Wolfe said. "Had the emeralds on him, *and* a bump key—one I'm sure will match the locks at Patrick's apartment and the storefront you were using, too. Tell me, did he approach you with this idea, or did you reach out to him?"

"I think," Anitra said quietly, "that's a question my lawyer should really answer."

"Have it your way. But there are harder questions coming, and not from me. The person you're ultimately going to have to answer to is your daughter."

The defiance on Anitra's face seeped away, leaving weariness and despair in its wake. "I know," she whispered. "I know. I was doing this for her. I couldn't stand her living one more day in a crappy, run-down apartment, growing up thinking it was *normal*, it was all she could aspire to. I wanted to give her her dreams . . ."

"Instead," Wolfe said quietly, "you took away her mother."

18

CHRISTMAS DAY DAWNED GRAY AND CHILLY in Miami, though Horatio knew that later hours would bring higher temperatures. He'd gotten up early, despite not getting home until late; he'd still been at the lab when Wolfe had come in with the news about the Santa bust. Horatio had congratulated him and then told him to go home, feeling just a little like Scrooge sending Bob Cratchit off to his family.

But Scrooge had found his redemption. Horatio still felt as if he were searching for his.

He went in to work, though the building was only minimally staffed; most of the rooms were as empty as a high school during spring break. The labs seemed as sterile and cold as the morgue.

He had gone over the Pathan case until his head pounded, but there were still questions he simply couldn't answer. He wound up looking at the other cases his team was working on, just to distract himself.

The Santa bust was solid; Wolfe had recovered both kinds of antidepressants from Anitra Farnsworth's hotel room, and her accomplice had been arrested in possession of the stolen jewels. Her daughter, Coral, was still at the hotel; the staff had volunteered to take care of her until relatives could pick her up tomorrow.

Horatio sighed. Christmas morning would never mean the same thing to one little girl again . . .

The door to Coral's room opened slowly. She wasn't asleep; she'd woken up fifteen minutes ago and had lain there, eyes wide-open, almost quivering with excitement, ever since. She was waiting, very patiently, for her mother to tell her it was time.

She sat bolt upright in bed—but the figure standing in the door wasn't her mom.

It was Santa Claus.

"Ho, ho, ho!" he boomed merrily. "Merry Christmas, Coral! You've been *very* good this year, so I came to give you your gifts in person!"

"Santa!" she squealed, jumping out of bed. "Mommy, Mommy, Santa's here!" She ran forward, scooted around Saint Nick, and darted into the next room—the one with the big Christmas tree and all the presents under it.

And waiting for her was her mother.

She was dressed kind of funny, in a bright

orange jumpsuit and a Santa hat, but Coral had gotten used to that—ever since her mother had started hanging around with those people who took pictures of her all the time, she'd had to wear all sorts of silly costumes. Sometimes Coral got to wear a costume, too, like the time they both dressed up like cowboys and rode horses.

She ran over and jumped into her mom's lap. "Merry Christmas, Mommy!"

"Merry Christmas, sweetheart," her mother whispered.

Coral was so used to the film crew she hardly noticed them anymore—but today they were nowhere in sight. There was just a man Coral didn't recognize, a man in a black suit with red hair.

"Where is everybody?" Coral asked. "You said there'd be lots of people."

"Not today," her mother said. "Today is just for us. Me and you and Santa."

"That's right!" Santa said, striding into the room and picking up a present. Coral thought he sounded a little like Mister Keppler, but happier. "Now who's this present for . . ."

"Who are you?" Coral asked the man with red hair.

"Me? I guess I'm one of Santa's helpers. I just came along to make sure you have a very, *very,* merry Christmas. You think you can do that?"

"Okay," she said.

And then her mother looked at the man and said, "Thank you," in a voice Coral recognized—it meant she was going to cry. Coral looked at her mother anxiously, but she didn't seem sad; there was a big smile on her face.

"I didn't do it for you," the red-haired man said.

Coral started opening presents. The next time she looked up, the red-haired man was gone, but there were more presents to open and she forgot about him pretty quick.

Until he came back later and told her her mother had to go away.

Calleigh found Horatio in the break room, sipping a cup of coffee and studying a file.

"There you are," she said. "Now why am I not surprised to find you here on Christmas Day?"

Horatio smiled. "I had a few things to take care of . . . but I didn't expect to see you here."

She pulled up a chair and sat down. "I snuck out early, told Dad I forgot something at work. He understands."

"I think I do, too."

"I see you're reading the Villanova file. Checking up on me?"

Horatio looked pained. "Calleigh, I have the utmost faith in you. You know that, right?"

"I—of course I do, Horatio. I'm sorry, I was just teasing. To tell the truth, the case is the reason I'm here."

His smile came back. "Duly noted. Actually, I was looking over this case file because I was feeling frustrated about the Pathan investigation."

"Looking for a little second hand Duquesne insight?"

"I suppose I was."

"Well, you've got the real thing, now—but I don't know how much inspiration I can give you. I'm stuck in a cul-de-sac with Hector Villanova, and I have *no* idea how to get out."

It was strange, Horatio would think later, how inspiration—seeing a connection between two or more things that previously you hadn't—worked just as well when that connection was made by coincidence instead of analysis. At the same moment Calleigh said "cul-de-sac," his eye fell on a single word in the report—and suddenly, it all came together.

"Calleigh, did you notice that Delko found trace amounts of cellulose in the chemical burns on Villanova's arms?"

"Sure. The body was found in a swamp—no shortage of plant matter there."

"True—but he didn't find any lignin, which should have also been present if the trace came from natural plant matter. Cellulose on its own suggests something else."

She frowned, thinking about it. "Paper?"

"Not just paper," he said. "A paper *sack.*"

* * *

"Mrs. Villanova," Calleigh said as the woman walked into the interview room. "Thank you for coming. This is my boss, Lieutenant Horatio Caine."

"Mrs. Villanova, I would like to extend my deepest sympathies," Horatio said. "I know this process has dragged on, and I apologize for that. I just wanted you to know that we've devoted as much time and effort to finding out what happened to your ex-husband as humanly possible."

"Thank you, Lieutenant." Solana Villanova was dressed all in black and had made no attempt to hide the dark circles under her eyes with makeup. "Do you have any answers for me?"

"I'm afraid we do," Calleigh said. "Solana, your husband committed suicide."

For a second, it didn't register. She frowned, as if she hadn't heard her correctly. "What? But the body—there was no head, no hands! The coroner told me explosives had been used, chemicals—"

"They had," Horatio said gently. "By Hector himself. He held a crude bomb in his mouth and put paper bags filled with crystalline drain cleaner around his hands, probably several layers thick. When the bomb went off, his body fell into the water. Water plus sodium hydroxide turns into a very strong corrosive base; as a plumber, he was familiar enough with the chemical to know how much to use, enough to eat away his fingerprints first and eventually dissolve the paper bags. He used another bomb with a longer fuse to sink the boat."

"But—but why would anyone do such a terrible thing?"

"That's what we couldn't figure out," Calleigh said. "It looked as if someone had murdered Hector and tried to prevent his body from being identified—but when we investigated, we discovered nothing that would implicate Hector being involved in criminal activities."

"Of course not," Solana said. "He was a *good* man."

"Yes, he was," Horatio said. "What my team did find was that Hector hadn't done much since he came to Miami. Despite what he told you, there was no business opportunity. The only significant actions Hector took were to buy a boat . . . and give himself a farewell dinner. He went to a local Brazilian restaurant and had them prepare *ceia de natal.* According to the staff, he was happy—as if he were celebrating something."

"Happy? But surely those are not the actions of one who is planning to kill himself?"

"Actually, Mrs. Villanova," Calleigh said, "it's not uncommon for suicides to display a sudden burst of uncharacteristic cheerfulness. It's not because their outlook has improved—it's because they've given up. They think they can finally see an end in sight to their pain."

"I don't understand. I don't understand." Solana fumbled in her purse for a handkerchief. "Why? Why would he go to all this trouble?"

Calleigh glanced at Horatio, and he gave her the slightest of nods. "We think he was trying to erase himself," Calleigh said. "It's why he came to Miami. Disappear in a foreign country, make sure your body can't be identified . . . and sever prior relationships in such a way that no one comes looking."

"The argument we had," Solana said softly. "The fight. Now I understand . . . he wanted to drive me away. To hate him. So I . . ."

"So you wouldn't blame yourself," Horatio said.

She nodded, her gaze turning distant. "I see. He must have been in pain, such pain. All he wanted was for it to end. But to do so would pass that pain on to me . . . and that, he would not do."

"He must have loved you very much," Calleigh said.

"I didn't know the depth of his love," she said. "Pain makes one selfish, no? But not Hector. It was not enough to give me my freedom; he tried to give me the gift of innocence, too. Of not knowing."

"I'm sorry," Horatio said.

Solana dabbed at her eyes with the handkerchief. "It's all right. It is your job to find things out. And I'm glad I know—for all his good intentions, Hector never really understood me. It's not my fault he killed himself; that was his choice. And as for the other things he did . . . well. Who would not be proud to know that someone loved . . . loved them . . . that *much*—"

And then Solana Villanova gave her ex-husband the only thing she could—the one gift he'd never wanted.

Her grief.

Christmas Day was notoriously slow for news, aside from the usual spate of attacks in the Middle East and the pope's annual speech from St. Peter's. So when something newsworthy did occur, it got even more coverage than it usually would.

Like the daring escape of a kidnap victim from his captors.

Abdus Sattar Pathan was found, bleeding and battered, wandering along the Tamiami Trail with a handcuff still locked around one wrist. A patrol car found him, picked him up, and took him to a Miami-Dade police station, at which point the FBI was contacted. Someone in the station leaked the story to the media, and the building was soon besieged by reporters.

Horatio got a call, too.

He drove over to the Miami FBI field office, where Pathan was being debriefed. Agent Sackheim was the one who'd called him—more out of smugness than any sense of professional courtesy, Horatio thought—and had agreed to let him interview Pathan about his ordeal. On Sackheim's home turf, of course.

Horatio endured the multiple checkpoints and security measures stoically. He gave up his gun without complaint and signed his name more than once. He had his fingerprints scanned and he walked through a metal detector. He almost expected them to ask him to remove his shoes.

Finally, he was ushered into an interview room. Sackheim was already there, sitting across the table from Pathan. Pathan was sipping carefully from a large mug of coffee and looked terrrible; one eye was swollen shut, there was a cut on his lip, and he still wore the bandage on his neck. Horatio nodded to Sackheim. "Dennis."

"Lieutenant."

Pathan eyed Horatio mildly. Despite his physical condition, he seemed at ease. Horatio thought he knew why.

"Lieutenant Caine," Pathan said. "I didn't expect to see you here."

"Of course you didn't." Horatio regarded Pathan incuriously, a slight smile on his lips, but said nothing else.

After a moment of silence, Sackheim cleared his throat. "Mister Pathan has had a most exhausting ordeal. If you have any questions for him—"

"I don't have any questions," Horatio said. "But I do have a request. A very simple request. Its relevance might not be immediately apparent, but if you wouldn't mind indulging me?"

Pathan shrugged wearily. "If I can. As I've already told the FBI, I learned very little about my captors—"

"This isn't about them. This is about you . . ."

Horatio reached into his coat pocket and pulled out a short length of rope. He held it in his closed fist, curled fingers up, an end poking out of either side of his hand. "I'd simply like you to do something that almost all magicians have done at some point in their careers. It's a tradition almost as firmly entrenched as pulling a rabbit out of a hat, or asking someone to pick a card."

Pathan's face broke into an incredulous grin. "You want me to perform a *trick*? I hate to tell you this, Mister Caine, but most magic relies on preparation. I can't just wave my hands and make something *disappear*."

"I don't want you to perform a trick, Abdus. I want you to demonstrate a very simple physical task. And it's *Lieutenant* Caine."

Horatio opened his fist. The rope had a knot tied in it.

"I want you to blow on this," Horatio said.

Pathan hesitated for just a second, then his smile grew even broader. "Is that all? A somewhat bizarre request, but for you, *Lieutenant*—I would be happy to oblige."

He began to lean forward—but Horatio drew his hand back.

"Not so fast. After all, this wouldn't be a proper scientific test without verification . . ." Horatio reached into his pocket and pulled out a small plastic film canister. He popped it open and pulled out a single, fragile object.

A tiny, downy, white feather.

Horatio stood. He placed the feather carefully on top of the knot.

"Have you lost your *mind*, Caine?" Sackheim asked.

Horatio leaned forward, holding his hand in front of Pathan's face. "Not at all, Agent Sackheim. I'm simply calling Mister Pathan's bluff."

Pathan's grin had faded to a smile. His eyes were locked on Horatio's, but they were no longer filled with amusement.

They were filled with hate.

"Go ahead," Horatio said. "One simple exhalation of breath. Surely the Brilliant Batin can complete a ritual performed by thousands of magicians at kids' birthday parties every year . . ."

Pathan said nothing.

"What's the matter?" Horatio asked. "A second ago you didn't have a problem—but then, a second ago you could have pretended to blow on it. And now you can't."

"All right, Lieutenant, you've made your point," Sackheim said. "Though I have no idea what you're trying to prove."

"What I'm trying to prove, Agent Sackheim, is that Abdus Sattar Pathan is a liar." Horatio pulled his hand back, closed his fingers into a fist around the knot again. "And I don't just mean he's lying about being kidnapped. I mean his whole life is a lie. You see, the Brilliant Batin *isn't* a magician."

"I never claimed to be," Pathan said.

"No, you didn't," Horatio said. "You billed yourself as a master of amazing feats and prestidigitation. You've never claimed that what you do is anything more than skillful sleight of hand and clever illusions. Which puts it in the realm of science—not magic."

"I'm sorry," Sackheim interjected, "but I don't see the relevance—"

"Bear with me," Horatio said. "Mister Pathan's home contains no photographs and no music, only a stereo tuned to a talk-radio station and a TV he probably never watches. He doesn't drink alcohol. He uses toothpicks instead of a toothbrush. Even the playing cards used in his act aren't actually playing cards—he has them specially made, with numbers and an abstract design instead of face cards. Why? Because, Agent Sackheim, none of those things are allowed under certain fundamentalist interpretations of Islam. Abdus Sattar Pathan is a Muslim—and a quite devout one. Despite the fact that magic is one of the things expressly forbidden."

"And the feather?"

"It's the knot that's important," Horatio said. "The Quran refers to magicians as 'the ones who blow on knots.' Mr. Pathan has spent his whole life constructing the illusion that he's a magician, but he's been very careful to follow the rules. Blowing on a knot would break them . . . and jeopardize his very soul."

"My soul," Pathan said, "is forever beyond your reach, Lieutenant Caine."

"Your soul isn't what I'm after, Abdus."

Sackheim got to his feet. "Lieutenant, do you have any evidence to offer that Mister Pathan has actually committed a crime, or did you just come here to criticize him for his religious beliefs?"

"No criticism of his beliefs is intended," Horatio said. "Only of his actions. I may not be able to prove you faked your own kidnapping, but I'm certain of it—and sooner or later, a jury's going to agree with me."

"Then I suppose," Pathan said, "that this isn't over."

Horatio dropped the knotted rope on the table in front of him.

"Mister Pathan," he said, "I'm just getting started . . ."

"You," Agent Sackheim told Horatio flatly, "are *done.*"

They were in Sackheim's office, a space every bit as neat and organized as the man himself. His desk held a lamp, a blotter, and a yellow legal pad with a single sharpened pencil centered exactly above it.

"I don't understand you, Horatio. You were the one reading me the riot act for not showing any compassion toward the victim—and now you're haranguing him for his *religion*?"

"I told you, it's not about that," Horatio said patiently. "It's the fact that he kept it hidden."

"So what? Not everyone's comfortable wearing their beliefs on their sleeve. You said yourself that Muslims aren't supposed to practice magic—no doubt that's the reason he kept it secret."

"That doesn't add up, and you know it. Hide your faith and flaunt your sin?"

"Maybe it has something to do with his father." Sackheim leaned back in his chair. "Family dynamics don't always make sense from the outside."

Horatio paused. He knew firsthand how true that statement was, and just how violent and unstable that dynamic could become; his own relationship with his father had come to an ugly and very final end. "None of this makes sense," Horatio muttered.

"Doesn't it? Abdus and his father have a major conflict over religious beliefs. Abdus later converts, but he's too stubborn to admit it—or accept protection from his family. Somebody finds out how much he's worth and snatches him. Abdus gets lucky and escapes."

"And the convenience-store assault?"

"You said he was devout. It makes perfect sense that nude pictures of a Middle Eastern woman would make him angry."

"So after years of maintaining a perfect illusion, he suddenly throws it all away? I don't buy it— any of it. Kidnappers who go to elaborate lengths to have me run all over Miami but don't make any ransom demands. Kidnappers who use an Iraqi land mine to kill a federal officer. Kidnappers who leave a crime scene splashed with blood but no other trace of their presence. Kidnappers who supposedly almost kill their target in the first place—and then let him get away. This case has more contradictions than a mobster's testimony, Agent Sackheim."

"I haven't forgotten about Hargood," Sackheim said. "But you're wrong about there being no cohesive pattern. Khasib Pathan's wealth and position make him a prime target for terrorists, and that land mine is exactly the kind of weapon they have access to. My people are tracing that mine back to where it came from right now—because, unlike your 'artificial heart' theory, the mine is hard physical evidence."

Sackheim leaned forward, clasped his hands together, and rested his elbows on his desk. "It's been a long day, Horatio. Go home. This is the Bureau's responsibility now—and we take care of our dead."

"So do I, Agent Sackheim," Horatio said. "So do I . . ."

When Horatio got back to the lab, somehow he wasn't surprised to find Delko waiting for him.

"Well," Horatio said. "Doesn't anyone around here know the meaning of the word *holiday*?"

"Merry Christmas to you, too, H," Delko said, grinning. "And I'm not staying—my folks'll shoot me if I'm not back in time for dinner. I just figured I'd give you your present in person."

"Oh?"

"In a manner of speaking. I did a little extra snooping concerning the Afterpartylife nightclub—the one where the land mine went off."

"And?"

"And I looked into the background of the consortium that owns it. Kind of a twisty financial trail, but I finally figured out who owns the controlling interest in the company."

"Let me guess . . . Khasib Pathan?"

"You got it. Looks like you were right—Abdus was trying to cause trouble for his father, all along. But I found out something else, too." Delko told Horatio about the phone call Abdus made from the hospital.

"He called his home phone? And someone answered?"

"Phone records say yes. Whoever it was, they didn't talk long."

"So the mysterious Francis Buccinelli was in the Brilliant Batin's house—but we didn't see any signs that he had a houseguest."

"Maybe he wasn't staying there."

Horatio shook his head. "I don't know, Eric. But whoever Buccinelli really is, he's the key to all of this. I think everything Pathan's done was simply to keep our attention focused on him instead of on the initial case. But smart as he is, he made a mistake."

"Yeah," Delko said grimly. "He tried to murder you."

"No, Eric. All that means is that whatever Pathan is covering up is serious enough to risk a federal investigation. The mistake he made was in not following through on a ransom demand—it proves that this was never about money."

"But we still don't know what it *was* about."

"Not yet," Horatio said. "I just came from seeing Abdus himself. I told him I knew he faked the kidnapping and I intended to prove it."

Delko frowned. "But, H—I thought you said Buccinelli is the key."

Horatio smiled. "He is. But the Brilliant Batin isn't the only one capable of misdirection . . . and until we find out what's really going on, I want Pathan to think *he's* the focus of our investigation."

"And if he tries to kill you again?"

Horatio smiled. "I suppose," he said, "I'll just have to rely on the people around me to keep me safe . . ."

His phone rang. "Caine."

"Merry Christmas, Horatio," Alexx said. "I just thought I'd call and—well, just to say Merry Christmas."

"Merry Christmas to you, too, Alexx. I'm glad you called . . ." He gave her the details on the resolution of the Villanova case. Halfway through, Delko tapped his watch and made an apologetic shrug. Horatio nodded and shooed him toward the door silently.

"Oh, Horatio, that's so sad," Alexx said when he finished. "He went to that much trouble, just to avoid causing her pain. With suicides, it's usually the other way around."

"Suffering can bring out the best in people as well as the worst. It all depends on what you do with it."

"What about what *we* did, Horatio?" Alexx's voice sounded troubled. "I know it's our jobs to uncover the truth—but in this case, I wonder if it wouldn't have been better if Hector had succeeded."

"I don't think so, Alexx. No matter who he was or what he did, Hector Villanova had a life. He affected the people around him. To deny that, to try to just slip away unnoticed, is to do not only himself but everyone who knew him a disservice. No one's life is entirely their own . . . and if you're going to end that life, you owe the people who love you more than unanswered questions."

"You're right, Horatio. Pain is just part of the package, isn't it? Doctors spend so much time trying to relieve suffering that sometimes they lose sight of that."

"Not you, Alexx."

She sighed. "I should get back to my family. *A*

Christmas Carol is about to start, and I always watch it with my husband."

"Holiday traditions are important," Horatio said. "Take care."

"You, too."

After he hung up, Horatio sat for a while in silence. Alexx's mention of the old movie had stirred up memories of it; the scene that came to mind was of Scrooge, all alone in his dark, empty house, huddled in front of the fire and eating his dinner— until the ghost of his former partner, Marley, showed up wrapped in chains.

"I wear the chain I forged in life," Marley told him. "I made it link by link, and yard by yard; I girded it on of my own free will, and of my own free will I wore it . . ."

Chains, Horatio thought. Hector Villanova had wound chains around his body to weight it down . . . but their weight was nothing when compared to that of the chains already wrapped around his heart.

"Is its pattern strange to you?" Horatio said out loud. "Or would you know the weight and length of the strong coil you bear yourself?"

No answer came.

Horatio turned out the lights and went home.